To Jeannette

Best Wishes,

Bridge Tender

[signature] 2021

D1521139

Carol Ann Ross

1

IRONHEAD PRESS

COPYRIGHT 2016 by Ironhead Press

Cover design by C.A. Ross and Connie Pletl.

This novel is a work of fiction. Names, characters, and incidents are a product of the author's imagination and are used fictitiously. Any resemblance to actual events or persons living or dead, is entirely coincidental.

Acknowledgements

This story could never be complete without the help of so many people who are there when I have questions or need technical support.

I want to thank the following people for putting up with me and offering answers to the little things that add truth and substance to the pages of this novel.

Yogi Paliotti, Lou Wilson, Patti Blacknight, Bruce Blacknight, Faye Batts, Gigi Oberlin, Janine Davis, Diane Edens, Shari Bruce, James Brown, Todd Thomas, Tim Thomas, Connie Pletl and Lee and Debbie McKnight.

Dedication

To the true locals of Topsail Island

Introduction

Hank leaned back in the captain's chair, propping his legs high on the railing of the small docking pier. He ran a finger beneath the hem of his white shorts; they looked florescent against the tanned brown skin of his leg.

Biting into his bottom lip, penitent thoughts filled his head—summoned, they seemed, from some dark recess.

How long had it been now? he studied the marsh; the setting sun muting the colors of the cattails and coarse grasses zigzagging with the sloughs and little creeks bordering its edge.

His eyes lazily followed the line of land southward to a sloop traveling slowly through the water, its sail tinted red in the evening light.

The sail luffed a bit and he watched as the man aboard tacked, dodged the boom and brought the sail to stand staunchly against the breeze.

How long had it been? he thought again, his eyes still fixed on the tinted colors of the scene—it brought to mind the words of an old song—the one about red sails in the sunset.

It doesn't seem that long ago—time didn't seem to have any meaning anymore. Hank envisioned his wife's lips forming a smile; the image coaxed one from his own.

There she stood, her long frame leaning against the bowsprit of his sloop. Emma was so beautiful against the red of the sky, her sandy colored hair blowing wildly about her face.

That face—the sun always brought out the freckles on Emma's face. And though she always scoffed about the sepia specks, Hank saw them as little badges of beauty. Each one made her more unique.

A heavy breath flowed steadily from his lips as he closed his eyes, recalling his deceased wife and the argument on the way out to sea, only a couple of miles past Topsail Inlet.

That day was supposed to be a day of celebration. Emma had just found out she was pregnant.

Hank was ecstatic; elated to a feeling he had never felt before. He had packed the gear early that morning, pulled the Jeep around and loaded it up with Emma's favorites, caviar, fresh bread, artichoke hearts—he saw her coming from the neighbor's house. For a moment it puzzled him. Why should she be at Orey's?

"Had to tell someone, I'm so excited," she had shrugged, responding to his puzzled look.

If it hadn't have been for Orey. His jaw tightening, Hank ran his hands across his face, and damned the one-time friend. *He's the bastard who gave her that bag. I should have known then. I should have found out and done something about it **then**.*

And when he'd caught her in the cabin doing a line, he lost it—screamed, threatened—how can you do this, you're having our baby!

"Just this once won't hurt. Come on baby, just this once." She'd held out the rolled bill, encouraging him to join her.

He slapped it from her hand, his chest rising and falling in angry pulses. He want to slap her, but didn't—instead, his eyes searched hers for reason, for some bit of sanity. Hank could not comprehend how Emma, his wife, his love, could take even the smallest chance with their child.

He studied her face; it was just as beautiful as always, but this time, Hank found her profoundly disgusting—just for that moment.

Cursing her, he grabbed at the remaining cocaine in the bag; Emma snatched it away and ran up the galley way stairs.

Hank followed her, and standing by the mast, watched as she pressed herself against the bowsprit.

"Throw it into the water!" he called angrily, steadying himself against the roughening seas.

Emma tensed her body and held on tighter to the stanchions of the sprit as the sloop bowed into a deep trough.

The sloop climbed another swell, then rolled down again. One after another, the swells came, the boat crashed against the rolling water.

Emma's eyes grew wide with fear, but Hank would not call to her, *Emma is wrong; she has no business doing coke—not when she is pregnant. Especially when she is pregnant with my child.*

If she's going to be an idiot, if she's going to act like a selfish bitch, then I'm going to scare the hell out of her. Maybe that's what she needs. The vague recollection of thinking these things, saying those words, flew through his thoughts.

Was I wrong to say that, to feel that? Hank questioned those reactions so long ago. His eyes found the lone sloop moving silkily through the sound waters—he had purposely turned the boat just so, making it slam a bit harder into a wave—the recollection disturbed him as the image of Emma's eyes growing wide with fear and her face turning ashen, settled in his mind.

"Drop it into the water," he'd called out, waiting for her to drop the bag of cocaine. He wanted her to do it, now, and then to ask for his forgiveness—he always did forgive Emma when she did wrong. "It will be okay then, just drop it."

The boat slammed into another wave, Hank watched Emma's trembling lips as the boat dipped—it had been so difficult not to call lovingly to her.

Nodding her head, Emma pursed her lips into a kiss—it was now a game.

Hank teased back, removing his shirt, puffing out his chest. Emma tossed her long hair to the side and pursed her lips again.

He knew he'd won as she dangled the bag of coke over the side.

The sloop had bowed into another trough, and then rose for another wave, a much steeper one. The boat pulled to the side, Hank struggled to right it as he kept his eyes on Emma. Then he saw the smile he'd been waiting for—that acquiescing smile. She winked at him as she released the bag held in her hand.

Another deep trough, another steep wave—Hank pulled against the wheel, his eyes darting to the growing swells, then back again to his wife. But she was not there.

That instant in time was a fresh as the day it happened. The agonizing feeling of loss had become memorized, etched in his brain. And though most of the images had become blurred somewhat by time,

Hank could not let go of the guilt and pain the memories brought him. In fact, he had come to welcome them.

With the memory, Hank felt the color fade from his face—even after all the years, *that* day still tore at him.

Searching for the sailboat he'd been watching, he finally noticed it making its way just south of where he stood.

The man had taken down the sail and was now motoring farther south.

Hank swallowed the lump in his throat as he closed his eyes. Again the vision of Emma swept into his mind. But this time her features seemed less clear. "No!" he screamed aloud. The thought of losing her image startled him. Concentrating, determined to find her face, his brows pinched together—and then it came, the clear points of her chin and cheek bones. "There you are," he whispered.

He needed to hold her, if only in his memory, she mesmerized him so, she always had. From the very beginning she'd taken his heart and soul.

A distant cousin, he'd met her at a Saturday afternoon family event, a hog killing and picnic an uncle had urged him to attend.

He'd never really wanted to go; since his parents' passing he'd found it difficult to socialize, and this country bumpkin outing would have never been something his parents would have attended. But Uncle Henry persisted—Hank reluctantly acquiesced.

At the gathering of aunts, uncles and cousins, he barely acknowledged in public, he milled about, nodding to the distant relatives, smiling back at those who smiled at him.

Feeling uncomfortable, Hank strolled to the backyard where men were swabbing a hog with sauce as steam rose from the grill. The aroma was enticing and he walked closer, he could feel the saliva accumulating in his mouth, but he wouldn't stop to taste the meat. Continuing past women huddled together gossiping and laughing, Hank heard his stomach growl. Tunes from a guitar and violin played in the air as little groups of people sang along.

He felt so out of place and continued past the hog and people, toward a small shed and overturned dory on chocks. His eyes perused the wild flowers, tall pines and squirrels scampering about the trees—and then he saw her—a young woman leaning against a sprawling oak as if she owned it.

Her arms folded behind her back, she stood barefoot, her sand hair cascading about her shoulders, her blue eyes beckoning Hank to speak to her.

Had he spoken first or had she? He recalled her lips forming the word, Emma. And then she smiled. What was it he'd asked her? Hank's memory blurred again for a moment. Whatever it was, Emma had responded with an emphatic no.

There hadn't been many girls who had said no to him; her response and the look in her eyes bewildered and bewitched him.

Why would anyone say no? He was good looking, came from one of the more wealthy families of the area. He could have any woman he wanted.

Most of the local girls hadn't had a meal served on a tablecloth, or one that hadn't been poured out from a bucket for peeling or shucking.

He could afford to take a date to a nice restaurant— one of the fancy ones in Wilmington, twenty miles away. He could afford to buy little baubles and candies. He could have any girl he wanted—they all seemed to want him—always commenting on his hazel eyes and so enthralled over the light blue Jaguar he drove around the community.

Despite all the attributes, Hank prided himself on not letting his personal wealth go to his head; that's one thing his mother had reinforced throughout his childhood. "We're like everyone else, we just have a little more; all people, even if they're in rags, should be treated well."

However, Lucinda Butler always added the caveat, "Just don't bring them home with you."

Hank did treat all women with respect, regardless of their station in life, but he never got involved, at least for very long, especially with those certain types of which his mother would not approve.

So when Emma, the distant cousin from the side of the family that was a little less refined, said no without blinking an eye, Hank was compelled to pursue her. He believed it would be a quick romance, and then he would move on, but it didn't turn out that way.

There was no Momma Lucinda to reprimand him, or make him feel guilty for dallying with the white trash—no one to point him in another direction or bribe with a new car or money.

Hank found something reassuring in Emma—something fulfilling in this new woman and despite echoes of his mother's warnings, he proceeded to fall in love.

Emma made him laugh and in many ways loosened some of the bonds that had restricted him. He felt free or at least freer than he'd ever been; he found more depth to his life as he and Emma grew closer.

They flew to New York one weekend, to Tahoe another. Emma schooled him in the fine art of crabbing and fishing; Hank taught her which fork to use. Within a few months, they eloped and moved into a small house on the property his parents had left him in their will.

Life was good, especially that first year when Hank and Emma traveled the world, visiting Italy, France, England, the Far East. They were a picture of happiness and Hank seemed another person.

One of his aunts commented that his mother would certainly not approve of his choice in a wife, nor his lifestyle. But Hank was happy for the first time in his life. Emma gave him the freedoms his parents had denied him—she took away the restraints of judging others—or at least made Hank loosen up a bit judging others by the way they dress, their station in life, or the cars they drive.

There were few things Emma wanted, it didn't matter to her how much money Hank spent on her; she asked for little and expected nothing.

Except for the sloop. She loved sailing—when she found out she was pregnant the first thing she wanted to do was celebrate on the ocean.

"If I hadn't have gone, if we'd taken the power boat instead of the sloop, if Orey—damn Orey." Hank spit into the brackish water below where he stood on the pier.

"I made him pay, Emma. I made them all pay." Balling his fists, he slammed them onto the railing. "Damn it, it wasn't my fault." Hank felt the doubt, the guilt—and knew it was he alone that carried the blame. He shouldn't have tried to scare Emma, he should have been more patient, more understanding. He should not have lost his temper.

"If Orey hadn't given her the coke, if I'd trusted my gut when I saw her leaving his house, if…freaking hell, it doesn't matter what happened." Digging his fingers into the hair of his chest, Hank pulled sharply, opened his clenched fist and released the strands of hair into the wind. "But Orey's gone, been gone a long time." He grinned. "An overdose will do that to you every time—he's the one, it wasn't my fault, Emma, Orey's the one that took you from me."

The corners of his eyes gathered in soft folds of tanned skin. "Sarah, Reggie and Mick…" Hank's fingers drew to his beard; he tugged gently on the hairs. It was still difficult for him to imagine himself as a bearded man. He'd always kept himself neat and clean-shaven.

Several minutes passed as he reflected on the changes in his physical appearance.

And the other changes? Have I changed so much since Emma? Since last fall?

Looking into the darkening sky, Hank studied the stars; he counted the ones in the big dipper and then the seven sisters of the little dipper. "Maybe there have been a few changes," Hank acknowledged as he considered the strength, the will power it had taken him to commit the acts he had. "I'm a stronger person, more self-assured." He said aloud, nodding, his hand against his chest.

His brow furrowed as confusion swirled for a moment in his head. *Why had it been so important to avenge Emma? Why not just Orey? Why Sarah, Reggie and Mick?*

He pondered the questions; they finally blurred into emptiness as the image of Mick's body lying prone on the deck of his Robola powerboat emerged. He'd tied a line around Mick's still breathing torso. As he motored through the inlet, he dumped it over the transom. The thunk of the body hitting the propeller echoed before letting out the line beyond the swirl of the outboard prop.

Hank towed Mick nearly all the way to Sears Landing, over a dozen miles, and then down into a creek. He cut the line; Mick was a tangled mess.

"That bastard won't be selling cocaine to anyone, ever again," Hank hissed, recalling that night at Topsail; he pulled his legs from the railing and stood. His eyes focused on the reflection in the sound waters. He pulled again on his beard and scowled.

Killing Mick wasn't that hard, that distasteful. Hank's cheeks swelled as he grinned broadly. "I should have done that bitch Sarah and Reggie myself instead of letting Mick have all the fun. I didn't even, didn't *ever* like him. He was so damn hollow…so vulgar…had no respect for women…just a flagrant prick…he thought I liked him." Hank laughed loudly, "And that phony British accent. What was that all about?" Again the feeling of strength and confidence swelled inside him. "I could never like anyone so loud, so gaudy and crude. He didn't have an ounce of modesty or respectability about him."

Scraping his fingernails against the wooden rail of the pier, he pictured Mick drinking the sparkling grape juice he'd served him that night. The feeling of control surged inside him; a tinge of regret peered from some recess into his thoughts, but Hank quickly brushed it away.

Digging his nails even deeper into the wood, Hank winced as splinters poked from the tips.

Turning the palms upward, he studied the tiny shards of wood protruding from his fingers and from beneath his nails; he watched intently as the blood oozed from them.

Mick never suspected a thing. Mick didn't think I had what it took to kill. Hank glimpsed a recollection of Orey sitting on his couch with a needle hanging from his arm.

"But I didn't kill Orey." Hank's lips curled at the corners as memory found the handgun in his lap. "Orey chose to die a less violent death. I gave him the option."

Hank studied his reflection more intently as he leaned against the railing. "Mick was a slob—and look at what I've become."

In the last nine months, since leaving Topsail Island, he gained forty-five pounds. Hank patted his stomach. "Lots of fast food burgers, macaroni and cheese, and beer." He shrugged and continued gazing into the ripple-less water. He rubbed an aching hand across the top of his baldpate, then ran his fingers through the hairs of his goatee.

Much to his surprise, he liked the beard and took great pride in keeping it trimmed just so.

With the extra weight about his face and body, the beard and fresh tattoo on his neck, tiny gold hoops and metal bar through his right ear, he barely resembled the man he once was—the clean shaven, always neat, preppy looking man.

Touching his fingers to the hammerhead tattoo, he nodded and stroked the gold hoops in his ear lobes.

The man with the hammerhead tattoo—that's me—the new me—bold—daring—in control.

Grinning, Hank's jaw tightened as he lifted his head skyward and away from the reflection in the water.

The sloop he'd been watching was now nearly out of sight. He sighed. The grating pain of losing Emma tugged at his heart.

Sloops always did that to him—reminded him of his wife—his deceased wife—and of that day when she'd disappeared into the rough swollen waters near Topsail Inlet.

No other woman could ever measure up to her. No other woman had ever come close to captivating him as she had. He would not allow that memory to fade.

He leaned against the railing again, the evening breeze felt cool against his shaved head. His thoughts alternated back and forth between Emma and those he felt deserved killing. A small voice tugged at him scolding him for them; another praised him for the accomplishments of retribution.

"Emma would be proud I did all that." Hank stood back from the pier's edge and placed his hands on his hips. "Emma." Her image colored his presence for a moment more before disappearing. Replacing it suddenly was the picture of the three women he'd met when he'd first come to Beaufort. Laughing as he walked along the wooden planks leading to the house, Hank spit again into the water. His pace quickened as the sound of tires against gravel met his ears. *But this one is different, she's more like my dear sweet Emma.*

Chapter One

Carrie flipped the on switch for the open sign to her lane, without thinking, she raised a forefinger to her mouth and began biting at the nail. Quickly she pulled it away, reminding herself that she did not need to start another nasty habit.

It had been three weeks since her last cigarette, it was tourist season and the stress was getting to her. She'd packed on thirteen pounds since quitting and the waist of her trousers cut into her stomach. She'd already popped the button three times, each time sewing it back a little farther along on the waistband.

"Excuse me for biting my nails," Carrie apologized to Mrs. Lloyd, a long time customer of Grocery World.

Carrie liked the older woman; she was always so polite and patient. They had become friends, sort of, at least Grocery World friends.

"That's okay honey; I know you're trying to quit smoking." The woman leaned in a bit, lowering her voice, "It's a bitch. I remember when I quit, I was mean as a snake and I gained forty pounds." She tittered as she continued plucking canned goods from her cart.

"Thank you, Mrs. Lloyd, it's one of the hardest things I've ever done."

"Well," the woman winked and smiled, "you hang in there honey and before long you'll forget all about those nasty old ciggies and then you can concentrate on the weight."

It shows, I guess, Carrie thought as she patted her tummy and returned Mrs. Lloyd's smile.

Undertones of muffled voices caught Carrie's ear. "These people down here are so slow. I don't see how in the world they'd be able to make it if we didn't come here and spend money. They wouldn't even be able to make their mortgages. All I can say is they should be grateful we come at all.''

Carrie glanced quickly at the couple behind Mrs. Lloyd, she wasn't sure if they'd meant to be heard or not, either way, the statement riled her.

Tourists, Carrie's eyes met Mrs. Lloyd's.

The older woman shook her head, "I heard them too, sweetie," she whispered, she winked and patted Carrie's hand.

"Thank you, y'all come back now." Carrie stressed her southern accent even more as she waved good-bye to Mrs. Lloyd.

Heaving a sigh, she turned her attention to the thirty-something couple, unconsciously her fingers flew to her lips. She felt her teeth tear into a thin strand of nail. Quickly she pulled her hand away.

"Ahem," the man cleared his throat.

Focusing her attention on the couple, Carrie spoke, "Sorry 'bout that...I've quit smoking and..."

"We're in a hurry if you don't mind," the woman lifted her head and looked off in the distance.

Oh my gosh, I can't believe these two, forcing a smile to her lips, Carrie spoke, "Welcome to Grocery World," she smiled broader and began checking the items on the counter.

The man's eyes shifted from Carrie's fingers to her mouth, he sneered then slid a snide glance to the woman beside him.

She rolled her eyes and looked quickly at the pump bottle of disinfectant next to Carrie's register, then back to Carrie.

Geez, you'd think I was picking my nose or something, grudgingly Carrie reached for the disinfectant and pumped a glob into her hand. She could feel the heat rising in her neck as she rubbed her palms together. *So YOU pay my mortgage for me, fat chance.*

"See, all clean now." Carrie raised her eyebrows and drew her lips upward into an exaggerated grin.

Oh, I'm going to get fired if I don't quit being so snippy to customers, she thought chastising herself. *Damn I need a cigarette.*

Scanning the items quickly, she pushed them down the conveyor belt, bagged them, then continued scanning until groceries, eyeing the whole-wheat loaf

21

of bread at the end of the order. Carrie's lips tilted upward again.

"Y'all here for vacation?"

"Yes," the man nodded.

"Have y'all been to Topsail before?"

The couple ignored the question as they exchanged a glance.

Stepping back a few paces the woman eyed Carrie, then folded her arms.

Wow, she's rude-they're rude. I'm just trying to be nice. But I guess I should be oh soooo grateful they are helping pay my mortgage. Carrie's smile turned into a sneer as she placed the bread in a bag.

Her fingers firmly folded around the center as she squeezed tightly. Lifting her eyes to the couple she said, "That will be seventy-three dollars and fourteen cents."

The man retrieved a card from his wallet and swiped it through the card scanner. He shook his head in disgust and sneered, "humph, *you people.*"

Carrie handed him the receipt, "Thank you for shopping Grocery Word." She added an acerbic, "Y'all come back now."

Smiling smugly to herself, Carrie watched as the couple exited the sliding glass doors of the store, once again her fingers sped to her mouth, but she caught herself before biting down. Pushing her hands into the pockets of her trousers, she turned to welcome the next customer.

"Welcome to-"

"Turn your light off," Fern ordered.

Carrie shot a perplexed look toward the store manager as she edged in front of her.

Pushing Carrie to the back of the station, Fern drew her attention to the next customer in line. She grinned politely, "I'm sorry, this lane is closed. Lane four is open and the clerk there will be glad to help you."

"What?" Carrie studied Fern's face curiously, "Why are you-?"

"I saw what you did."

"What?" Immediately Carrie realized that Fern must have caught her squeezing the customer's bread. Her face reddened; again her fingers flew to her mouth.

Following the store manager into the office, Carrie mulled over excuses; *I didn't mean to, they were so snotty, you should have heard what they said about Southerners.*

"Ah hell, Fern," came out of her mouth instead. She plopped firmly on the chair next to the manager's desk. "It won't happen again."

"No, it won't happen again." Fern tapped her pencil on the desk blotter.

"I've quit smoking and…"

"I've never put one of those nasty things in my mouth," the manager interrupted. "So, it doesn't matter to me if you're smoking or not. You don't get to be sarcastic or angry with anyone, that's the bottom line and this isn't the first time. We both know that."

Carrie scrambled for one of the excuses she'd been thinking of, "But you didn't hear what they said about Southerners."

A defiant hand flew in front of Fern's face to silence Carrie. She slowly shook her head no and tightened her jaw. "You're fired."

23

Chapter Two

"It's the first time I've ever been fired from a job," Carrie could feel the tears welling in her eyes.

"Oh, don't start crying. Getting fired isn't the end of the world. It just means you're not a robot." The scowl on Paula's face softened as she watched Carrie tear a strip of nail from one of her fingers.

"You're going to have to stop that, though."

"Things have been...*weird*, for lack of a better term, since...you know."

Paula nodded. "That episode with Hank and-"

Carrie brushed the air with her hand and shook her head no. "I can handle that."

"Sure doesn't look like it." Raising an eyebrow, Paula continued, "A lot of things have happened to you in the past year."

"I don't like thinking about it," Carrie waved her hand through the air again. "Maybe all the tourists-*terrorists*-whatever you call them, are right. We do need their money. I don't know how I'm going to make it without a job." She pulled her Chihuahua Bella close to her and stroked her gently. Joey stood near her feet, staring jealously as his master stroked the little dog's fur.

"That is a stupid thing to say. Regardless of where you go, the person doing *any* job relies on the patron's dough, and that's in any town, U-S-A. We live in a capitalist country, honey, and the whole world uses money." Paula crossed her legs and leaned back in the recliner. "We don't owe tourists any more than the guy working behind the McDonald's counter in Chicago owes the guy who buys a big Mac." Shaking her head, she pushed back farther against the recliner. "You haven't been the same since last summer. Are you sure what happened with Hank isn't still bothering you?"

The small room filled with silence as Paula looked quickly at her friend relaxing on the divan. She felt badly for Carrie, who hadn't spoken even to her about events from last year, the murders and Hank nearly killing her. Paula wondered if Carrie had gotten any help, if she'd talked to anyone like a psychologist, counselor, or any professional at all.

Breaking the silence, Paula cleared her throat and began, "You know, if you ever decide to sell this thing, let me know. It's the most comfortable chair I've ever sat in."

"Nope, can't sell that one. It's the only reason I get company. But I have to disagree." Carrie stretched her legs as far as she could and rolled ankles from left to right, waiting for the popping sound. "This, my

Cleopatra couch, the divan, is the most comfortable chair in the whole world."

"It's not a chair." Paula rebuked.

"Well, la-tee-tah. Seat, this is the most comfortable *seat* in the whole world." Carrie pulled her knees up to her waist and turned her face away.

Paula groaned, trying to get Carrie to open up was not going to be easy. "Hey, I was teasing."

"Umm." Shrugging, Carrie settled her hands behind her knees.

"You better get out of this funk or whatever you call it, girly. Don't get too comfortable feeling sorry for yourself. You're out of a job and it's summertime, tourist season and most of the places around here have already hired all the help they need."

Stretching her legs before her, Carrie groaned, "I know, I know. But I just can't seem to get motivated."

"You better, you don't have a choice unless you've suddenly come into a lot of money."

Carrie rolled her eyes, "I simply can't believe I got caught and I can't believe Fern didn't let me off the hook. For goodness sake, she knows how the terrorists treat us. She knows it's hard to keep from saying anything to them, especially when they're so obnoxiously rude."

Shrugging, Paula reached for the soft drink resting on the end table. "Who knows what motivates ol' Fern? Personally, I think she canned you because she knows she can." Paula slid a cutting glance toward Carrie. "Me, I don't need that piddly job. I'm part-time help and-" Paula hesitated, taking a long gulp from the can of cola, "I'm leaving."

"What?" Carrie swung her legs from the divan. "You're leaving? Where are you going?" Who am I going to talk to?"

"Don't get so bent out of shape, I'm not leaving town," Paula chuckled. "I've been offered a job at the bridge."

"I know you don't need the Grocery World job, but what about fishing? Are you giving up commercial fishing? When summer's over, that's what you always go back to."

Paula pursed her lips. Her chest rose and fell slightly as she patted the chair's armrest. "I've been fishing ever since I can remember, I love it. There's nothing like watching the day break on a palette of blue and green," she exhaled softly through her parted lips. "But the restrictions and regulations are getting to be too much for me. I need time to think, time to regroup."

"But bridge tender? That's a pretty sedentary job, isn't it?"

"And standing in one place for eight hours, isn't?" Paula leaned forward pulling the recliner upright. "I'll try working at the bridge for a while. At least I get to be near the water and you know how I *have* to be near the water."

"Church…it's your church."

"Something like that," nodding, a calmness settled on Paula's face. "And it can't be too difficult working on the bridge—besides, that little operational house is air conditioned."

Both women paused as they listened to footsteps creaking along the outside porch. Joey jumped from the divan, raced to the screen door and started barking, the hair on his back rose. Bella leapt from the divan as well, stood near Carrie's feet and yipped unenthusiastically.

"Oh, it's just me, you little ankle biter," Mindy scratched on the screen, infuriating Joey even more.

Giggling, she peered into the room through the screen.

"Arf, arf…arf, arf. Your little muttkins have me sooo scared." Mindy jiggled the locked door. "Carrie, Paula? I heard what Fern did to you."

Padding across the floor to the screened door, Carrie lifted the latch and pushed Joey aside with her foot. "I guess everybody knows by now."

Mindy nodded, "Yep, news travels like wild fire at the *World,* especially when it's bad. I heard she caught you squeezing some touron's bread."

"That's a new one—touron—is that what we're calling them now?"

"Fits," answered Mindy.

"Let me guess, tourist plus moron gives you touron." Paula scoffed.

"You got it. After that last thing, you know, I told you about it." Mindy looked from Carrie to Paula. "Remember, I had turned at the stop light and was going south. There were around four cars in front of me and I saw an ambulance coming with its lights flashing and the siren on. Well, me and three of those cars pulled to the side to let it pass, except for this one moron who speeds up and passes everybody and makes the ambulance slow down. I tell you, it really burned me up…*touron.*

And the license plate was definitely out of state." Mindy shook her head, pulled a loose strand of wispy hair behind her ear and looked at the two liter bottle of cola on the table, "Do you mind if I have some Pepsi?"

she nodded as she moved into the kitchen. "I'll just have a small glass, I can't stay long. I've got to get over to Miss E.J.'s and dog sit while she's out of town."

"Help yourself, the ice-maker's not working, but there's a bowl of ice in the freezer." Carrie returned to the divan and settled herself against the soft fabric. Joey and Bella jumped up to curl next to her legs.

Pulling one of the kitchen chairs into the living area, Mindy sat down and sipped gently from her glass. "Gal, I'm sorry Fern got you. Mr. Sanders was in the next lane and he told me he heard every word that couple said to you—said they were rude—said he didn't blame you one bit, since they were so snotty and all." She nodded her head and giggled. "Nope, I don't blame you at all, but ever since you've quit smoking you've been a little edgy. You don't seem to want to *talk* to anybody—you kind of *bark*. Sometimes you even snap at me and I'm your friend, girly." She took another sip from of the cola, "Mr. Sanders said he couldn't believe you squeezed that bread right in front of Fern, she wasn't standing four feet away from you."

"I need a cigarette. Will one of you go to the World and get me a pack? " Carrie ran both hands through loose strands of strawberry blond hair, pulling it back sharply from her brow. "Damn," she looked from Paula to Mindy.

"I thought you *quit*." Mindy snorted. "Seems kind of silly to start again now that you've lost your job because of stopping."

"Oh, shut up." Looking from Paula to Mindy, Carrie groaned. "This stinks, I can't get anyone to help me out here. I try to do something good—try to improve my health—it makes me nuts and *this* happens—I get fired. Maybe everything will go back to normal if I start again."

Paula shook her head, "Honey, you're a mess—and nobody's going to buy you cigarettes. You're going to have to tough it out, just like everyone else."

Paula's scolding tone annoyed Carrie; she folded her arms across her chest.

"If Mindy can quit so can you, Carrie."

"You should have done the vaping instead—I told you it would be too hard to stop all on your own." Holding her e-cig between her fingers, Mindy raised it to her lips.

"Humph." Rising from the divan, Carrie walked into the kitchen, opened a cabinet and pulled out a box of cheese crackers. "If no one is going to buy me cigarettes, I guess I'll just get fat."

Mindy and Paula exchanged knowing looks.

"Your problem isn't so much the quitting smoking, it's that policeman." Paula pulled herself upright in the recliner.

"Ever since that thing with Hank and those people he killed, you've been…touchy," added Mindy.

"You seemed wrapped up in the detective after that and then—who knows what happened there? You never talked with us about it." Pulling her feet up into the seat of the chair, Paula strummed her fingers on the end table. "You won't talk to anybody about anything. And then you decide to quit smoking. Did you do that for Detective Don?"

"Going through all that crap you went through with Hank—I mean—you went to bed with him and all." Mindy blew a vanilla scented cloud of vapor into the air.

Carrie shot her a heated glance.

"Well, it's true," Mindy shrugged.

"You both did too," A cynical glare exploded from Carrie's eyes.

"Hank wasn't killing people then." Mindy sneered and pulled her e-cigarette to her lips again; another thick cloud of vapor released into the air.

"You haven't quit smoking—that thing has nicotine in it." Carrie retorted angrily.

"You don't understand. With the e-cig you can lower the intake of nicotine into your body."

"And?" Carrie cupped her chin in an open palm.

"A regular cigarette is like twenty-four milligrams of nicotine and with an e-cig I can go as low as three grams and then down to none."

"So what are you down to now?"

"I'm at about twelve."

"But you're still getting nicotine."

"Would you get off it? Don't you see, I'm lowering the amount!" Mindy replied defensively, her voice rising louder above Carrie's.

"Okay, okay," Paula stood; her hands opened wide before her. "Let's keep it down, we don't need to start yelling and arguing about this." She stared boldly at the two women and pointed to Carrie. "Mindy is right."

"What?" a look of betrayal swept across Carrie's face. "That thing *does* have nicotine in it—it does."

Her lips drawing into a line, Paula rubbed her brow, "I'm not talking about the damn e-cig, I'm talking about you going to bed with a man who tried to kill you and who killed three other people along the way."

"But you two both told me you had affairs with him—neither one of you seems to be bent out of shape over anything—even the killings."

"How would you know, you barely talk to us anymore," said Mindy.

"It's different, that was several years back—a *different* me slept with Hank. At least it feels like it." Pausing for a moment Paula sighed, "Granted, it bothered me some, but Carrie—"

"And I was drunk—it doesn't really count and besides, it was three years ago. It's no big deal." Mindy interrupted.

"Sex is never a big deal to you, Mindy. It's like shaking hands."

"Screw you!" Mindy barked.

"But to some people it's an intimate act, it means something—or is supposed to." Her face contorting in anger, Paula squared her shoulders, "and don't ever yell at me again."

Mindy frowned, took another sip from her glass of cola and fumbled with the vaporizer strung around her neck.

"You need to talk to someone about what happened last summer—about Hank. That was a bad time, Carrie. You could have been killed. You were pulled into the thick of some very sick and bad things."

"It started with the Hummels." Lowering her head, Carrie licked her trembling lower lip. "And Morgan Simpers."

"Yeah, whatever happened to Morgan? I haven't seen him in the store since all this happened." Mindy asked.

"He sent me a note, apologizing." A faint smile brushed across Carrie's lips. "I think he's too embarrassed to come in the store now."

"I bet Roz ripped him a new one," Mindy giggled. "I'm surprised she didn't divorce his butt."

"I feel sorry for him," Carrie's eyes softened for a moment.

"I blame Don, he let you get too involved."

"Yeah, whatever happened to Don?" Mindy blinked a wary glance toward Paula. "Mr. Hunka, hunka, burning love."

"He said he had to get away for a while."

"So he's not with the police force anymore?" Mindy's eyes widened. "Robby never said anything about that."

"I didn't say he wasn't on the force anymore, I just said he had to get away, something about his kid and everything being too much."

"So he dumped you." Blowing another vaporous cloud into the air, Mindy crossed her legs.

"I don't know," Carrie shrugged. "It wasn't like that."

"Regardless of whether or not Don dumped you, Carrie, you need to take care of yourself." Paula pushed her face forward, "I mean it."

"*He* was there for me; he's who I talked to after everything, after Hank." Lifting her head to meet Paula's gaze, Carrie lifted her chin. "It *was* scary. I was scared—scared Hank would come back—for *me*. Everything, nothing made sense, it was horrible, especially when I found that English guy."

"He wasn't English, he was only pretending to be—at least that's what Robby said," blurted Mindy.

"I know that," retorted Carrie. "But everybody thought he was, so…"

"We know what you mean." Paula nodded, encouraging her friend to continue.

"I guess I sort of drifted away from y'all. And you, Paula, you'd started doing your commercial fishing and I just didn't see you that often, at least often enough to talk to you."

"You sure as heck weren't talking to me either, Carrie." Mindy pouted.

"Sorry about that Mindy. I just didn't want to talk to anyone after that. And Don was coming around, we were—I was confiding in him. He listened, he cared—and I thought I had it all worked out—that I was past it, that everything was going to be okay."

"And your detective in shining armor dumps you."

"It's not like that, I said! He didn't dump me."

"Were y'all hitting the sheets?" Mindy asked casually.

Paula groaned, "Mindy…" she drew her lips into a line, preparing for a reprimand.

"No," Carrie reached out her hand and shook it at Paula, "it's okay. She can ask that. And the answer is no. Believe it or not, *no*."

Mindy and Paula exchanged glances. Mindy raised an eyebrow as she drew another long pull from the e-cig.

A gentle giggle fell from Carrie's lips, "I know neither one of you believe me, but Don and I never went to bed. The man's a saint, I tell you. We just got to be good friends."

"Did he kiss you?" Mindy asked eagerly.

"Yes, we kissed a couple of times, but we both decided that getting physical was not a good idea, right now anyway."

"But he's gone…out of town?" Paula queried.

Nodding, Carrie sighed, "I miss him. He's such a good man and whenever I needed to talk with someone, Don is the one I called. He's been there for me."

"*Was* there for you," quipped Mindy.

"So that's why you've quit smoking. You want to be a better person for Don." Paula shook her head.

"Something like that. He's kind of impressed upon me that I can weather anything and that I should be proud of who I am." A grin played across Carrie's lips. "So you see, I am okay with what happened last summer—sort-of--for the most part. I know I'll probably *never* be totally over it. It's just the smoking; it is really making me wacky. I want a cigarette *really* badly, and I want to quit. Instead, I eat whatever isn't moving and bite my nails. So, when Don comes back, I'll be fifty pounds heavier and have ugly fingernails but I will no longer be a smoker."

Both Mindy and Paula leaned back in their chairs; they exchanged looks of exasperation.

"Huh," Mindy slapped her thigh. "You keep at it, gal, and maybe by the time he comes back you'll be through with smoking and I can give you a few pointers on losing all that weight you've gained."

Setting the box of crackers down on the counter, Carrie walked next to Mindy; she settled an arm around the girl's shoulder. "You know, you really have a way, not a subtle one, mind you, but you do have a way of putting things into perspective." Carrie rolled her eyes and winked at Paula.

Shrugging, Paula nodded, "Try the e-cig, Carrie. Just give it a try. Maybe you won't feel so *wacky,* maybe you won't bite your nails anymore and you won't be so grouchy. No one is going to hire a grouch."

"Okay, okay. You two have me convinced. I'll give it a try."

"And," Mindy tittered as she exhaled a plume into the air, "I came over here for a reason. I didn't come here *just* to remind you that you've been a real bitch lately and that you're getting fat."

"What reason is that?" Paula leaned forward, propping her head in an opened hand.

"The Upper Deck is hiring. My friend Tillie from there says a girl quit this morning and if you hurry on over you can pick it up. They're really busy and need someone A-S-A-P."

Chapter Three

Sliding from the faded gray Dodge Charger, Don welcomed the Avis (or one that delivers) agent and inspected the bright yellow Mazda parked before him. It would have to do and from the looks of other cars in Joyce's Bar and Lounge parking lot, it fit in well, but then, so did his Charger. "Thanks man," he handed the young agent a ten-dollar tip. "You don't know of a good garage around here, do you?" He caught the name embroidered on the pocket of the man's shirt, "J.T.—one close by, that can tow the Dodge for me."

"Sorry, today's my first day and I don't know squat about the place. I'm originally from Maryland."

Don nodded and wished he had asked first before handing the money over. "So I guess you don't know much about this dive either, huh?"

"Nope, except that it looks like one." The young man laughed.

"How about a beer, my treat." Pausing, Don checked out the boy's youthful grin. "You are twenty-one, aren't you?"

"Twenty-five, I just got that baby face thing going on. At least that's what my wife says—but yeah, I'll have a beer."

Being polite always costs me money, Don thought as he entered the bar and relaxed on a bar side stool.

Nodding a thank you, Don slid another ten toward the bartender, "You haven't seen a guy around here—say, around six foot, salt and pepper hair, kinda clean cut?"

The woman shook her head no, "What's he done?"

"Nothing, I'm supposed to meet my friend Hank here for a fishing trip."

"We got a fellow named Hank comes in now and then, but I haven't seen him in a couple of weeks. But he sure isn't what you call clean cut—tats and piercings."

"Probably not my friend." Don swallowed a few sips from the beer and leaned against the bar, his eyes slowly scanning the walls of Joyce's. Like most bars, it was dimly lit; a jukebox stood against a far wall near several booths and tables. A couple sat holding hands at one, a lone patron sat at the end of the bar texting on his cell phone.

It was obviously an older establishment with dusty knotty pine paneling; a few deer heads on the walls evidenced that at least a few of the patrons were hunters. He stood and walked to study the framed pictures scattered here and there. Most were older, at least fifteen to twenty years; a few were present day, their color less faded.

A chuckle exited his lips as he studied a photo of three women, related it seemed from their resemblances. Scooped necked sweaters revealed cleavage; their hair was teased high and for today's mores, they wore too much make-up. It was as if they'd walked out of the 1980s. *Probably not too much here,* he thought as he walked back to the stool. *Hank wouldn't hang around a place like this. He's long gone, if he was here at all.*

J.T. thanked him for the beer and left; the bartender asked if he'd like another, Don declined and toyed with the nearly empty bottle.

"That's a good kid," she commented. "Just got out of jail."

"Really?"

"Yeah, you know there's a minimum security prison right up the road in Harlowe, don't you?"

Don tilted his head, focusing on the woman's eyes, "Oh yeah," he nodded, vaguely recalling the jail. "Are you Joyce?"

The woman guffawed, and without offering any explanation or her own name, replied, "Joyce sold the place twelve years ago."

"Oh," Don watched as she bent bend to retrieve bottles of beer to stock the refrigerated cases. *Not real friendly here either, are they.* Rising, he walked through the door and out into the sunlight.

"I guess you're waiting for me," Don spoke to the Mazda parked in the dusty lot. "Guess I'll get something to eat." Thoughts of Carrie's ham and cheese casserole entered his head, "I should give her a call."

****

41

Carrie sat across from Blythe, the owner of The Upper Deck, and listened as the woman rattled on about what she expected from her employees.

"Clean white shirt, black skirt—not too short, or slacks. Black shoes—no opened toes, and you must pull your hair away from your face—none hanging in your eyes." She paused, pursed her lips and tapped the pencil in her hand against the wooden table.

"Normally," the woman continued in her strong New Jersey accent, "I wouldn't hire anyone without checking them thoroughly, but Tillie says she's known you a long time and that you're a good worker…and I need someone now." Blythe Goodfellow again drummed the pencil eraser rapidly on the wooden table. Slowly eyeing Carrie's appearance, she added, "I'll give you a chance. You'll make good tips here, but you'd better be on your toes. I know you girls down here in the South don't move too fast…" Blythe's grin faded as quickly as it had appeared, "…and I don't put up with any sitting around, there's always something to clean, put away or wash."

Inhaling deeply she laid the pencil on the table, rolled it back and forth a few times then placed it behind her left ear. "Be here tomorrow at three."

Rising from the seat, Blythe walked abruptly into the kitchen. Instantly the sound of pots hitting the floor rang out. Shrill reprimands and colorful language debasing the help followed.

Geez, do I really want to do this? Carrie asked herself rhetorically as she rose and exited from the main entrance door. *I heard she was really hard to work for—a real slave driver.*

Her face feeling the warmth of the sun against it, Carrie shook her head; "I really need a job, so I guess I'll have to put up with the Yankee bitch, for a while anyway." She whispered the words as she stepped on the loose gravel of the parking lot.

Slipping into the seat of her car, Carrie tried to remember if she had a white blouse. "I know I've got a couple of black skirts but they might be too short according to Blythe." Edging her car close to the road, she looked both ways, then hit the gas to move out into the slow moving traffic. "But I do have some black pants that will do."

As she pressed the button to turn on the radio, Carrie leaned back against the vinyl seat to listen as Mark McGrath crooned one of her favorite oldie tunes. She always had liked that song; she remembered dancing with her children, Jeff and Missy, so long ago in the living room of their home in Florida. It *did* seem so long ago. Now, they were living their own lives, both doing well—both still happily married, she hoped it stayed that way for them for a long time. Carrie smiled as she thought of her children; she was thankful they had chosen their paths wisely.

If only I had waited to get married later in life, maybe I could have gotten some sort of degree, something beyond a high school diploma, I wouldn't be working these low paying menial jobs. She shrugged, "I can't live life over again, at least, that's what Don's always says." Breathing in the warm salty air of the island she drove slowly toward her home, "Well, it is what it is and at least I live at the beach. Can't get much better than that."

Carrie pulled the e-cig from her pocket and lifted it to her lips. "Yep, this beats going cold turkey." She blew a plume of cherry scented vapor into the atmosphere, "and, unlike Grocery World, at The Upper Deck there is no bread to squeeze."

Pulling into the lane leading to her home, Carrie peered deeply through the bushes lining the drive. She hoped she would see the dull gray Dodge sitting there parked in front. But it wasn't there.

She missed Don. And she wondered if she would have gotten more romantically involved with him, had he stayed, or at least shared more information about where he was going and when he might return. At least she hadn't hopped into bed with him like she had with Hank.

Carrie's head spun for a moment at the thought of the monster—that's what he was—what he must have been. Calmly she inhaled and exhaled, releasing the tension; erasing the dark feelings that even the thought of Hank conjured.

Her mind pushed through to thoughts of Don. He'd been gone for almost a month now. She glanced at the dashboard clock. It was nearly four-thirty. She'd turned her phone off for the interview with Blythe and forgotten to turn it back on. Sliding her hand into her purse, Carrie fumbled about for it.

"Damn." She gritted her teeth. "He called twenty minutes ago."

Quickly she dialed his number, it rang; then switched to voice mail. "Hi, call back or leave a message."

He sounded so curt and cold in the recording; Carrie shook her head thinking how opposite Don really was. Smiling, she considered whether or not to tell him about getting fired from Grocery World and her new waitress job. "Sorry to have missed your call—was busy and didn't hear the phone ring. Hope everything is going well for you. Call back when you can. Bye." She decided against telling him.

Leaning back against the seat of the car, Carrie slid her phone back into the purse. She wondered how Don would react to her losing the Grocery World job. "It's not like it's a career or anything," she told herself. "It's just a piddly cashier job."

She blew a quick breath and exited the car. Joey and Bella were bouncing up and down at the window; they always made her smile.

"Okay, okay," Carrie leaned down to pet the little dogs, moved to the kitchen counter and opened a bag of dog treats. "Y'all are so good, I sure do love my puppies."

Chapter Four

"Been thinking of how you helped me out last year. Would like to repay you for all you've done. How about coming up for a few days?" Hank texted the words on his phone, then hit the send button.

Slipping it into his pants pocket, he stepped lightly across the deep pile carpet of his rented home, he wondered about the recipient of his text. Would she respond immediately or would it be a few days. Usually the former was the case; Emma's mother always took her time responding. Sometimes she didn't respond at all.

"I'll give it till Wednesday," he muttered aloud as he opened the refrigerator door and retrieved a bottle of Saint Pauly Girl beer.

"That old woman—can't figure her out." Pausing, Hank stood before the open glass doors of the room.

He walked slowly out onto the deck and leaned against the railing.

From his creek side home, he could see lights from a small vessel as it glided along the darkened waters of the waterway.

Walking out to the dockside pier, he studied the thick marsh grasses growing between his house and Pamlico Sound. They stretched maybe a hundred yards before him.

The area was very reminiscent of Topsail but it *was* different. There were fewer homes along the waterfront-fewer piers fingered out into the briny expanse. Still, it reminded him of his home. But then, any place along the southern Intracoastal Waterway had that feel of life beginning and dying. It was there in the marsh and the tides, the smell of what wasn't any longer, what was and what was going to be.

All along the coast there was *that*. So being there among the reeds and grasses, close to the water felt somewhat like home, just that it wasn't.

He longed to go back. He missed his home and the routine he'd carved out for himself there. Sometimes he wondered why he had even left, but then a pall would come over him and the thought would vanish.

In his heart, Hank knew he could never leave the coast. It was like being wrapped in life and everything that had ever meant anything at all. The smells, the sights, nothing else in the world, nowhere else in the world, could compare.

Feeling the pang of homesickness, Hank lifted his head toward the distant sound of a powerboat moving slowly through the water. He let the weight of his body lean forward against a railing and peered downward to watch flecks of light dancing on the brine. *I want to go back.* The familiar distorted reflection stared back at him through the ripples-a feeling of self-loathing settled in his belly.

Gritting his jaw, Hank dug his fingers into the wooden rail, spat into the reflection of a bloated face and baldhead.

Lost in thought, he was startled at the words that seemed to come from the wind.

"So, there you are."

Hank turned immediately, hidding the fingers of his right hand tightly against his left to hide what he knew must be damaged, perhaps even bloody.

"I was wondering where you were. You look so lonely out here."

The word's poured from her lips like warm caramel, soothing Hank, relaxing him with welcoming familiarity.

She leaned against the wooden railing, her long freckled legs crossed over each other; her arms folded against her breasts. "You stood me up."

Hank glanced at his wristwatch and shook his head, "Damn, I apologize, Estelle…Essa…it's just…"

"Save it, big boy. I learned long ago that if something is important enough, you don't forget. Obviously, I'm not important enough."

Chuckling, Hank slowly approached the woman. "Then why are you here if I don't think you are important enough?"

"Bastard," the word fell as a whisper. Estelle grinned. "Beats the hell out of me why I want to be with a fat bald man, anyway. But honey, you are such a treat in the sack; I had to find out what it would take for more."

"Oh, that." Hank slid his eyes over the young woman's body-it was beautiful. And he had always been partial to freckles. Emma had been sprinkled with them, but this woman was awash in sepia flecks.

Estelle moved slowly toward Hank, unbuttoning her blouse.

"Let's go inside," Hank slipped his hand into Estelle's and pulled her gently along the boards of the pier.

As they reached the glass doors, he grasped her waist and jerked her into the curve of his body.

Pushing him away, the tall woman stood before him and licking her lips, continued unbuttoning her blouse. In moments, she let the soft material slip from her shoulders to reveal amply rounded breasts, covered in small brown freckles.

She reached to her denim shorts and unsnapped the rivet. They hung loosely about her hips.

She's even built like Emma, Hank swallowed hard, he could feel his body shaking.

Reaching both hands to Estelle's head he spoke, "Just who are you?" he asked.

"I'm who you want me to be."

Hank threaded his fingers into her long, thick, curly hair, pulled her face close and covered her lips with his mouth.

****

"Tell me more about your oceanfront home," Estelle lay on her side, the bed covers draped loosely across her hips.

Reaching her bare toes to his, she rubbed the arch of Hank's foot, then wrapped her leg around his thigh.

"It's nice, has a fantastic view, but not *ostentatious*," he slid a glance to his companion. "You do know what *ostentatious* means?"

"You think just because I'm related to the three idiots—the V girls-that I'm as dumb as they are?"

Hank laughed; he touched a palm against her cheek, "No, you're very intelligent. That's why I like you," He stroked her hair and stared into her blue eyes.

Estelle nodded. "So you *like* me."

"Um hum...I could get lost in those eyes." *Tiny brown flecks, just like Emma's.* He felt his heart flutter, "Estelle,"

"Essa, call me Essa."

Tango eyed the woman lying next to her master. A growl rose from her throat as the woman pulled herself closer. Tango's tail swished to and fro, frizzing as she released another low growl.

Hank rubbed the cat's back gently, "Shh, she's fine."

Estelle reached a hand to pet the animal but drew back quickly as a raspy hiss and sharp teeth responded to her attempt. The cat's entire body frizzed as it reached a paw of extended nails toward her.

"Bitch, what a bitch. Your cat doesn't like me." Propping herself on one elbow, Estelle pushed her unruly mane to drape across her shoulders.

"She doesn't like women who cuss a lot." Hank narrowed his eyes; a slight grin played on his lips.

Estelle boldly met his gaze. "Working on it honey. I've been trying to please you." Her sarcastic tone changed to a more submissive one as she gently tugged on his chest hair.

Hank continued petting the cat, "Poor Tang is old; she must be around thirteen now."

"Cats live a long time. I had one that lived to be twenty-two. But she sure as heck wasn't as mean as this one." Running a fingernail along the bicep of Hank's arm, Estelle leaned into the crook of his neck.

Hank felt the warmth of her breath, the softness of her lips as they caressed the side of his face.

"You know, there's not anything I wouldn't do for you. You know that, don't you, baby. *Anything* you want." Her hand gliding along the side of Hank's body, avoiding Tango, Estelle kneaded her fingers into Hank's back. Slowly they traveled to his buttocks and then to Hank's thigh. She pulled her nails upward leaving red marks in the light skin where his shorts would have been, then ran her fingers along the line where the darker suntanned skin was.

Gently picking up Tango from his chest, Hank settled the cat on the floor. "Later, Tang, later."

Studying the contours of Estelle's voluptuousness, Hank caressed her skin, lightly touching the softness, covering the tiny colored spots.

"Anything," Estelle's eyes blazed steadily into his.

"Estelle…"

"Essa-I've told you to call me Essa."

"Essa."

"I meant what I said, I'd do anything for you."

"Essa." Hank cooed the name softly again, running his fingers along the splash of freckles along the woman's shoulders. "Essa," he closed his eyes. "Essa," *Emma.* The thought of his deceased wife startled him as his eyes flashed open.

"What's the matter?" Estelle asked coolly, "seen a ghost?"

Drawing her in closely, Hank closed his eyes again. "You're so beautiful."

Reaching for his hand, she studied the fingertips. "What have we here?" Estelle asked. "Did you hurt yourself?"

Hank's gaze burned, his jaw twitched. His eyes lowered for a moment before he resumed stroking the woman's speckled skin.

"You've been a bad boy, haven't you, Hanky?"

"I don't like it when you call me that," he growled.

"But you have, haven't you?" Estelle's voice purred softly as she stroked the side of Hank's face. "Tell me about it, sweetheart. I'll always love you, always take care of you." She stoked his cheeks again and pushed her body even closer.

Emma always told me that—she would always take care of me. Hank closed his eyes tightly to the memory.

Clasping his hands in hers, Essa squeezed the tips of Hank's fingers and watched as blood oozed from them. "I'm here for you," Estelle watched as Hank blinked; a tear slowly wound its way from his cheek to the pillow.

"Emma." The name was barely audible.

****

E.J. Rosell studied the texted words she'd received from Hank, raised and eyebrow, then flipped the cover to her phone shut. "The man is four quarts short of an oil change."

Lifting the overweight Siamese cat from her lap, she rose from the chair and padded into the kitchen, filled a glass with water from the tap and walked back. "What in the world does he want?" Her words aimed at the mixed breed dog still lying beside the chair. "There's nothing else I can do. I sure as heck shouldn't have done anything in the first place." She reached down to let the dog lick her hand. "Sure shouldn't have, huh, Nicky." She patted him softly on the top of his furry head. "Poor boy, you're getting as old as me." Puckering her lips she bent to kiss the air between herself and the dog. "You're such a good boy."

Her fingers manipulated the little seashells and bits of wire on the end table next to her, moving them into little patterns.

"Hmm, that would make a cute pair of earrings," she picked up a small shell, and a shark's tooth, threaded a thin wire through the hole of the shell and wrapped more wire around the tooth. "Hmm." Eycing her creation curiously for a moment, she placed it back on the table and rubbed her sore fingers then reached for the remote control to the television.

Leaning against the thick padding of her chair, Emma Jewel let her mind wander back to the night Hank had come to her.

Yes, she'd heard about the murders. No, it wasn't any skin off her nose if the damn Yankees were turning up dead; if drugs were involved, then good riddance. And that was the rumor; the three murdered people were part of a drug ring.

Of course, they would be from out of town. Northerners were always pushing their way of life on the one time little fishing town.

Still, nothing had been confirmed. No names had been revealed and the newspaper offered little information other than what she'd learned from friends in the community.

E.J. nodded as she recalled Hank repeating the gossip. They'd both agreed that drug dealers were bad news and then of course, it was broad consensus that Northerners were always bringing changes and most of them were not for the good.

Hank told her too, that one of the murderers was after him.

What were his words? She searched her memory. "One of them is after me. Just because I happened to know the Englishman, he thinks I must be involved in some way. I've been getting phone calls, Emma Jewel. You have to help me, hide me please."

"He acted so scared, like he needed me. Like his life depended on me." Emma Jewel toyed again with the shells on the side table. Mildred the cat jumped into her lap and E.J. stroked it softly as she continued talking to herself.

"That's what he said, and I believed it. He sure must have thought I was stupid—guess I was. Yep, I sure was stupid to believe him." She sighed, "There always was something about him that wasn't right. I tried to tell Emma, but *no,* my little girl had to have *him—and* I felt obligated to her to help her husband. Wasn't he the love of my dear Emma's life?"

Nicky groaned lazily as he shifted his weight and stretched out his legs on the floor next to E.J.

"You always knew there was something squirrelly about him, didn't you boy?" Emma Jewel leaned forward to look at the old dog. "Uh huh, always something squirrelly. You were always leaving the room when he came over here with Emma—he was always so proper, never a hair out of place. A real fancy man from the uppity side of the Butler family—

used to having things a bit easier than my Emma ever had them.

She was always such a tomboy. Just what in the world did my little girl see in that man? What did he want with my baby, my only daughter?"

I wish I'd never seen him, never met him. I wish my Emma had never met him either.

All of his begging for help, crying about someone wanting to hurt him had persuaded her and she met him in the woods near her home. They drove to her place north of Topsail Island—to the cottage nestled in the woods near Pamilco Sound between Beaufort and Havelock. She'd bought the house several years earlier as a get away from the ever increasing summer crowds. It took about an hour and a half to drive there from Topsail.

As she and Hank drove the lonely road there, Hank endeavored, a few times, to explain about the people, the ones who'd been killed, and what he did or didn't know about them. It all sounded so innocent, so confusing. He shook his head in disgust about drugs and about the people who sold and used them.

At that moment E.J. felt sympathy for him, he looked scared and alone. And she wanted to believe in him, to trust him.

The little brown house with the green shutters stood hidden somewhat from view along a winding creek. Palmetto bushes grew thickly about the exterior of the house, a magnolia stood to the rear, near where E.J. had planted flowers long ago. Pine trees sprinkled the yard along with a few scrub oaks.

She'd bought the get away for the solitude and it served that purpose well, being three miles from the nearest neighbor. It was a lovely little retreat, with all the greenery about and the thick marsh grasses, egrets, osprey and otters. There was always a critter or two hanging around. Emma Jewel had spent hours watching them. And days upon days enjoying the peace and quiet when she and her daughter would visit for extended periods of time.

Now Hank was there in her sacred place.

The thought sent shivers through her body. Nine months had passed since she'd seen him last. She'd learned a lot in those nine months. She supposed that Hank was aware that she knew the truth. That thought scared her too.

For a long time she didn't hear anything from him and hoped he was gone, that he'd gotten tired of using the generator to supply electricity. He never had been good with gadgets or appliances. But in the last several weeks she'd gotten texts from him, she'd answered only a couple.

"What to do." Emma Jewel leveled a heavy sigh through her nostrils. "For nine months I've been wondering if I should tell the cops. Thought I wouldn't have to. Thought that squirrelly weasel had enough sense to leave my house and me alone. Now I'm an accessory. *What more of a debt do I owe Emma?* she thought as she ran her fingers over the old flip-style phone.

"What in the world does he want?" she spat angrily as Mildred's purr deepened. "I just want to know what in the hell that bag of worms wants?"

Chapter Five

Carrie balanced the tray on her arm and lifted it level with her shoulder. She looked out to the far corner of the dining room where the family sat facing the large glass windows over looking the water.

She did have to admit that The Upper Deck offered a fantastic view of the Intracoastal Waterway and the swing bridge.

As she made her way to the customers, her eyes followed the glide of a sloop as it veered right to stop and wait for the bridge to open. There were two other boats waiting in line for the bridge, a trawler and a powerboat.

Carrie always loved watching the boats go through the bridge and watching the old steel structure turn to allow passage.

Her lips curled a bit at the corners. Losing her concentration, a hip slammed into a seated patron, Carrie held the tray slightly, glanced at the man seated at the table and nodded, "So sorry, sir."

"No problem, honey. Glad you didn't dump all that food on me and my wife," he drawled in a slow southern accent and reached a hand to touch the woman's next to him. She smiled too, "Sweetie, you're doing just fine, but I'd love it if you could bring me another sweet tea."

"Yes ma'am," Carrie smiled back to the couple and continued toward the corner table. *I cannot afford to lose this job,* she thought as she concentrated on not spilling the contents of her tray. The idea of unemployment frightened her as she fought the urge to look once again at the picturesque scene through the windows.

Greeting the table with a smile, Carrie settled the dinners and asked if there was anything else she could get for anyone.

"Everything looks delicious," a man from the table nodded. "We're fine, thank you."

This was her third evening working at the fancy The Upper Deck restaurant. So far things had moved along easily—no problems, no run-ins with customers, no disasters. *Now, if things will just continue this way. I could stay her for a while, maybe even get to like it,* she thought.

Leaning against a kitchen workstation, Carrie studied the cooks rushing to prepare foods, earnestly trying to arrange the dishes in a pleasing appearance as possible.

There's only so much you can do with a dead fish, Carrie held back a laugh.

"You're up," a voice called to her.

Setting three large plates on her tray, Carrie slipped through the swinging door of the kitchen into the dining room and stepped across the wooden floor to another table of evening diners.

She settled their plates in front of them, grinned and asked the usual. All smiled in return, nodded and turned their attention to their meals.

I guess when people have food in front of them, they're less likely to be grouchy. Carrie thought of the inconsiderate customers who had frequented Grocery World. *At least I don't have to put up with such rude and arrogant people here.*

Out of the blue she heard snapping fingers and a deep monotone voice calling, "Lady, lady."

Carrie turned; a man's arm was raised above his head as he snapped his fingers.

"Yes, you. *You*," The man's voice grew louder, more short and more authoritative. "Hey, now."

Making her way toward the man seated at a table near the center of the dining room, Carrie stepped lightly but quickly with her tray by her side. "Yes sir," she stood next to the man, "May I help you?"

"We ordered clam chowder not this bowl of white garbage."

I guess the honeymoon's over; Carrie caught her breath for a moment. Holding the smile steadily on her face, she apologized and asked the man if she could replace the soup with another item from the menu.

"Do you have any soup that doesn't come from a can?"

"Our chef does make a wonderful collard soup."

"What the hell is that?" the man asked sharply.

"It's a very popular southern dish…"

61

"Sounds ghastly." He pushed the bowl of soup farther away and grunted, "And this stuff," his fingered dabbed at the shrimp and grits on a neighboring plate. "What the hell is this?"

"Sir, the lady did order shrimp and grits." Carrie thumbed through her order pad.

"I don't care if she ordered it or not. It tastes like shit and I'm not paying for crap like this. You people down here can't cook worth a damn and you certainly don't know how to make clam chowder."

*Well sir, You're not in New England and we have our own way of cooking. If you don't like it, please get your sorry ass back up north, s*he thought. A smile, plastered on her face, Carrie listened to the customer complain. She nodded and then said she would talk to the manager.

Blythe glided to the table, schmoozed an apology, steak dinners all around with everything on the house.

When the circumstances called for it, Carrie noticed, Blythe sure did know how to kiss butt.

****

"It's a damn infestation, I tell you. Just a damn infestation. Like cockroaches, if they're in one room, they're in all the rooms." Pulling her fingers through her hair, Carrie plopped down on the divan in her living room.

She unbuttoned the buttons of her white shirt and untied the string from the black apron about her waist.

Bella and Joey, both looked longingly up at her from the floor.

"I'm sorry, y'all, but I think I may have gone from the frying pan into the fire." Patting the sofa, she beckoned the dogs to join her.

Both jumped up, sat on either side of her, continuing the longing looks.

"What is it? You act like you want something." Carrie looked around the room, stretched her neck to view the kitchen where the dog bowls were kept. Everything looked as it should. There appeared to be plenty of water as well as a substantial amount of food.

"Okay, you thought this job would be less stressful- that and I would come home cheerful and slather you with love and affection." Sighing heavily, Carrie buried her face in her hands. "I'm sorry, I was hoping for that too. But I don't think there is any shortage of rude and ignorant people. I must remember that." She tapped the side of her head. "Like Don always said, 'it's up to me to learn to deal with situations.' And since I am in a profession—and I say that word lightly—I have to learn not to take criticism so harshly. You'd think I'd have learned that at this stage of my life."

Carrie moaned softly and raised the palms of her hands to her eyes, "Oh Lord, I need help with this." The words fell sincerely from her lips and she reached a hand to caress the little Chihuahuas sitting next to her. "I really need some help with this one, puppies. Or I'll never—let's see, in the last year, I've been dumped by a man who later threatened to kill me, found a dead body, fell head over heels for another man who, without *real* explanation, simply got up and left, and I've been fired."

Peering deeply into Joey's brown eyes she asked, "Now what else could go wrong?"

Joey wagged his tail and moved his snout closer to Carrie's face; his pink tongue licked her cheek.

"Oh, thank you Joey, you're always so attentive. At least I know you love me—and you too Bella." She reached to pet the smaller dog.

Carrie reached for the vaporizer in the pocket of her apron; she examined it to make sure there was plenty of liquid still inside.

Drawing it to her lips she sucked gently on the tip, filling her lungs with the soothing steam.

"At least I don't smell like a cigarette all the time," she patted the dogs again. "But Don said he never could smell the tobacco on me…probably just being nice."

She released a cloud of orange scented vapor into the atmosphere; the dogs' ears perked.

"No, it's not food. You can't eat it." Carrie grinned to herself and chuckled, "I guess I could really get you two going if I got steak scented vapor."

Closing her eyes for a moment, Carrie pictured Don, his smile, his physique. She sighed once, then again more lightly, closing her eyes, she fell asleep.

CHAPTER SIX

The months he spent in the Topsail area searching for Hank had proved a waste of time. Even with the help of surrounding county law enforcement, no leads had been produced. It was as if Hank had vanished into thin air.

So why did I hang around so long? Why did I keep telling myself the bastard was around there? Don Belkin raised a hand to his thick blond hair and scratched his scalp. "I need a bath." He rubbed his stubbly chin. "I still think somebody knows something, I'm sure of it. Those people stick together, even if they don't like one another."

"Humph, just like clams, they all were eager to talk about the dead *Yankees,* but they ain't going to squeal on a Butler. I knew that after the first week." *So, why did I stick around so long? Carrie, that's why. If I want to be honest with myself, I could have left in January.*

Even if the locals weren't talking, Don had the feeling that part of what they were saying was true—no, they didn't know where Hank was. And no, they weren't hiding him—and they had no idea where he may have gone. But they knew something more, at least, that's what he felt in his gut.

It was in the cadence, the hesitation, folding of arms when he approached or asked questions—something was missing or too much was being said—someone or all of them were not being forthcoming. And if they weren't, then he'd have to find the answers elsewhere.

Searching his memory, the times he and Hank had gone fishing, Don tried to recall conversation that would lend themselves to clues, to anything that would suggest a place where Hank would feel safe. Nothing came to mind. But then, one early spring evening as he and Carrie walked along the beach, he, half listening as she chatted vivaciously about the visit with her son, Jeff and their journey to Clawson's Restaurant in Beaufort, it came to him.

Before all the murders, Don had been to Beaufort a few times. He liked it fine—another nice quiet place with lots of nautical ambiance.

Last fall officials in the area had been sent an alert to keep a lookout for Hank—nothing ever came of that.

In his mind's eye, the image of he and Hank relaxing against the transom of Hank's boat, cleaning the reels after a day on the Gulf Stream, appeared. "Emma and I went to a place near the Outer Banks a few times—real peaceful, a cozy place between New

Bern and Beaufort. We used to go there a lot, to get away from the summer crowd."

"Yes, Hank had said that, *Beaufort*." He hesitated for a moment, *But everybody goes to the Outer Banks. The fishing there is the best.* "No more excuses," he said aloud. "I need to check that out."

It was that image, that memory that prompted him, no, compelled Don to begin a search north of Topsail, near the Beaufort area.

The next week he said good-bye to Carrie. Did he love her? He was sure of it.

That same week he enrolled his son, Phil, in a military academy. "I won't apologize for this," he'd explained stoically, "There's evil in the world, but evil doesn't think it's evil. It feels justified in its actions." He pulled Phil in for a quick hug and handshake, "I do love you, son. But I have to do this."

Choosing between right and wrong was not easy. Knowing what was right or wrong was even harder.

****

Moving the footrest aside, Don rose from the overstuffed chair where he's spent the night. His head ached, so did his left upper thigh.

He shook his head, thought back to the previous evening and the three sisters he'd met at Joyce's Bar and Lounge, Veda, Vela and Vera. "Oh hell," he grimaced, rubbing his head. "Did I really do this?"

His stomach growled, a belch found its way to his throat and he tasted the remnants of a too greasy chicken fried steak dinner from a local eatery. He remembered going back to Joyce's after the meal and before finding a hotel room. All he was expecting was a cold beer and a chance to kick himself in the butt for coming all the way there based on a *feeling*. Now, the Dodge was broken down and he was stuck.

The older sister had sat perched on a bar stool, sipping a mixed drink; he settled himself a few stools down from her. Initially she ignored him, but within a few minutes she was leaning his way, her head wobbling as she steadied herself against the bar. "Hi, I'm Vera," she grinned broadly as she caught his eye.

Don politely nodded, "Don," he spoke his name confidently, reached to shake her hand and smiled back.

It was the wrong thing to do—Vera mistook his gesture as a sign that he was interested. Gathering her purse, drink and napkin, she moved to sit next to him.

Slurring rambling words, Vera dabbed at falling tendrils of teased hair held by a pink banana clip. She ran a finger to the corners of her lips and began talking about riding horses and picking fresh fruit from trees when she was a child.

Don recognized her from the photo on the wall he'd seen earlier, he smiled as she spoke, endeavoring to be polite, but not too polite.

"Daddy owned over fifty acres and then he sold it to that damn developer," The woman reeled in her seat, Don reached a hand to steady her.

"But I guess it's okay, I got one of them new-built houses in the place—*Cedar Way on the Green*. What a stupid name." She smiled for a moment, "but they did put a freaking golf course out there." She sighed heavily and raised the glass to her lips. "But—oh—I miss the farm so much. It was so--" she lifted her head quickly and dabbed at the spittle on her lip. "Sorry 'bout that—but things *change*, don't they?" Her large brown eyes begged the question. "*Change*, humph-- and then Hank left me too." Breaking into sobs, she rambled on about the man named Hank, the past and how changes had wrecked her life.

Again Don tried to comfort the woman, allowing her to lean against him, he patted her shoulder.

"But, you just don't understand," Vera's head wobbled from side to side as her eyes searched Don's for sympathy. "He really understood me—correction, he really understands me. He'll be back, I know it, he loves me." Vera looked pleadingly into Don's eyes. "Maybe I'm wrong—you do too, don't you? You understand me—huh ?" She cooed, stroking his thigh.

Pushing her face toward his, she repeated, "huh?" Vera's breath reeked of bourbon; Don pulled back.

"What is it, sweetie? Ain't I pretty enough?"

Lowering his eyes, Don nodded his head, "You're very pretty, it's just--"

"Hey, I've been with men—*real men*—better than you, buddy boy. Men with a lot of money who know how to treat me right." She jerked away from his touch.

"I'm sorry; I didn't mean to insult you."

"Hank'll beat the crap outta you!" Vera bellowed as she stood, wobbling and holding on to the side of the bar.

"Hank?"

"Yeah, Hank Jordan." Finding her footing, Vera inched away from the stool and bar.

Don caught her by the arm as her body slid to the floor.

"She lives down Hummingbird Circle, a little over a mile from here." The bartender tapped the counter.

Don reached into his pants pocket and pulled out a twenty. "You know her?"

"Only from here. When she gets like this, whoever she's with ends up taking her home or one of her sisters does." She nodded toward a table near the restrooms. "That's them over there."

Holding Vera closely, Don moved her to a booth, settling her there as comfortably as allowed by the wooden structure, then walked to the table where the sisters sat. "Your sister," he motioned toward Vera, "is passed out—just wanted to let you know." He turned to leave.

"Hey, don't go, good looking. Sit down and chat a bit."

Don eased himself into the chair nearest the woman with short black hair; a bright red bow sat starkly in the center of her hairdo. "What about your sister, Vera?"

The other sister pulled her chair closer to Don's and giggled, "I don't think she's going anywhere right now." She turned back to her sister, "Do you, Veda?"

Looking from one woman to the other, Don forced a grin; he felt uncomfortable and straightened himself in the seat. "So, your sister is named Vera and you are Veda...and you?" he nodded to the thinnest of the women.

"I'm Vela. We're Veda, Vela and Vera." Vela swished her shoulder length hair aside to reveal a butterfly tattoo. "We're the 'V' girls. At least that's what everybody calls us." Vela giggled again.

"I can see why." Relaxing in his chair, Don motioned for the waitress to bring him a beer. "I bet your momma is Victoria and your daddy is Victor."

"Close," Veda replied. "Daddy is Virgil and Momma is Viola." She took another sip from the glass in front of her, licked her lips and released a long soft breath of air. "You know, Vera is the oldest."

"By far," added Vela. "She's way older than we are."

"Twins?" Don queried.

Laughter spilled into the table space, "Well—yes, but we try to avoid looking like it. Can't you tell. I've got black hair and she's got that cat puke red hair." Vela's raspy voice rang out almost too loudly.

Veda turned sharply to her sister and scowled. "It's auburn-dark auburn."

"It's still red—cat puke red."

"It's not, it's what's in. All the people in Hollywood are dying their hair red. It's the new blonde."

"Crap, if all the people in Hollywood were jumping off cliffs—"

"Shut-up," Vela scowled at Don. "Our cousin has *real* red hair. Just as natural as all get out."

"Had, she *had* red hair, that pretty color until a couple of weeks ago."

"Oh yeah, I forgot. She went and dyed it some dishwater color-calls it medium blonde or something like that."

"Why in the hell she did that, beats me. But it's pretty and she's tall too, with freckles all over the place." Veda smirked. "She's the one who broke poor Vera's heart."

"We was all sitting here like usual a few weeks back—Hank was with us and that bitch walks in, sauntering and swinging those hips of hers."

"And you'd of thought angels from heaven had come through the door, 'cause Hank near 'bout fell outta his seat." Veda sucked her teeth and tugged at a hoop earring.

"That was the end of Vera and Hank. I mean he dropped her like a sack of cement."

"It took a few day, it wasn't right then," Veda chided.

Vela rolled her eyes, "Was too, by the next day."

"Damn you, you think you always know everything."

Don folded his arms across his chest and watched the two women bicker back and forth. Barely listening, he turned to check on Vera. She was still propped against the back of the booth.

He imagined that in a couple of hours Veda and Vela would be in the same condition. Rising from the table he walked to the bar and asked the bartender to repeat Vera's address, then paid for another round of drinks for the twins.

"Oh thank you," Veda paused, speaking as she reached for the glass of bourbon and Coke.

"He's such a gentleman," Vela added. "Oh my goodness, I just never can get over some of these men." She looked intently at her sister. "I mean, he's so much like that Hank guy."

"I know, I know, he's just like him." Veda inched her face close to Don's. "I bet you open doors and pull out chairs too, don't you?"

"And paying for stuff," Vela added." You ain't rich are you?" Lifting her chin, she grinned boldly.

Still standing, Don shook his head no, "How about your friend Hank? Is he?"

The women shrugged and sipped from their glasses.

"Is Hank from around here?" he asked casually.

Dabbing a finger into the corner of her eye, Vela examined the little glob of mascara at the tip, "I don't know much about him, but he was nice and he always bought drinks for us."

"But we girls, you know, we are sisters and when one of us gets our sights set on a man, it's hands off for the others." Veda tittered, "And Vera was all over that man, like white on rice. She had—"

"What do you mean, she *had,* Vela sneered, "she *has* it bad for that bald headed man."

"Baldheaded?" Don leaned into the conversation.

"Yep, bald as a cue ball, and chubby. Really, I don't see what she sees in him."

"He ain't chubby," Vela guffawed, "that man's fat."

Shrugging, Veda took another gulp from the bourbon and coke, rattled the ice around and held it high in the air, "I need another one over here."

"He ain't been around for a few weeks. And I don't know what Vera saw in him anyway. He was sort of snooty—uppity, if you ask me. I just think he wanted to get in her pants."

"I thought you said he was a real gentleman?" Don's brow creased; he rubbed the stubble of his chin.

"Yeah, he was. But then it just seemed the gentleman stuff was for show."

Veda swirled the remains of her mixed drink in the tumbler. "He was all smooth and giving her compliments all the time. I kept telling her that he'd dump her once she gave in, but no, no, no. Not my sister, Vera, she thought they were in love and she went to bed with that jerk."

"I told her she needed to get him to spend some money on her before she did that," Vela looked over her glass to Don and winked.

"And it wasn't long after that, he was done with her."

"Umm," Don shrugged and sipped from his beer before setting it on the table. "I think I'll give your sister a ride to her house, while you two ladies enjoy yourselves here. I hate to see her sprawled out like that." Don shifted his eyes from Vera back to the sisters.

The twins giggled loudly.

"Guess we'll help you, don't want our sister taken advantage of while she's in such a compromising position. But I promise, we won't stay long." Vela winked again.

As he drove to Vera's, Don thought of Hank's M.O. Wasn't that what Hank was known for, being a gentleman? Being charming and then once he got a girl into the sack, dumping her?

It sounded very much like Hank, but bald and fat? That wasn't like him at all. Hank's vanity would never allow him to be anything other than perfect. He'd always taken pride in his physique, his thick salt and pepper hair and his charm. To alter his slim and preppy appearance, would certainly drive the man nuts.

"Well, there you go," Don whispered to himself, "the guy is nuts."

Don raised his fingers to the stubble that had been growing for the last few days; he brushed his hand over his own thick blond hair. *Wonder what else Hank had done to disguise his appearance?*

He looked to Vera, still silent in the passenger seat of his car. He wondered what Hank would want with a girl like her. It was as if she and her sisters were a mixture of a 1950s Marilyn Monroe and present day Lady Gaga—ostentatious, pretentious and self-absorbed. These were certainly not Hank's type of women. He seemed to go for the earthier women—uncomplicated—real.

He thought for a moment of Carrie. *She's about as real as they come,* a faint smile moved his lips to curl slightly.

"I'll hang around until Vera wakes up." He strode to the overstuffed chair after depositing her on the bed. Stretching his legs, his feet found the footrest. He yawned as Vela and Veda went on and on about one thing or another. He'd blocked their noise out and succumbed to much needed sleep.

He heard the whispered words between the two women, "He's passed out too," before hearing the door close as they left. He drifted into sleep but it was short-lived as Vera burst from the bedroom. Her light brown hair, half up in some sort of bun, fell heavily over her eyes. "I remember you." She moved stealthily towards him. "Ooh woo, you were so nice."

She leaned next to the chair, walked her fingers down his arm and toward his jeans, determined to unzip them.

Don shook his head and chuckled, trying to make light of her advances. But Vera was resolute; she struggled, her arms flailing about.

He was surprised by the woman's strength; she had to be nearly as tall as him and she was by no means thin. He was lucky the other sisters had left; surely he couldn't have fought off all three. He chuckled again at the thought.

The tousling became a sort of game to Vera, as she reached for his crotch and then for his shirt, over and over again, giggling with each attempt.

When she grabbed his thigh, he yelled in pain. The reaction softened her advances as she apologized for hurting him.

He thought the tug of war was over, but then she grabbed at her own blouse, tearing it open, revealing a sports bra overflowing with soft flesh. For a split second, Don considered giving in, but only for a split second. The wrestling began again, she pushed him to the couch and just when he thought he could resist no more, Vera stopped.

"The bastard dumped me," she blubbered. "And he never even gave me a reason why, just took up with that damn cousin of mine." Vera swept the loose hair from the front of her face. "I need a drink."

Don searched the counter and found bottles of vodka, bourbon and gin lined next to the toaster. He half-filled a tumbler with Coke and splashed bourbon into it.

"Double that would you," Vera cooed from the living room. "Geez, he was always so nice, so proper, treated me like he thought the world of me. But then, that damn cat, he paid more attention to it than me."

Yes, it sounded like much more than a coincidence. This man sounded a lot like Hank Butler.

"And that freaking cousin of mine, she's a witch." Taking a gulp from the drink, Vera tried to re-button her blouse, the expression on her face suggesting that she had no clue as to how it became unbuttoned. "My damn cousin, Estelle." She gazed angrily at Don, "She's done this crap to me my whole life—stealing my boyfriends."

Chapter Seven

After stuffing the last crumbs of a hush puppy into her mouth, Carrie tied the strings of an apron around her waist, then peered into the dining room of The Upper Deck. Already six tables had been seated and it was only five-thirty. It was going to be another busy evening.

"I don't want that damn thing around your neck, Carrie. I've told you before and if I have to tell you again, you'll be looking for another way to pay your bills." Blythe barked, sweeping in through the kitchen doors.

Quickly, Carrie unsnapped the cord around her neck and placed the e-cig in her pocket. "I always remove it before—"

"Sam! The next time I have a complaint about the seared tuna, you're out too. Got that?" Standing with her hands on her hips, Blythe scanned the kitchen for a moment then walked slowly about eyeing the workstations. "There are plenty of others who would just love to have your jobs, so keep on your toes." She brushed by the prep cook and another waitress then turned and burst through the swinging doors.

"Geez," Carrie muttered, "I bet flies are always landing on her."

"You better be careful, I'm pretty sure she has eyes and ears in the back of her head…she's probably not even from this planet." Sammy chuckled.

"How do you put up with her?" Carrie asked. "She is so demeaning."

"How did you put up with working at Grocery World for three years? I know you had to put up with all kinds of nasty people there. Here it's just every once in a while."

"Yeah, they're probably afraid you'll put something in their food if they aren't nice." Carrie laughed.

"No, there are no complaints because of the fantastic chef, and that seared tuna her majesty mentioned was not cooked by me. It was Royce, the prep cook filled in for me yesterday." Sammy brought the blade of a knife across a flounder, severing the head. "Besides, I have weapons of my own."

"Really?"

"Look, I've been here for three and a half years. It took me awhile, but I listened and found out a lot of things." Sammy reached for a skillet and turned the flame of the gas range on. "Oh, I'm on my toes, but I'm very fortunate. There have been lots of compliments about my food preparation; I even had a couple of write-ups in some local magazines and papers. If she loses me, and I go somewhere else…well, let's just say I have a little bit of leverage."

"Must be nice," Carrie grinned. "But Sally got canned a couple of days ago for spilling someone's drink. We waitresses have no leverage at all and I'm so nervous around Blythe—I'm afraid I'll screw up every time she gets near me."

"Tonight after you get off work, go over to Gerard's Pub. You might see something there that will diminish *Massa* Blythe." Sammy's light brown fingers continued rubbing spices into the fish before him.

Carrie raised an eyebrow, "Really? So that's where she hangs out."

"On Wednesday nights—karaoke night." Turning his attention to the tall woman entering through the back door, Sammy added, "The boss lady really puts on a show." He smiled and nodded to the woman.

"I'll be there!" Carrie studied her too as she stepped in front of the time clock. "Hi, I'm Carrie."

The woman smiled as she clutched her long hair and wound it into a bun. "Hi y'all, Blythe just hired me yesterday, so I'm a little nervous."

"It's not bad, you'll make good tips and most of the customers are easy going—some tourists can be a pain, but that's rare."

"I'm used to that sort of thing, I can handle folks like that." Her mouth opened in a broad smile that lit up her face; her blue eyes sparkled wildly.

Sammy eyed her and watched as she pinned back the stray hairs about her face.

Carrie always envied tall women. It didn't seem fair to be so willowy and able to eat anything you wanted. She watched as the new waitress straightened her skirt and smoothed her blouse. *My, she sure is freckly,* she thought, *she is striking.* "What's your name?"

Turning, the woman reached into her pocket retrieving a nametag. "Essa," a long slim finger underlined the letters. She reached her hand to shake Carrie's, "I might like to go to that place too, how about I tag along tonight after work."

****

"There she is," Carrie leaned in and cupped her hand to whisper into Essa's ear. "Sure is letting loose."

"Looks like she's having fun."

Carrie and Essa sipped their drinks, watching their boss toss back a mai tai, the paper umbrella tumbled to the floor.

"Eww," Carrie grimaced as she watched Blythe wrap an arm around the man sitting next to her and run her tongue into the folds of his ear.

"Geez, did you see that? She stuck her tongue in that man's ear and I know good and well he's growing a haystack in it. Even from here I can see the hair." Carrie shook her head, "And she's got the nerve to be snooty to *me*."

Leaning forward, Essa studied her employer, her lips curled into a faint smile. "Humph, well—she ain't shy."

Carrie sipped loudly on her straw, "They put more ice in here than anything," she scoffed. "I'm getting another Pepsi. Want another drink?" Carrie's glance grazed Essa's empty tumbler.

Reaching into her purse, Essa handed Carrie a ten-dollar bill. "My treat, you get the next one, just make mine another bourbon and Coke."

"Bourbon and Coke, got it."

It wasn't difficult for Essa to notice Carrie's look of skepticism. She edged her eyes upward, settling a closed hand under her chin. "I can handle the hard stuff, sweetie. I don't need you looking down your nose at me. '

"I wasn't, I—"

"I saw the look, sweetie." Essa slid her eyes toward the crowd of people. "I could drink both you and ol' Blythe under the table."

Carrie eyed her new friend curiously; initially she'd believed they might form a friendship, but now she wasn't sure. She forced a shallow laugh, turned and began making her way to the bar, trying to keep out of Blythe's view.

Pushing slowly through the horde of people, Carrie finally found the opposite side of the bar; settling her elbows there, she studied the two bartenders busily trying to keep up with the requests for mixed drinks and beer.

She perused the crowd; all were engaged in conversation, nearly all swayed and bounced to the rhythm of the band's music. Men had their arms around women and those not paired into couples were laughing and drinking along with everyone else. Carrie felt out of place. The bar scene had never been part of her life. Her gaze drifted to Blythe, still rolling her shoulders and swaying her hips to the beat of the music. Her blouse was completely unbuttoned, revealing her dark brassiere, and as her head bobbed back and forth, she withdrew her arms, letting it fall to the floor.

Raucous laughter echoed from the bar where Blythe stood.

"Shake 'em, momma!" a singular voice rang out.

"Oh my gosh! Is she really taking off her clothes?" Carrie's mouth fell open. "I can't believe she'd do such a thing."

"She'll be on stage next howling into the mike, trying to sing," a warm voice fell upon Carrie's ear. She turned to face soft gray eyes looking directly into her own.

"The table right there, where that man and woman are seated—they're her business partners from The Upper Deck," the man spoke as he leaned in closely.

Carrie pushed back against the crowd of people to make room between her and the man, but she was met with a collective push back. "Sorry," she mouthed, as her face inched closer to his.

"No worries, my dear." He paused for a moment and lifted a bottle of water to his lips. "I'm Lev."

"Carrie, my name's Carrie." She grinned, and then scowled. The loud music and voices overwhelmed her for a moment. She tiptoed to see if she could catch a glimpse of Essa.

Yes, Essa was still at their table, but a husky bald man with a goatee had sat down across from her. Adjusting his sunglasses, he leaned in closer.

Wonder who that is? They seem to be rapt in deep conversation. Carrie drew her lips into a crooked smirk. Her eyes drifted then to Blythe, now on stage.

"Oh baby, baby. Let me…"

The off key words stung Carrie's ears.

"I'll be so good to you…"Shaking her aging body about; Blythe stepped out of her tight mini skirt. Black panties and bra were all that was left of her attire.

Sammy was right. There is no reason to feel intimidated by the boss lady. "What a fool," Carrie said aloud.

"You've got that right." Lev moved closer to speak again.

Carrie studied his casual dress and shaggy hair.

"She makes such an ass of herself and then acts like she's queen bee." He smirked and reached for her hand, "Come outside, I want to talk with you."

Carrie jerked her hand away, "I don't know you."

"Sorry, I just wanted to talk to you without having to yell."

"What about?"

"We have a mutual friend."

Carrie's curiosity allowed her to follow the man as he found her hand again and led her through the crowd. Pushing open the heavy door, a blast of warm humid air burst upon the pair.

Compared to the stuffy air-conditioned room, the night air felt refreshing; Carrie felt as if she'd been freed. She'd never liked crowds.

"So I take it, you don't like Miss Blythe Goodfellow." Lev leaned against one of the small outdoor tables.

"I work for her."

"Well, that explains it," he chuckled. "I can imagine she's not very easy to work for."

"That's an understatement. She's very bossy and very demeaning. She treats the help as if she owns them."

"In a way, she does." Pressing the water bottle to his lips, Lev nodded. The corners of his eyes gathered in tiny folds belying a smile.

Carrie slipped into the stool behind her, then immediately rose; her hand reached to the seat of her jeans.

"Can't decide if you want to stay or leave, huh? I won't bite. I'm a nice guy."

"No, I sat in something."

"Turn around," Lev touched a finger to her shoulder and pushed. "Looks like you wet your pants."

"Oh no." She ran a hand over the wet spot.

"It's not that bad, you can hardly tell it." He paused for a moment and grinned, "In fact, it looks pretty good."

Carrie flicked an upward glance and crossed her arms, *Geez, this guy is making a pass-can't believe it-but then, this is a bar.* "Look, I've got to get back in, I forgot to get my friend's bourbon and Coke and I don't have a drink either."

"But you're not really a drinker, are you?"

Her head cocked to the side, *how did he know?* "I need to go back in," she stammered.

"I'm sorry, I'm just playing with you—don't be so serious."

Her eyes blinking rapidly, Carrie steeped back.

"I've been watching you—no that sounds like I'm a stalker." Lev's face reddened slightly. "Sometimes I come on too strong—just my way of kidding around. I meant to say that I noticed you when you came in and sort of have been looking at you and your friend." He shrugged. "She swallowed her drink fast and has been looking all about the room checking everybody out—and you—you nursed whatever you've been drinking for the last thirty minutes. You and your friend seem like very different women, that's all I meant."

"My, but aren't you observant?" Carried pulled her lips in tightly.

"It pays to be observant, you never know what you'll learn about people."

Carrie rubbed a hand down her pants leg and moved toward the door, "I've got to go," she said, avoiding his gaze.

Stepping back, Lev let her pass.

"I really need to get that drink for my friend." She smiled and grasped the door handle.

Reaching above her, he held the door open and they both walked back into the throng of music and white noise.

"Took you long enough," Essa smirked as Carrie settled the bourbon and Coke in front of her. "I've been fighting off the men since you left."

"Yes, I noticed a man sitting with you. Looked like you were in deep conversation—find a boyfriend already?" she teased.

"Pfft, just another loser trying to get lucky."

She is pretty, Carrie thought. *I can see where men probably fall at her feet. And she's got that aura of confidence about her; a man would have to be very bold to approach Essa.* "I bet you *do* have to fight off the men." Settling herself in the chair, Carrie slid an envious glance to meet her new friend's eyes.

"Men...humph. They always want something."

Carrie lifted her glass of cola, "I'll drink to that."

Chapter Eight

This was the third time in one week Lev had come to The Upper Deck. So far, Carrie had done well avoiding him. But it was only three o'clock and she would be the only waitress there until four. She'd have to wait on him.

She eyed him curiously as he sat facing one of the large windows, his hands tucked neatly into his lap. When she'd greeted him and brought the menu, he'd said very little. And then when she came back to bring his water and ask for his order, he'd given it politely, adding only that he'd like to talk with her again.

I wish he'd just go away and leave me alone. Carrie thought as she studied Lev from the kitchen door.

"I think I have a stalker," she said, watching Sammy perform the finishing touches on the meal.

"Your order will be up in a few," he stated matter of factly. "And what makes you think he's a stalker? He might just like you."

Carrie shrugged, "Maybe I am being too paranoid."

"No, not you." Sammy teased as he placed a sprig of parsley on the plate and then walked quickly to peer out the door at the customer. "He's nothing special—got a nice bod, but who am I to judge. You're a big girl. But then again, maybe he is a stalker."

"Thanks." Carrie sneered and turned her attention back to Lev, inching the kitchen door open a bit more to study him again.

His broad shoulders tugged against the plain red tee shirt he wore. The dark blue jeans were tight as well.

She sighed, *maybe I am overreacting, but having him follow me is kind of creepy.* Biting her lip, Carrie noticed the chain about his neck; the pendant hidden beneath his shirt.

Still holding the kitchen door ajar, Carrie wondered if his dark shaggy hair was due to missing too many haircuts or if it was simply his style; she let the door swing shut, crossed her arms across her chest and waited for Lev's order.

"I thought you told me you had a boyfriend." Sammy snickered. "You've been checking that dude out since you brought back his order--hanging there with your nose sticking out the door—you better be careful, if Blythe walks in, you're toast. You know she doesn't like anybody standing around." Nodding toward a stack of cloth napkins he continued. "Wrap some silverware."

Shrugging, Carrie walked to the station and grabbed a knife, fork and spoon and began wrapping them. "I do have a boyfriend—sorta. And Lev—I met him the other night at Gerard's." She turned on her heels and stepped to the counter watching as Sammy ladled shrimp onto the entrée.

"Oh, he's got a name?" Sammy teased, "Lev, huh?" He slid the hot plate onto the counter. "There you go. If *Lev* doesn't say that's the best shrimp scampi he's ever eaten, there's something wrong with him."

Carrie grinned. "He'll like it." She grabbed a basket of hush puppies and settled it next to the plate.

"Here you are sir, Shrimp Scampi and hush puppies." She placed the items before Lev, avoiding his gaze.

"Are you free this evening?" he asked, his gray eyes searching hers.

Her brow pinched, Carrie responded, "Look, I'm not in a place where I can welcome any other men in my life—not right now—so no thank you." Carrie hoped the curt response would discourage him.

"Do you have a boyfriend?" He drank heartily from the glass of water, emptying it.

Carrie ignored the question. "Sure are thirsty, aren't you?"

Lifting his head, Lev found Carrie's eyes this time. "Yes ma'am, I am. I've had a long day—had to chase down a thief this afternoon, who led me through sand dunes and about four of those gigantic rental houses."

"So you're a cop." Closing her eyes momentarily, Carrie shook her head. "I thought you were a creep."

"I might still be." He chuckled.

"I'm sorry—for your lousy day. Did you catch the thief?"

"Of course I did." As Lev's eyes held hers, he leaned back in his chair, dabbing a napkin at the corners of his mouth. "So what about tonight—just a drink—a Pepsi. Okay?"

Before she could answer, Carrie spied Blythe making her way towards the table.

Blythe cleared her throat as she brushed by Carrie. Turning her head sharply, she shot her a heated glance.

The color left Carrie's cheeks, anticipating a warning or some kind of embarrassing reprimand. She swallowed hard and looked regretfully at Lev.

Immediately he snapped his fingers above his head and called out, "Hey! Hey lady. You! Are you the manager?" Pushing his chair back, Lev stood, glaring at Blythe. "I've been coming here for the last two years"

Damn he's a good liar, not a twitch, doesn't skip a beat, Carrie stifled a smile as she watched Lev lie to her boss.

"I've been mostly pleased with the service and food, but today," Lev continued, "But I noticed the potholes in your parking lot—"

"Mister, there are no potholes in my parking lot." Blythe's lips pursed as she moved closer.

"*Your* parking lot? So this *is* your establishment."

Blythe nodded. "You're mistaken. There are no potholes." Sliding hooded eyes to Carrie, she pursed her lips again.

"I was asking this waitress who to speak to about the holes, my front end is destroyed. I'll be sending you a bill, if you like or maybe the town needs to light a fire under your ass." He pulled out his wallet, flipping it open to show the badge. His mouth tightened into a straight line as he squared his shoulders. "Is that okay with you?"

Carrie watched her employer flinch as, Blythe's eyes lowered for a second before returning Lev's gaze with a grin.

"I apologize Detective—?"

"Gass, the name is Gass."

"I'll be sure to have that fixed."

****

"You really told her off-put her in her place." Moving the straw to her lips, Carrie sipped the cola gently. "You saved my job—I'm impressed."

"It pays to be observant," forming a steeple with his hands, Lev lightly tapped his fingers together, "I noticed a hole at the edge of the driveway when I drove in—it was in the far corner, but nevertheless, it's a pothole." Reaching a hand to touch hers, Lev tilted his head to the side, "I'm glad you joined me tonight. I'm not so bad." He opened the menu to peruse the listings, "get whatever you like." Looking over the top, he added, "And I'm not trying to—*get involved.*"

The last words startled her, and Carrie pulled back. "My boyfriend, Don, called the other day…"

"Don's a good guy."

Again, his words startled her. As her eyes narrowed, she leaned back, folding her arms. "Really?"

"Yeah, we were friends in the Marine Corps. We've known each other for decades."

A wavering smile played on Carrie's lips. "Then why are you—I mean—if Don is your friend—you come on like…"

He shrugged, "Just wanted to see if you were…"

"If I was fooling around on him, huh?"

Lev shrugged again. "Maybe I'm just looking out for you, Carrie. Don asked me to do that."

Unconvinced, she leaned closer to peer into the man's face. "How do I know you're telling the truth?"

He pulled a cell phone from his pocket and began tapping the numbers. Lev turned the phone toward Carrie.

"Hi, call back or leave a message," Don's voice echoed from the speaker.

A broad smile covered Carrie's face; she clasped her hands to her chest. "Oh," the word fell self-consciously from her lips. Removing her hands quickly, she settled them in her lap. "That's Don, that was his voice." Nodding, she released a brief laugh, "Oh, so Don has talked to you about me."

"Well, he didn't tell me your shoe size or anything like that."

"Funny, ha-ha," Arching an eyebrow, Carrie added, "What *did* he tell you?"

"Not much at all. He just asked me to keep an eye on you."

"Am I supposed to be in peril—like some damsel in distress—and you're going to save me?"

He stared at her, drumming his fingers. "He has a job to do, Carrie. Otherwise he'd be here. For now, I am."

What's that supposed to mean? She thought, irritated that she had been left alone by a man that had promised no future, but then she wasn't sure what she wanted either. "So Don is still looking for Hank and I guess you're here to fill in—so you know all about last summer—what happened—the murders."

"Yes." Lev toyed with the nearly empty glass of water, "I'm here to fill in," He nodded to the waitress that they were ready to order. "This is a small time police department here on the island, not a lot of full time residents. But it's growing and when Don told me the city was looking for another detective, I put in my application, I've had enough of the big city—time for a change."

"He never told me anything about you. About having someone check up on me."

"Don doesn't talk a lot about himself, he's got a lot of issues…if you want to call them that."

"I know—his son—his ex, yes, he has a lot on his plate right now."

"Then there's you."

"I don't think I'm that big of a deal."

"More than you know, honey. More than you know."

She could feel the color reaching her cheeks and she lowered her head, escaping Lev's steely gaze. She felt him studying her again. It was as if he was perusing her thoughts, her actions, everything about her.

"Relax, Don's okay. He's just doing his job."

"How close is he to getting Hank?"

Lev shrugged.

"Okay, you can't tell anything, but I'm not stupid."

He shrugged again and chuckled softly.

"Thanks a lot." Carrie curled her upper lip, "I feel like I'm in some sort of spy movie."

"It's not a movie, honey." Lev's voice lowered, "The man's a killer."

The coldness with which he spoke the words sent a shiver through Carrie. Her eyes widened. For the first time, even since last fall when all the bad things started, when people were showing up dead, even afterwards when Don consoled her, now, was the first time she had truly felt fear.

Chapter Nine

"Been thinking of how you helped me out last year. Would like to repay you for all you've done. How about coming up for a few days?"

E.J. read the text aloud. "It's still here," She barked. "That dag blasted message hasn't disappeared yet."

She reflected on the length of time she'd had the old flip phone before realizing she could send and accept text messages. *I still can't figure out how to erase things—delete—that's the term used; I haven't even learned how to delete things from this damn phone.*

E.J. didn't like cell phones, but hers had become a necessity. Traveling to the Outer Banks and then down to Kure Beach and Wilmington as often as she'd been doing in the last few years had made the phone a vital part of her existence.

There always seemed to be a double-edged sword quality to all things; she enjoyed the travels, but hated the technology required. She loved meeting the people who vacationed from all over the country, but hated sitting in the hot summer sun. It seemed everything was a compromise.

Making jewelry from beach glass and seashells she found on the beach had in the beginning been a past-time hobby, but it had blossomed into something more and now selling it was even more fun. Making money for it was even more so.

Several little shops along the southeast coast were purchasing it and with the extra cash she'd been making, she'd been able to buy a newer car and visit some of her relatives that lived farther inland.

But the phone—it was so complicated—so annoying—ringing at all hours. She hadn't even figured out how to change the ringing to a buzz or some other tone. A couple of friends had cute tunes play when their phones rang, that's what E.J. wanted.

Closing the phone, she tapped her fingernails on the kitchen table, then reached for the coffee still steaming in the mug in front of her. She flipped the phone open again to re-read the message, her eyes slowly scanning the words. "Hell, what am I going to do?" She stood and walked to the kitchen sink, leaned against it and peered out the window onto the sandy expanse before her.

It was early morning, a low tide, and a calm day. A good time to do some shell hunting. The waves lapping the shore, inching in, left cloud-like froth among the scattered bits of shells.

"Damn," she spoke aloud again, only this time more vehemently. "That man's gonna be the death of me." E.J. laughed cynically, "yeah, that's right. A freaking *murderer* is going to be the *death* of me." She shook her head, continuing the conversation with herself as the dog and cat followed behind her.

"Treats, I guess you want *treats*." The sentence had started out angrily, but ended in softness as she looked into the faces of her pets. "I sure do love my babies." E.J. bent to pet Mildred and Nicky, her long time companions.

She opened a cabinet door and pulled out two bags, "A kitty treat for my pretty kitty and a doggy treat for you." She tossed each pet a tidbit.

Opening the door to the screened ocean front patio, E.J. breathed the salty air deeply into her lungs. She looked left and then right, nodding and grinning, happy that the crowds had not yet begun to amass on the beach. "By ten they'll be there though," she scoffed.

If Hank had not been in the little cottage, she would have already been there to escape the busy summer months on Topsail.

She couldn't abide the crowds, not with all the memories of peaceful summer days when the island still felt like it was her own.

But like everything else, Topsail was changing. Even her little oceanfront house had changed. Once a hot spot for the young, the Sea Gull Restaurant had lost part of the roof and some of the outdoor patio to Hurricane Fran in '96. And rather than remodel and repair, Emma Jewel renovated it for her own residence. "Yep, the times, they are a changing." She sighed softly; her eyes searching the horizon, "not a swell in sight." They gleamed, as she moved to touch the screen between her and the air. Leaning against the door she shaded her eyes from the morning sun; Emma Jewel surmised that it was probably around seven o'clock. She grabbed the floppy blue hat hanging from a nearby nail, settled a green cloth bag in the crook of her arm and made her way to the shore.

****

"That man keeps coming around and he always sits in your station. What's up?" Essa tapped a pencil on her order pad.

"Guess he's got the hots for me." Batting her eyelashes rapidly, Carrie wiggled her shoulders.

"Sammy says you already have a boyfriend, some policeman—a detective."

Carrie shot a glance to Sammy and glared angrily.

He shrugged. "Well, you do don't you and he is, isn't he?"

"I'd say we're more like good friends. Her eyes shut for a second, an exasperated sigh blew from her lips. "And I really don't like talking about it."

"Sorry," Essa rolled her eyes as she slid several plates onto a tray. "Didn't know you were so *sensitive.*" Brushing against Carrie, she pushed open the swinging door to the dining room.

"Hey man, I didn't mean to gossip about you and what's his name. I guess it sort of slipped out—know what I mean?"

"I'm sorry, Sammy. I just don't want anyone to think Don and I were an item."

"Why not?"

She shrugged, "For one thing, it never got to that point and we really are just good friends. And the other thing, when ordinary people realize you're friends with a cop, they treat you differently." Ladling clam chowder into a bowl, Carrie added, "I don't remember telling you anything about Don and me. How'd you find out?"

"Everybody knows, Carrie. This isn't the big city of Charlotte or Raleigh, everybody knows everybody else's business here, especially yours—remember last summer?—you were front page news."

"Umm…you're right. I guess I shouldn't get so bent out of shape when someone mentions it."

Sniggering quietly, Carrie settled the bowl of chowder on a tray. "How about I bet you a dollar that the woman I'm taking this to complains about it."

"Where's your customer from?" He asked quizzically.

"Not down south." Carrie tittered.

"No bet. I'd lose it." Sammy scoffed," I don't understand why Blythe even has it on the menu. It's not a southern dish and I'm sorry, but we be in *de south*." He laughed heartily.

"We sho is…now, what do you suppose ol' Blythe would do if we started talking like that?"

"She'd fy yo ass, hunny chil."

Carrie burst out laughing, and watched as Essa waltzed gingerly through the door.

"What did I miss?" Her eyes widened as she searched the two faces.

"Oh nothing," Sammy grinned. "We're just goofing around."

Essa curled her lips and flipped her hand in the air, "Sorry about earlier, girlfriend. I have no business interfering in your personal life."

"That's okay. I shouldn't be so secretive. Like Sammy says, this isn't Charlotte or Raleigh and I guess everybody already knows I was seeing a detective."

"Look, I know the last time we went out, I wasn't the warmest and friendliest person around, but I promise I'll try to be better. I just want to be friends. How about after work we go to The Daily Grind, and get a latte or something—just relax."

"Sounds good to me."

****

"Cute car," Carrie brushed her hand along the rubber eyelashes attached above the headlights of Essa's red Volkswagen Beetle. "Real?" She asked, stepping into the passenger seat; she touched a hand to the vial by the dashboard holding a violet orchid.

Essa slid into reverse and backed from the parking space, "Every morning I stop at the Surf City flower shop and get an orchid, my favorite flower."

"They are pretty," Carrie watched as Essa stepped on the clutch and moved into first, then second gear. "I bet this car is fun to drive."

"I love it," Pressing again on the clutch and then harder on the gas, she moved swiftly down the road.

"The whole car smells like flowers," Carrie leaned to smell the orchid. "My favorite is daffodils."

"Umm," Essa scowled as the car pulled in front of the coffee shop; the two women exited into the thick night air.

"Daffodils? Really, but they're so ordinary," Essa commented loudly as she closed her door.

"Carrie's an ordinary girl, not simple, just not flashy, like some people tend to be." Paula wrapped an arm around Carrie in a welcoming hug, "good to see you. Where have you been hiding? Haven't seen you in a while."

"Oh," Carrie looked from Paula to Essa, "I'm sorry, I've been so wrapped up in work—but—Paula, this is Essa. She works at the restaurant with me."

The women nodded to one another; Essa straightening her shoulders to tower over Paula's five foot, eight-inch frame, loosened her hair, shaking it about to settle wildly beyond her shoulders.

"You're new here." Paula commented.

"Uh huh," Essa checked the buttons of her blouse, running her fingers along her exposed cleavage." Yes, I drove down from the Banks a couple of weeks ago and was lucky enough to get a job right away."

"So you're the one who drives the little red Bug?"

"Yep."

"Cute car. I've seen it coming and going across the bridge quite a bit lately."

Carrie ran her hands over the faux eyelashes. "Paula used to work with me at Grocery World, she's working as a bridge tender now. She's a local girl, has her own boat."

"Well, aren't you special—your own boat and everything," the words mocked as Essa haughtily tossed her mane and smoothed her hands along the contours of her waist and hips. "I never did like going out on the ocean, but to each their own." Essa glared at Paula.

"Yes, to each their own." Paula repeated as she held the door open to The Daily Grind.

The women were quiet as they stood in line to order coffees, Carrie could feel the tension and offered grins to both.

Essa nodded in return and pulled a cell phone from her purse, "Damn, I forgot all about that appointment." Without any further explanation, she exited the shop.

Carrie watched through the window as Essa opened the door to the Volkswagen and slid behind the wheel, a scowl covering her face. "There goes my ride home."

"Don't worry, I'll take you."

"Oh, I'm not worried about that. I can walk, but she's the one who suggested we get a coffee—wonder what that call was all about." She shrugged as she approached the counter to order. "Essa suggested coming here. Said she wanted to make amends for the other night when we went to Gerard's and was bitchy."

Paula tilted her head a bit and raised an eyebrow, "Oh."

"Yeah, we went to Gerard's to watch the boss lady make a fool out of herself."

"I could have told you that. Dancing on tables again, was she?"

Laughing, Carrie sipped from her coffee, "Made me lose all respect—my fear of her, rather, and I am no longer intimidated by her." She took another sip and leaned forward in the little coffee shop chair. "If I'm not mistaken, it seems to me that you don't like Essa very much."

"I don't."

"Why? You don't even know her."

Paula ran a finger around the rim of her iced coffee, "I can't put my finger on it yet." She paused for a moment, "there's more to her—I've seen that little car go back and forth in the dead of night. When people come and go like that, something's usually up—and don't tell her what I just said. Don't tell her that I've

102

seen her with a man. Sometimes she has a bald headed man with her."

"What's the big deal? So she's got a boyfriend—he's bald. What's so bad about that?"

Taking a sip from the plastic tumbler, Paula looked away and drew a breath, "There's something, Carrie—I don't trust her. Just don't get too friendly."

"She did leave in a hurry and she was the one who suggested we go out for coffee after work. I think *you* make her uncomfortable. You aren't jealous of my new friend, are you?" Carrie giggled.

"Maybe so—anyway—it's not fair that anyone could look that good and not be in the movies," Paula offered a crooked smile, "and believe me, she knows it."

"You're right about that."

"The car she drives is hard to miss, it comes and goes at all hours of the night and this guy I've seen her with looks really rough. And then *this*—inviting you to go out for coffee—the excuse—an appointment at this time of night? Now come on, that was strange. She left because she felt uncomfortable."

"Maybe," Carrie shrugged, "I agree, she is strange—and you know what else is strange, or rather stupid."

"What?"

"Drinking coffee at ten-thirty at night."

"Yeah, I was wondering why you were drinking coffee." Paula laughed.

"I know why you are, you're getting ready to go to work, right?"

"Yes, I have about thirty minutes before I have to be there."

"Well, how do you like working at the bridge so far. Are you bored yet?"

Paula chuckled lightly, "I wish I was getting bored, I'd love to catch up on my reading, but so far it's been interesting."

"Lots of boats going through in the middle of the night?" Carrie asked.

"Not really—not so much at night—the night is pretty quiet; it's the early morning hours that seems to be the busiest, with the shrimp boats and fishermen heading out. This time of year, most of the yachts are already in Florida, but a few come through now and then." Relaxing into her chair, a slight grin played on her lips, "I see lots of things, Carrie. Some of those fishermen don't bother wearing cloths—some of the people on those fancy yachts don't like wearing them either, especially when they're making love."

"Oh my word, you mean to tell me that you've seen…"

Nodding, Paula giggled, "Yes ma'am, some people don't care and some, I guess have no clue."

"I guess things would not be boring if you're watching all that."

"There are other things too."

"Like what?" Carrie sipped from her cappuccino, raising an eyebrow.

"Who goes out with whom, who is sneaking back home, who's driving whose car—all kinds of things. And you would be surprised at how some of these goody two shoes slink around at all hours of the night."

"I envy you, at least your job sounds exciting. The most excitement I get at The Upper Deck is when a customer throws a fit about the clam chowder or complains about grits and other southern food."

"Same old thing, huh, Yankees complaining about the south. Makes me so glad I don't have to put up with it anymore." Paula spread her hands on the table and drummed her fingers rapidly against the glass. "Have you heard anything from Don?"

Carrie shook her head no, "but there's this man that I met a few nights ago at Gerard's and he's…"

"A new boyfriend—potential one?"

"No, nothing like that," Carrie's mouth formed a quick grin. "Although, there is something about him. He's not a tall fellow, not even that good looking, but there's something about him." She cocked her head and peered guiltily at her friend.

"And?"

"He says he's looking out for me—for Don—that Don asked him to keep an eye on me."

"And Don is where?"

"I have no idea where he is at. All I know is that he is still on the police force and looking for Hank."

"That's another thing, it's so odd that Hank would disappear like he did. Somebody here on the island has got to know where he's at."

"Don said the community clammed up after everything happened last year. Nobody knew a thing." Carrie shook her head.

"Somebody did. They're just not talking."

Chapter Ten

Emma Jewel pulled her green Dodge Durango into the circular pine straw driveway of the cottage. Two parked cars were positioned to the side of the driveway; E.J. pulled behind them. She recognized the Chevy sedan, it stayed parked in the shed by the cottage and was used when she visited or by friends who came along on occasional weekends. She'd given Hank the freedom to use it when needed. But the other, the Volkswagen, she wasn't sure about. More than likely the little red Bug behind the Chevy belonged to a woman.

For a moment E.J. thought about honking the horn; she certainly did not want to walk into an uncomfortable situation. But she decided against it.

Shaking her head, E.J. shrugged off the unsettling feeling of her son-in-law's womanizing. She'd seen so much of it since her daughter's death. But he seemed to have no shame. Hank felt fully justified in seeing and being with women. After all, he was a single man and had been for years.

E.J. understood that. No man was going to do without, that much she knew. It was the amount of women that he ran through and the gossip that followed—gossip about his strange sexual behavior—and she'd heard about the cat, too.

Perhaps it wouldn't have bothered her so much if Hank had been subtler, or even re-married. But seeing him go through so many love affairs was disturbing.

Curling her upper lip, Emma Jewel brushed by the Volkswagen Bug, noticing the wilted orchid near the steering wheel and the eyelashes above the headlights. *Haven't I seen this car on Topsail?*

Her purse held tightly in the crook of her arm, Emma Jewel studied the lighted windows as she slowly made her way to the front door.

Still in the shadows of the house and surrounding scrub oak trees, she listened as the tinkle of laughter filtered through the night air. E.J. stopped, straining to hear what the female voice was saying.

"She's so plain, I can't see you being with someone like that."

"It didn't mean anything." Hank's voice strained remorsefully, "I'm so sorry, it will never happen again my darling… *Emma.*"

Emma? E.J. grasped the side of the building, trying to see to whom Hank was talking; two tall shadowy figures meshed together in the dim starlight. Unable to discern who was who, she strained to hear

108

the last few words, but shook her head as the whispers blurred into the wind. *I better get out of here,* she thought as she turned to slowly make her way back to her SUV.

Finding her way in the dark along the winding lane, Emma Jewel finally turned on the headlights as she reached the highway.

Who were they talking about? She wondered. *Emma? Has he found a girl named Emma?* Looking into the rearview mirror she expected to see headlights. *Did they hear me? Is he coming after me?*

There were none. Except for hers shining in the darkness, the road was vacant. Chills radiated up her back. *Why in the world did I come out here at night? The man's a damn murderer.*

As E.J. turned on the radio, she could feel her heartbeat relax from its rapid beat. She rolled a window down and let the cool salty breeze wash over her. "Emma," she whispered the name of her daughter, Hank's deceased wife. Her lips slightly parted, she blinked rapidly to stay the well of tears she knew was coming.

"It doesn't make sense...Emma. I would have never thought he would be with another woman named that. I've even heard that he has turned women down after learning they have my little girl's name."

She drove in silence for a few moments, *I don't think I need to ever see him again.* E.J. felt her jaw tighten. "But the rent. That bag of worms owes me rent. I can't just let him stay there free."

As she drove Highway 70 to 17, E.J. considered the possible ways of getting rid of Hank—getting him out of her little cottage—her summer refuge.

She considered calling the cops, but wasn't she an accomplice now, hiding him for so long?

"I could say that I didn't know he was here." Grimacing, she tapped a finger against the steering wheel. "I've been doing that all along, haven't I?"

****

Carrie pulled the bottom to her new tankini bathing suit up over her abdomen. The blousy top covered her mid-section, billowing in ruffles; she looked in the mirror and patted her stomach. "Getting it off is always a lot harder than putting it on." She frowned at her reflection in the mirror.

Curling her lip, Carrie grabbed the loose fitting cover-up she'd purchased the day before at Surf City Gifts, the little gift shop next to the IGA. She slid her arms into the thin orange fabric and fastened the top three buttons.

Outside, Essa waited in her VW Bug, Carrie pulled a curtain aside and eyed the woman holding a cell phone close to her ear. "She's always on that phone." Carrie said, "Wonder who she's talking to. The last time I asked her about it, she nearly bit my head off."

Slipping her feet into a pair of orange flip-flops, Carrie grabbed an oversized straw bag and stuffed a beach towel, sunscreen and a bottle of water inside. "I don't really think she likes me." She looked in the mirror again to ask herself rhetorically, "So what are you doing hanging out with her? Dummy."

"You don't look so bad," Essa smiled as she shifted into first; her foot still on the clutch. She stifled a laugh; her eyes examining Carrie for a long moment, watching her as she threw the straw bag in the back seat. Sighing, Essa added, "You look…*cute*."

"I know what *cute* means, Essa, *cute* as in *not* pretty. *Cute* as in the Pillsbury dough boy."

"I don't understand how you could let yourself go…"

"It's only fifteen pounds, it's not like…"

"You're too sensitive-AND paranoid."

Carrie flipped a hand in the air, "Look if you're going to start demeaning me, trying to make me feel like there's something wrong with who I am and how I think, then I can get out of the car."

"Sorry." The word, laced in sarcasm, bit hard into Carrie as she lowered herself into the seat. Essa slid into first.

"Let's just have a fun day." Carrie's tone lightened as she struggled to ignore Essa's tone.

"So touchy, so sensitive—you know, you might want to go to a shrink about all your insecurities."

As they approached the stop sign, Carrie's hand pulled on the door handle. "Life's too short for…"

"Okay, okay. I'm sorry. I won't say anything like that again."

"Why do you do that?" Carrie stared hard at Essa. Her brow pinched heavily, "You're always saying such nasty things to me. If you don't like me the way I am, then please leave me the hell alone—I didn't seek out a friendship with you, I've got plenty of friends."

Essa's eyebrows drew upward, her chin quivered as tears welled in her eyes. "I can't believe you're saying these things. I'm only trying to help you." Her hands covered her face; her shoulders shook.

The car engine clunked to an abrupt stop as Essa's foot released the clutch, leaving them parked at a side street intersection.

Indifferent to her sobs, Carrie watched the woman for a moment before reaching a hand to stroke Essa's shoulder. "She does have a heart." The words fell carelessly from her lips.

"Of c-course, I have a h-heart. What m-made you t-think I d-didn't?" Essa's suppressed sobs distorted her words. "Y-you're the one who doesn't h-have a h-heart."

"Ah geez," I'm sorry…okay, let's just get going. But I'm not letting you or anybody belittle me. I'm very aware that I've put on a few pounds, but they are coming off and I've quit biting my nails." She scowled, "and it's not the end of the world if I don't look like a damn stick model." The words hissed from her mouth. "For your information, I've been told by many that I'm a pretty girl, nice looking anyway." Carrie breathed a heavy sigh, endeavoring to relax, "there are many days that I don't feel pretty at all."

Essa straightened in the seat and turned the key in the ignition to start the car. "I'll take you home if you want."

Carrie exhaled noisily, "I want to go to the beach. You asked me to go to the beach."

"Okay, we'll go to the damn beach," Essa shifted into first and turned right, then shifted into second.

"This is ridiculous."

"Let's just forget it," Essa turned into a driveway and pulled the gearshift into reverse.

"Yes, let's forget it. I'll forget the other day when we were supposed to go to the Daily Grind and you backed out. I'll forget your rudeness at Gerard's. I'll forget about how rude you are. Honey, you have some deep seated problems and if you hadn't of begged me again to spend time with you. I wouldn't be here."

Essa's chin dropped as she released her foot from the clutch. "There's just been things. I haven't been myself." Essa explained. "But I don't want to talk about those things." She turned and grinned sheepishly. "I'll do better, okay?" her eyes pleaded.

"Okay, we'll try again." Carrie sighed and changed the subject quickly; "This is the first time since last summer that I've gotten a chance to even get in the water. I'm really looking forward to getting some sand between my toes."

In the few minutes it took for the women to find a place to park, get out of the Bug, and settle the beach paraphernalia onto the sand, Carrie made an effort to keep the conversation light. For the next hour or so the prattle consisted of The Upper Deck, Blythe and some of the more obnoxious patrons.

"It's not so bad, compared with Grocery World. There seems to be less snooty people." Sitting on the blanket, Carrie lathered sunscreen on her legs and arms.

"Oh, don't let them fool you, sweetie. "They're just afraid you're going to spit in their food. That's why they're so nice, and—they're always nice to me, a little bit of cleavage goes a long way."

"What?" Carrie pushed up from the blanket.

"The men, I make sure a couple buttons are undone, and I lean over a lot." Licking her lips, Essa rubbed her hands over her freckled breasts, pulled into a sitting position and handed Carrie a bottle of lotion. "Would you mind, sugar. I'm going to roll over and I need some of this on my back."

She had to admit it. Essa was gorgeous. It didn't seem fair to be that tall and well, not thin, but not pudgy, in any areas except the breasts and rear.

And that hair, what I wouldn't do to have thick curly hair like she has. The Lord sure did bless her with beautiful features...or was it the devil? She rubbed the lotion across the woman's shoulders and back, then handed the bottle back.

"What about my legs? Aren't you going to do my legs?"

"You can reach them, can't you?"

"I thought you'd *want* to."

Fumbling with the bottle of sunscreen, Carrie drew back, her nostrils flared as she glared at Essa. "I don't do that." She shook her head.

"I guess it's mixed signals, then, because you're always looking at me."

"Envy, pure envy. You're tall and pretty, but..." She rose from the blanket. "This is all wrong. I don't think I like you or trust you. Paula's right."

"Paula? The bridge tender? So she doesn't like me either." She glared at Carrie, her mouth pursed. Suddenly Essa's chin dropped, her voice quivered in tearful breaks, "n-nobody likes m-me...and uh...Garth l-left me, I have lost everything."

Carrie's eyebrows squeezed together; her eyes narrowed. *Is she for real? I don't know if she's lying or if she's just really screwed up.* She stood hovering over Essa for a moment, *one more time, I'll give her the benefit of the doubt one more time. Maybe Garth is real.*

"I'm sorry that things have been so bad for you lately, Essa, and I want to trust you. I know what it's

114

like being new in a small town and how hard it can be to make friends.'

Lifting her swollen red eyes, Essa mustered a feeble grin, "I've been a mess since Garth dumped me…he beat the hell out of me…broke my nose…busted my lip." She rubbed a closed fist over her heart and held out a hand to pull Carrie back to the blanket. "It was bad, Carrie, real bad."

"So sorry you had to go through that, sweetie. Have you been to a counselor or a woman's shelter or talked with someone about it?" A guarded Carrie searched for the concern for others she'd always found so easily. "You need to talk to a professional."

"That all costs money, Carrie. I just try not to think about it too much." Essa squeezed Carrie's hand, "Let's just forget I even brought it up. Okay?"

Carrie watched as Essa adjusted the strings to her bikini and rolled sideways to riffle through her handbag. She studied the large leather purse. It had been hand painted. A mermaid with long tendrils of hair streaming about her, floated beneath the sea—a seahorse, an angelfish and an octopus glided alongside through the sea grasses. "Oh, I love that bag, I saw it in that little shop, The Mermaid's Purse, a few weeks ago and…"

"I've had this thing forever," Essa admonished, "I bought it in a store in Charleston."

Carrie studied the bag, if she recalled correctly, the designer had told her it was a one of a kind piece; she looked closely to the corner beneath the mermaid, were the initials, PB had been etched in black. *PB, Patti Blacknight. That was the name of the designer.*

Suppressing the urge to speak, Carrie grinned, *What kind of reaction would she have if I confronted her in this lie?* Carrie pulled back and nervously rose from the blanket.

"I think I'll take a dip." She turned from Essa and walked toward the small waves lapping the shore.

"Don't let any sharks get you, I heard they're out in droves this year." Essa called. "They'll tear you to shreds."

****

Tilting her body against Hank's, Essa brushed her lips against his, "You know my name isn't Emma. You keep calling me that."

Hank studied her features slowly, "In lots of ways you are like my wife."

"But we're not married, I'm not your wife."

"I mean that you are like her in ways…" He ran a forefinger across the bridge of her nose, "spots, little freckles—and the shape of your face." Hank cupped her face with both hands, "Your shoulders," his hand caressed Essa's neck, moving gently along her arms to grasp her hands. "You are very much like Emma. You don't let me dominate you."

"So your late wife was a strong woman who didn't let you take advantage of her."

"I think she was a lot like my mother—a no nonsense kind of woman. Momma would have liked her. Emma kept me in line."

"And did she—really? Did she really keep you in line, Hank?"

"Yes, except once. That one time." Hank's eyes glazed, his chin drooped as he turned away.

"Tell me…my darling. Tell me." Essa cooed, pressing her lips against his neck.

Pulling the woman with him, Hank settled himself on the damp wooden planks of the dockside pier. He drew his knees close to his chest; it rose and fell heavily.

Essa curled her legs to the side and nestled close to him. "Tell me. How—when did you disappoint her?"

"She was going to have our baby." Hank's eyes begged as he searched hers. "We went out on the sloop to celebrate and…"

Recounting the incident, the events leading up to Emma's death, Emma's anger—the games they always played—forgiveness. Hank retold the day she'd fallen from the sloop.

Essa watched as his hands dug into the wooden planks as he told the story. "It was my fault—wasn't it?" His head fell to his chest, his hands dug deeper into the splintered wood of the dock.

"Come back again with me—to Topsail." She murmured.

"I do miss living there."

"Nobody even recognized you in Gerard's."

"I rarely went into bars, Emma. I rarely hung around people that did."

"But *she* didn't even recognize you."

"Carrie?" he nodded.

"She didn't even know it was you and she even mentioned she saw a man sitting and talking with me when she went to get our drinks. So you see—nobody recognizes you and nobody will."

"Maybe, let me think about it."

"You do that, think about it. There are lots of things to think about." *Like how to get you to Topsail, how to get rid of the mother-in-law who holds the strings to your money and land. Getting you to marry me will be easy—and then getting rid of you will be easiest of all.*

Chapter Eleven

"Who are you?" Vera leaned against the kitchen counter, her elbows splayed as her hands held up her head.

Don roused and turned to her, "So, you're finally up."

"I asked you a question. Who are you and what are you doing in my house? Now, if you were in my bed, I'd know what you were doing in my house, but..." Vera squeezed her fingers into her temples, massaging them gently.

Rising from the chair, his bed for the night, Don walked into the kitchen and opened a cabinet above the sink. "Here, I took these earlier, maybe they'll help." He shook a couple Tylenol into his palm, then filled a glass with tap water.

"Thanks," she swallowed the pills, "but you still haven't answered my question.

Don reached for another glass and turned on the tap, "I was at the bar last night and you passed out so I brought you home."

"And you're not in my bed…" She looked quizzically at him.

"I don't take advantage of women when they're *not themselves*."

"Oh boy, another *gentleman*."

"That's what you were saying last night. You kept talking about some guy named Hank and him being such a gentleman."

Vera rolled her eyes, "some freaking gentleman, he ran off with my cousin Estelle."

"I'm sorry to hear you were treated so badly, Vera, but I'm not Hank."

"And you want to make things all better. Don't you sugar?" Vera sneered.

"If I had wanted to, I could have last night." Don opened a nearby loaf of bread and tossed a couple of slices into the toaster. "I'll make breakfast. You go ahead and wash your face, you'll feel better."

Shaking her head, Vera pulled her robe tight and tied the sash, "another gentleman, making breakfast for me. Hank did that—two—no, three times before he met my lying, money grubbing cousin."

"Why do you call her that?" He cracked four eggs into a pan of hot grease and began scrambling them.

"Because, that's what she does. She goes after men she thinks have money." Vera stretched her fingers into a cat-like pose and hissed, "She's just like a cat, selfish, concerned with nobody or nothing but herself. And don't let her fool you, she can lay it on thick, so thick that you can't even tell she's lying. She'll make you think she loves you, that she cares, but she'll sneak up from behind and pounce—that's what she did to me—to Hank. She came sashaying around, buddy-buddy like every time Hank was around and then—true to form—whoosh! Just like the damn no good--"

"Sorry to hear that." Don interrupted as he smeared oleo on the slices of toast, setting each next to the eggs on the plates before him.

Flopping his frame on the couch, he gestured for Vera. "This Hank person must have been some kind of catch."

"I guess so—I don't know—I know he was crazy about me—for a few weeks until *she* walked in. I should have known better than to let her get around my man. Especially when he started talking about going out to the Gulf Stream on his fancy *boat* and his beautiful ocean front *house* and all the farm *land* his family had." Vera scooped a fork full of eggs into her mouth then moved the plate to the end table, hunching sideways to eat.

A few minutes of silence ensued as they ate the eggs and toast; familiarities of the man Vera was talking about and Hank the killer gnawed at Don and when the front door suddenly burst open, he stood quickly. Vera, without raising her head, guffawed, "It's just the twins, don't worry about it."

Cautiously he studied the women, then settled back onto the couch, still thinking of Hank. He was, it was too much of a coincidence, their Hank had to be his. He was almost sure of it.

"You're still here," Veda's eyes widened, her head wobbled as she blew air through her teeth.

"Did y'all have a *good* night? *Sleep* well?" Vela waltzed around the side of the sofa and seated herself next to her sister. "Scoot over, big sis." She pushed her hips against Vera, encouraging her to move closer to Don.

"Get your ass up, I didn't do anything with *him* last night." Rising, Vera moved to the overstuffed chair and curled her feet beneath her. "He ain't my type."

Veda and Vela turned their attention to Don, studying him as he sat helplessly alone.

"Did you hurt my sister?" Vela hovered close behind the couch.

"I hope you didn't hit her, I'll knock the living shit out of you if you touch—"

"He didn't touch a hair on my poor little pea picking head, he's been a perfect *gentleman*." Vera pulled a pack of cigarettes from the robe pocket and tugged on the end table drawer.

"Holy shit, don't tell me you're going to light one of them things up."

"I can't stand it when she smokes," Vela pushed her face forward toward Don. "You don't smoke do you?"

He shook his head no.

"I stopped smoking about six years ago, best thing I ever did." Veda touched a hand to her over teased hair and straightened her blouse.

"And look what it did to you, Crisco, fat in the can," Vera snarled.

"I'm glad he doesn't smoke." Sweeping past him, Vela perched herself on Vera's chair and grabbed the cigarette out of her hand. "You need to quit. No man is gonna put up with a woman who stinks like a damn cigarette."

"I bet that's why Hank ditched you." Veda added to the rapid banter.

Vera retrieved another cigarette from her pack, touched a lighter's flame to it and released an audible plume of smoke into the air. "Screw you."

Vela touched Don quickly on the arm, "You know, that Hank fella was nothing to look at. You're a lot cuter than he was."

"Is, than he *is*." Veda added.

"What do you mean?"

"I mean I saw him driving down the road with the bitch, our lovely cousin, in *her* car." Veda's lips curled.

"Where?" Vera asked.

"On highway seventy, it looked like *cuntusabundus* was going south."

Don stretched his legs out to reach the coffee table as he leaned back against the sofa. "I keep hearing all these remarks about your cousin Estelle, yet I haven't even met her—it's not very nice to slander someone when they're not around to defend themselves."

"No one in this room is going to defend that damn whore." Veda tugged at the waistband of her jeans.

"And that's exactly what the bitch is," Vela growled expletives, then added, "she sure is a whore."

Anyone who watched movies or even television was bound to hear a myriad of coarse expressions used without reserve and Don realized it had worked its way into the vernacular of American culture. Still, he found he could not get used to hearing so much vulgarity, especially from women. He hadn't been raised to speak that way; however, in his line of work it was commonplace. He nodded and listened as if unaffected by the base repartee as he guided the "V" girls to spill all they knew about Hank and the cousin, Estelle.

"She sounds like some kind of witch casting spells over men," Don teased. "She must be a real beauty."

"I swear, I think we have another man gone ga-ga over that bitch and he hasn't even met her." Vera's hand, with an extended middle finger, flew above her head.

"Whoa, I didn't say I wanted to meet her. She just sounds like a real piece of work—kind of intriguing. Sounds like the kind of woman I'd steer clear of. But—in her defense…"

"She just lives down the road a ways, I could…"

"No, no. I don't think I want to meet her." Don stressed, "I haven't even gotten to know *you* fine ladies yet."

Vela giggled, "You hear that? He called us ladies."

Nodding, Don avoided their eyes, *my big toe is more of a lady than these filthy mouth wackos.* "I apologize for crashing in your chair last night, but I'm worn out. I'm on my way down to Wrightsville Beach and my car's transmission sounded funny, so I thought I'd stop in your little town and seek out a garage." He turned unflinchingly toward Vera, "Where's the best place, Darlin'?"

"Darlin', Dar*ling*, that's what that bastard called me." Vera slinked into the kitchen, reached into the cupboard for the bottle of bourbon and poured some into a tumbler.

"Kind of early, isn't it sis?" Vela asked snidely.

"She's got it bad." Veda whispered.

"Well, he did always call me darling…" Vera tilted the glass and threw the contents down her throat, "It was the way he said it, you know, *dah-lin.*, like they say it down there in South Carolina or Louisiana." Closing her eyes for a moment, she caught a shallow breath and poured again from the bottle of bourbon.

"Seaside Auto, that's the best place to take your car," Vela rested against the kitchen counter. "That's where I take mine."

"Do you have a place to stay?" Exposing her cleavage; Veda crossed her arms and leaned forward against the couch. "I've got an extra room at my place."

A short laugh fell from his mouth as Don stood, "As nice as that sounds, I must confess that I do have a girlfriend and I'm not the cheating kind."

"What'd I say?" Vera's words slurred, "A real gentleman, a real freaking gentleman."

****

"So, if you're watching out for me, are you checking in with Don—telling him I'm okay—and how often?"

"It varies. So far I haven't talked with him much—nothing to tell. You seem to be doing just fine." As he tilted the bottle of root beer back, Lev studied Carrie's face. "You haven't heard from Hank have you?"

"No, he's never bothered me, never made any contact at all. I've hoped that he drowned or disappeared somehow into some sort of vast expanse."

Lev chuckled, "out of sight, out of mind?"

"Something like that."

"Guess he scared the hell out of you." Relaxing into his seat, Lev watched as Carrie rubbed her fingers nervously with her thumb. Lifting her shoulders, she brought the e-cig to her mouth.

"You should talk to someone about last summer, these kinds of things can mess with your head."

"Don and I talked a lot about that. He helped me work through all the fear and paranoia." Carrie rested her hands beside her body. "My friend Paula is a good confidante, too. I'd swear she has a degree in psych."

"Paula?"

"Yes, we worked together at Grocery World and now she is a bridge tender."

Lev nodded, "The one who has the fishing boat?"

"Yeah, but how did you know?"

"Detective—small town—duh."

Carrie's cheeks flushed red, "I keep forgetting that. Sorry."

"I've noticed her leaving the bridge early in the morning. She lives down Mill Creek. Doesn't she?"

Again Carrie nodded.

"Why don't you introduce me to her sometime?"

Carrie rested against the bar, an obvious smirk covering her lips. "So you want to meet Paula. I assume it's business—police business."

"Yeah, what else would it be?" Lev teased.

"Oh, I don't know. It's just the way you ask—the way you present yourself. I was sure the first time I met you, that you were coming on to me."

"Maybe I was."

"See what I mean, I don't know how to take you."

"Anyway you like, honey."

"Oh geez, get off of it. You're getting boring now."

126

"You're wondering if I come on to all women under the pretense of doing my job."

"I guess so."

Lev touched a finger to his ear and smiled broadly, "Yes. Yes I do."

"You're a dirt bag."

"I'm a sweet dirt bag. One hundred and seventy pounds of twisted steel and sex appeal."

Chapter Twelve

"I think I've got him, or at least it sounds like him." Don held the cell phone to his ear as he closed the door to the hotel room. "I've got a gaggle of scorned women up here who have just about described our friend to a tee."

"Just about?"

"Seems Hank, if it's him, has shaved his head and packed on a few pounds."

"That'll work." Lev chortled.

"Anything down there?"

"Nope. Carrie says she hasn't heard a word from him. I believe her. I don't think she's hiding anything."

"She wouldn't."

"She's going to introduce me to her friend Paula."

"And…?

"She's a bridge tender."

"Oh yeah, that's right. I'd forgotten—Carrie did say something about Paula working at the bridge now." Don nodded, "She's a cool headed sort of gal—no

129

nonsense and there's a bird's eye view from the bridge. Nobody gets on and off the island without her seeing them."

"He could come by boat." His legs dangling from the dock, Lev fiddled with the line wound around a cleat. "You know that girl really misses you, I could take advantage of the situation."

"If she lets you do that, then she's not my girl." Don shot back quickly.

"That's kind of cold, don't you think, old buddy." Lev could hear the sigh from the other end of the phone.

"I got lucky up here, really wasn't expecting to find anything, but the "V" girls seem to know quite a bit."

"The what?"

"The "V" girls, three sisters whose names all begin with the letter "V. They were talking about this guy who's seeing their cousin. Except for the baldhead and weight, he sounds like our man. And get this—he's using his real name—Hank—but a different last, Jordan or something like that." Pausing, Don threw his pistol on the bed and loosened his belt. "Tomorrow I'm going to talk to the one named Vera again, if I can keep her from passing out."

"A real lush, huh? You're not taking advantage of that, are you?"

"Only if I wanted to go dumpster diving, but not much of a chance of that."

"Oh," Lev laughed, and skipped a stone across the still dark waters.

A long silence lingered between the two men. Don, sat on the bed and kicked off his shoes. Lev skipped another stone across the water.

Breaking the quiet, Don spoke, "You be careful with Carrie, I like her a lot, maybe even more than that."

"Really?" Rising from the dock, Lev said, "You've always had tenuous relationships, pal—I think she's too good for you."

Again, a long silence ensued.

"Maybe."

Lev forced a laugh then continued, "Good luck. Hope he's the one you're looking for and remember, call me if you need some help. He pressed the phone off and slid it in his trouser pocket. *So he listened to Carrie, helped her work through her PTSD. Who's helped him with his?*

His fingers folded behind his head, Don lay prone on the worn hotel mattress; he stared at the ceiling. His thoughts moved tensely between his son Phil, Carrie, his ex-wife Maggie, and Sarah Chambers. He couldn't say that love was the connection. There certainly had been no love between him and Sarah. And Maggie—looking back, that couldn't have been love either. *Maybe—I* was *young—she was gorgeous.* He grinned, *love for a few minutes.*

The strange connection they all shared, playing such intimate, involved parts in his life left him feeling uneasy—like a nightmare that just wouldn't quit.

Why can't I just live a normal life? He felt the tension growing in his shoulders, "I got to get out of here," Don sprang from the bed, grabbed his gun and wallet and left the hotel room.

A speed limit sign zipped past him as he drove the lonely road; the image of a young Maggie held his attention at a local dance, he suspected she was high on something, but he wasn't sure. *I should have known then.* Another sign zipped by, Don glanced the illuminated dashboard and eased off the gas, and tried to rationalize that there was nothing he could have done for a dependent personality, Maggie was lost in a pharmaceutical world of prescription drugs and who knew what else. If she hadn't have been Phil's mother, he would have no use for her. Maybe because she was Phil's mother he had no use for her. She was the exact opposite of Carrie.

Carrie, she was a relationship that offered peace—maybe even hope. Don closed his eyes, relaxing into the possibility of having a life with her—having a normal life, if there was such a thing. He pictured himself with his arm around her and Phil—as if in a photograph.

His head buzzed with *what ifs* and *whys*; *Phil, did I do the right thing?* "It's the best military school around," He justified, "It's the best thing for that boy." He felt the tug of loss, realizing he had never really known his own son.

"Damn, Reggie, damn Sarah. Damn Hank—but that bastard did do me a favor—he took care of them, got me out of having to deal their freaking drugs—I guess, I could say he kept me out of jail. *But he'll use it, sooner or later, he'll throw it in my face.* He's the last tether to last summer. After he's gone, I'm free."

He searched for a clear radio station and strove to push thoughts of Hank and his son away.

Where he was driving, he wasn't sure—*maybe the coast,* he thought as he headed east. He wanted to level his foot to the floor, fly through the small towns and country-like landscape. Hitting the accelerator again, he sped forward to nearly eighty, then eased off the pedal, slowing to the fifty-five speed limit and then even slower as he drove through Riverdale and Croatan.

Succumbing to the rural areas Don relaxed into the bucolic atmosphere; warm air rushing from the window seemed to melt away thoughts of the crimes he was investigating. The cloudless sky, twinkled hope and peace; a smile gradually formed on his lips, his shoulders relaxed and Don found himself feeling something he hadn't felt in a long time. *I could just go away, forget all this crap. Get a job at...*

"Humph," his hands grasped the steering wheel more tightly, *I have to do this. I have to find that murdering son of bitch, I **have** to. I will never be free until he's dead—or at least behind bars—no, he's got to go.* Braking for a light in Havelock, Don watched as a stray cat darted across the highway; a red Volkswagen speed through the intersection, just missing it. *Carrie wouldn't be safe and Phil—I owe my son the best.*

****

"Why did I ever let you talk me into this?" Paula scolded as she adjusted the bodice of her dress. "I don't even know what to wear on a date, and a dress? I haven't worn a dress in ages. Do I look okay?" She asked, fiddling with the buttons. It's been so long since I've been on a date."

"You look fine and it's really not a date. Lev just said he wanted to meet you. I'm supposed to see him here at Gerard's tonight and you're just going to *happen* to be with me." She glanced at her friend's feet, "But why heels, aren't you tall enough already?"

"I don't know what to wear," Paula's face contorted into an exaggerated grimace. "And you gave every indication that this was a *real* date—you said he couldn't wait to meet me and so I assumed he knew I'd be here. You did tell him I was coming."

"Sort of."

"You're acting like Mindy, this is something she would do—this is a very *teenage girl* thing to do. I feel like a fool."

Carrie sucked softly on the tip of her e-cigarette, "Oh shut up, you're just bent out of shape because you're going to meet a man. Now act like you're relaxed—he just came through the door."

Sidling next to Carrie, Lev settled his hand on her shoulder and turned to Paula. "Hi." He nodded, and then turned away.

Paula nodded in response as she looked past her friend, "Hi." *For someone who wants to get to know me, he sure is acting cool.* She took a sip from the glass of wine before her and stared at the line up of various liquor bottles behind the bar.

Carrie rolled her eyes, "Humph, is that all you're going to say, 'hi?'" You're always so forward. What's up?"

"She's taller than me."

"What?" Carrie giggled, "So, all that bravado is a put on. Ha, ha, ha." She stared angrily at him, "So what if she's taller than you." She studied his face for a moment, "It's not just the height is it, honey?"

Lev shrugged,

"Paula does have that air of *don't mess with me* about her. But you're being rude."

"Then *introduce* us." His glare admonished.

"Okay, okay." Leaning back, allowing a better view, Carrie began, "Lev this is Paula, my dear friend. And Paula, this is Lev, whom I really don't know at all."

Paula shot her a puzzling look, then met Lev's eyes. "Well, that was a *nice* introduction. I guess I can assume that *my friend* is very concerned about my well being since she's setting me up on dates with strangers."

Lev chuckled, "I'm sorry, I guess I put Carrie on the spot," He reached his hand to shake Paula's and led the way to a table.

Paula did tower over Lev and now felt a wave of self-consciousness as she stepped next to him.

"I forgot to tell you he's a cop, a detective," said Carrie.

"Oh. That's why you wanted to meet me, huh?" Paula glanced away as the three settled into a booth. "Since I'm a bridge tender," she sneered, "I know exactly what you are going to ask me." Her steely gaze penetrated the distance between she and Lev. "You want me to let you know about the comings and goings of the residents and visitors to Topsail—if anything looks odd." As the words left her lips, she suddenly felt foolish for having dressed for the 'date.' *I should have known, the only reason a man wants to spend time with me is business.* She relaxed her body against the back of the booth and kicked off the sling spiked heels from her feet. "I've seen *you* coming and going." Her eyes teased, "What is it with detectives and their vehicles? They're either faded and full of dents or faded and old as dirt—or both."

Squaring his shoulders, Lev leaned slightly to the right and grinned, "Gets me from A to B—and uh, let me ask you, just how fast do you take Mill Creek when you go home from your job at the bridge?"

"So you know where I live?"

Lev shrugged. "It's hard not to notice that bright red Camaro zipping up and down the roads."

"If you know so much about me, why did you bother to have Carrie introduce us, if that's what you want to call it."

"I wanted to see you in something beside jeans and a tee-shirt."

Ah, there he is, the man who comes on strong. Carrie rolled her eyes.

Paula drew her lips inward, "If I wasn't an open minded woman, I'd say that's a pretty sexist thing to say."

"But you *are* an open minded woman."

"Don't patronize me."

"I'm not, it's just an observation."

And it pays to be observant, Carrie recalled Lev's words from a few days ago. She watched the flow of conversation between the two. In a way she envied Paula's strength, or was it coolness? She hadn't paused or succumbed to anger during their repartee. She hadn't gotten up and walked out either.

In the few years Carrie had known Paula, she'd never seen her so intensely involved in conversation with the opposite sex. Usually she found a reason to excuse herself, especially if the man seemed flirty or aggressive.

"You're just another transplant, coming here from who knows where—trying to tell everyone what they should do and what is wrong with the way we live."

Lev drew his lips in to take a deep breath. He stared at Paula for what must have been a good ten seconds. "Are you going to be able to help me out or not?"

"Shouldn't be a problem." Paula pulled a card from the small beaded bag by her side and handed it to the detective. "Text, don't call."

Taking the card, Lev rose, nodded to the women and walked to the bar.

"You were a little rough on him, weren't you?"

"Carrie, I just don't…"

"You thought he wanted to meet you because he was interested."

"That's the impression I got from *you*. And well, it's obvious that he is not. This is strictly business."

"And you're going to make sure that it stays strictly business, right?"

"I have no reason to believe it is anything else and did you see how uncomfortable he was with my height. I have to be at least a couple of inches taller than him."

"Take off the damn shoes and it won't be so noticeable."

Paula swallowed the remainder of her wine and moved the empty wine glass about nervously. "I think—oh," She paused and nodded toward the door. "We've got company."

"Who?" Carrie smiled as she watched Mindy stroll toward their table.

"Hi y'all." The younger woman bent to give the others a hug. "I haven't seen you in ages—well days." She gently pushed her hand against Paula's shoulder. "How's things at the bridge?"

"Mornings are gorgeous and so are sunsets."

"So the view is great. I knew you'd like it."

"I didn't say I liked it, but it's better than nothing, better than what you do." Paula teased.

"Yes ma'am. But I bet it's not quite as challenging." Mindy rolled her eyes.

Smiling, Paula pulled Mindy close, "One of these days you're going to get the snot beat out of you. I've seen you tailgating those Yankee cars and shooting them the bird."

"If they are going to pull out in front of me and make my purse spill all over the floor, then I'm going to ride their tail as far as I can and honk the horn every time they stop."

Mindy eyed the man walking toward the table, "Ooh, hunka, hunka." She licked her lips, "My, what big biceps you have." Mindy looked deeply into Lev's gray eyes. "Is this for me?" She winked, "I mean—is this beer for me?"

Lev settled a bottled water, Michelob and two glasses of wine on the table. "Yes, my dear, the Mich is yours and for these two lovely women, the wine."

"Water for you? Don't you drink?" Mindy asked boldly.

"No, I don't." He watched the look shared between the women. "If you're thinking that I'm an alcoholic, I'm not. I just choose not to drink—it's a health thing."

"Oh," they all said at once.

"No big deal, glad you're drinking healthy—if that's what it is." Wrapping her fingers around the beer Mindy asked, "How did you know I drink Michelob"?

"I usually know what women want."

Carrie covered her face with her hands, "Oh my word, that is the cheesiest thing I think I've heard in a decade."

"Yeah, I know, kind of tasteless. But then..." Lev shrugged. "I don't know anymore what is the right thing to say. Some women are offended and others are not. I guess I should have known…" he turned to Paula. "that you ladies…"

"Are politically correct." Mindy tossed her thin light hair away from her face as she lifted the beer to her lips. "As for me, sweetie, I don't mind if you talk un-political to me—I'm an Independent—and if my friends aren't going to introduce you to me—" she batted her lashes, "I'm Mindy."

Lev grasped Mindy's hand, "Nice to meet you."

"Nice to meet you too." She ran her fingers over the large biceps of an arm. "Sugar, you sure are built."

"Thank you," Lev smiled broadly.

"Where you from, sweetie?"

"Arizona."

"Good googamooga, that's a long way away— way out west. "Are you a cowboy?"

Lev tipped a make-believe hat and nodded. "Grew up on a ranch."

"What's it like out there?"

"Grand Canyon, lots of desert, dry, miles and miles of nothing that goes on forever and ever." He gulped from the water bottle, "I guess you're a local."

"I sure am."

"Are all of you ladies locals?"

"We're all locals, but you're not a native unless your grandma is in the graveyard." Mindy giggled, "Mine and Paula's in the graveyard."

Lev chuckled, "I know just what you mean," If you're not from here, you're from somewhere else."

"By gosh, I think he's got it," Mindy giggled and tipped her beer against Lev's water bottle, "I think this fella might be one of us."

"Now that we're all friends, and everybody knows everybody" Paula added sarcastically, "why don't you two sit down—Mindy, fill everyone in on what's happening at Grocery World."

"As if we care," Carrie sniggered.

"No, no, I'd like to know what goes on in the quiet little towns of Topsail Island—all three of them—Surf City, Topsail Beach and North Topsail."

Mindy wagged her tongue, "See," she settled herself in the booth and began, "Fern is still lording over everyone. But it's so funny, the girl she hired to take Carrie's place, what's her name—uh Te-ah, Tee-ja, something like that. It's spelled like the stuff you drink but sounds different—well, she does the same thing you did Carrie—she squeezes bread. I nearly busted a gut when I saw her do it," Mindy blew a cherry scented plume of vapor into the air, "Of course, when I asked her, she denied it." Reaching to pat Carrie's hand she added, "she's not nearly as nice as you are, sweetie. She's been there for three weeks now and she won't warm up to anybody, just does her stuff and goes home."

"Maybe she's shy," Carrie said.

"Maybe, but she needs to get un-shy if she wants to make any friends."

"Maybe she just doesn't want to make friends," added Paula.

And why would that be? Carrie studied her, realizing that perhaps Paula was just as vulnerable as the rest of them.

Lev seemed to read her mind, and met her eyes in affirmation. Gently he nudged Paula with his elbow, "Yeah, why would someone not want to be friends?"

"Friends don't play head games."

"Who are we talking about now?" Mindy looked from Lev to Paula, then to Carrie. "I'm lost."

"You came in too late and missed all the good stuff." giggled Carrie.

****

"Taking the boat out today?" Lev leaned against the marina gas pumps and gestured with an outreached hand for Paula to toss him the line as she motored her boat close to the dock. Catching it, he quickly secured it to a cleat.

"Thanks," Paula nodded, avoiding eye contact.

"Is it your day off?"

"My week off."

"Must be nice."

"It is."

"I heard you're the only woman captain here on Topsail."

"Yep."

Lev waited for her to continue. After a few moments, he asked, "You been doing this for a long time?"

"Yep."

"Is that all you can say?"

Paula pulled a bumper into the boat and turned away. "I told you the other day that I'd keep an eye out for curious activity, but I really don't know what you want. At Gerard's the other night you weren't very specific."

"You left before I could get specific."

"I don't like staying out late."

"You work late hours."

She shrugged, "Just wanted to go home."

"But we were all having such a good time." Standing on the dock, Lev extended a hand downward to help Paula from the boat.

She ignored the offer, "Just hand me the nozzle to the gas pump."

"You looked pretty." The words bolted from his lips as he reached for the nozzle.

"You don't have to say that." She stood watching him, studying him.

"I'm not afraid of you," His gray eyes twinkled.

"What?" Shaking her head, Paula leapt from the boat, grabbed the nozzle and leapt back.

Lev followed behind her, quick to unwind the cap. "You act so tough—so unaffected. But I know you like me."

"No I don't."

"You just think you don't. Everybody likes me." Crossing his arms, Lev looked watched as she shoved the nozzle into the gas receptacle. "Let me help you."

Surprising even herself, Paula handed the gas nozzle to Lev. Her eyes grazed his biceps; she noticed a partial tattoo hidden by the sleeve of his Guy Harvey tee-shirt. Forcing saliva down her throat, she turned away. "Would you please leave me alone."

"Just promise to take me fishing. I've never been fishing on the ocean before."

She looked coyly his way, "Really?"

"Yeah, really."

"Maybe I will."

Chapter Thirteen

"Layfayette Bishop—Fate!" Emma Jewel called out as she pulled into a Grocery World parking slot. "Hold on, I need to talk with you."

A broad grin settled on his lips as he turned to close the door to his truck. "Hey E.J. Where's your dog?"

Tilting her head sideways, E.J.'s brow furrowed in puzzling contemplation. "What do you mean—where's my dog?"

"Every time I see you riding around you've got that hairy dog of yours sitting next to you." Adjusting his thick black glasses, he added, "It ain't you, unless your dog's sitting in your lap."

"Oh," She laughed, "Nicky's at home. He's getting too old to jump in the truck like he used to."

Fate nodded, "Ain't we all." He leaned against the grocery cart and ran a hand through his still thick hair. "So, what's up?"

"I was wondering if you wanted to do a little fishing tomorrow. I'd like some company."

"Tomorrow's Sunday, gal, you know I'll be in church."

"What about after church. I'd really like to talk with you about some things."

"It ain't about that son-in-law of yours, is it?"

E.J. slid her eyes to the pavement and shrugged, "Maybe."

"Did he contact you?"

Shrugging again, Emma Jewel said, "I just would like to talk with you, Fate. Can't I talk with my brother?"

Brother, she hardly ever calls me that. He studied her expression; one he saw rarely—one that told him she was worried. It was uncommon for Emma Jewel to worry or at least express worry. "I'll be over around two. How's that?"

"I'll fix us a late lunch," E.J. smiled and walked back to her truck.

****

"I had this dream—it was so real—Hank was seeing some woman—a tall one."

"Now, E.J. you know Hank sees other women." Fate brushed the air.

"But he called her Emma."

"In the dream?" Fate raised an eyebrow and smirked a crooked grin. "And you believe this *dream*?"

144

E.J. stared at him, her hand on her hips. "That's what I said."

"Okay, but I don't think you're talking about a dream. I think there's something else."

She stared into Fate's eyes, pursed her lips and sighed, "Okay. There was no dream."

"You were always a bad liar."

"No, I was a good liar—just not to you."

"So what about this woman and Hank. Where'd you see them?"

"I went up there—to my cottage the other night and saw him."

"What did he have to say?"

"I didn't talk with him, Fate, I just saw him and this woman out on the pier."

"And you didn't let him know you were there?"

E.J. shook her head. "But he called her Emma."

Fate raised his brows, "Your daughter is not the only female on the planet named Emma."

"I don't know Fate, it just didn't seem right. It didn't *sound* right—not the way he said her name."

"You're getting real mysterious now, you say you saw Hank with a woman named Emma—and you didn't talk with him—what's up?"

"It was all so strange—Hank sounded so *strange*."

"Hank is not the kid we knew way back when; he grew into someone totally different. To tell the truth, I don't think we ever knew him."

Emma Jewel shook her head as she set a plate of crab on the table; she pulled a chair next to him and sat close, touching Fate's arm with hers.

Toying with the food, he spoke, "I know it's been hard for you gal—losing the only daughter you had. But I thought you'd come to terms with that."

145

She stared soulfully into his eyes. "Sometimes—it is, sometimes it's not. When I see him—Hank—and the way he is around women—I hate him for *her*."

"You haven't forgiven him, have you?"

Emma Jewel jerked her head softly from left to right, "I never did really like him, didn't trust him, always so goody-goody and just plain spoiled by his momma."

"We all knew that, his momma and daddy gave him whatever he wanted, they always *did* think their shit didn't stink." He stuffed a forkful of crab salad in his mouth, chewed for a moment then added, "He loved her though, E.J. I know for certain, he did love Emma."

"What's love, Fate?" She struggled for a second to keep her tears at bay, breathed in and continued, "He took my baby, both my babies. I should be playing with my grandchild who'd be a teenager now, chasing him around, yelling at him for playing too many video games or what ever it is these kids got their noses stuck in these days." She smiled and speared her fork into Fate's salad. "Of course, if you'd of married me, we'd have a slew of children and grandchildren running around here."

Releasing a heavy sigh, Fate took a long gulp from the tumbler of water. "Brother and sister, we're siblings."

"You always used that as an excuse, Momma and your daddy didn't get married until we were in our teens." E.J. frowned. "I always knew you loved me, now say that isn't true."

"Oh E.J. you were always like a sister to me."

"That ain't true either, you kissed me and that wasn't a brotherly kiss."

146

"We were teenagers." He pursed his lips.

"But it's true, I know you always loved me until—and then, after that you were so mad at me and then you went and got married, just to punish me. I know."

"Long time ago." Fate muttered.

"Sorry—I am—really," her eyes pleaded. "Sometimes I just dream about this little girl that used to be me."

"Can't live in the past." He grasped her hand in his. "We'll always be friends, good friends."

"You're just not ever going to forgive me, are you?"

"I forgave you a long time ago, Emma Jewel."

"It's been four years since your wife died."

Fate touched his brow with a worn hand. "You can always count on me."

E.J. rose and padded across the bare boards of her home to the porch. She grabbed two fishing poles and nudged the two beach chairs leaning against the wall. "Get these, let's go fishing."

"Lord, I love surf fishing, haven't done it in ages," a broad grin stretched across Fate's face, "thanks for asking me to join you—kind of like old times, huh?"

She smiled back, "yeah, kind of—with you, anyway. So much has changed."

"Don't go maudlin on me, gal."

"Can't help it." Emma Jewel drew a long pause, "This," she nodded to the ocean. "is my guts, all my insides—my church. It's where I talk to God and damn it if He doesn't answer me." Biting her lips, E.J.'s eyes sparkled.

Fate nodded. "Our little slice of heaven has changed a lot though—going to keep on changing."

"I know, I hate that. I hate it so badly I want to scream, but I can't scream loud enough, so I don't scream at all." She grew quiet and cast her line into the breakers.

"We had the best, you know." Watching her face contort into a familiar stoic pose, Fate repeated the sentence. "We had the best, E.J., we had the island before all the development, when it was new and young, just like we were. And you got to admit it, we had one hell of a childhood—ain't nobody had it better than we had growing up on Topsail."

Fate drew his arm back, casting the line far out into the breakers; he settled the fishing pole in the stand and waited for E.J. to do the same. "So, what are you going to do?"

"Hold on, I'll tell you in a minute." She cast out again, then reeled in her line to check the hooks. "Yep, I thought I saw my bait go flying off." She giggled. "We did have the best." Turning to him, she winked. "Life is good, I know."

"Well then, you need to do something about *you know who.*"

"I know," E.J. plopped into the chair, releasing an exaggerated sigh.

"Um, shouldn't you be talking to the police?"

She shrugged and fiddled with the bag of faux shrimp.

"Shit or get off the pot, Emma Jewel, this is serious stuff."

Wading ankle deep into the ocean water, E.J. called back, "Mullet might be running today."

"Maybe, it's getting kind of hot for *good* fishing." Fate rolled his neck from side to side and stretched his legs out before him. "I know you heard me. This is serious stuff, Emma Jewel. You never should have hidden that man. I thought you might have done something like this, but I never would confront you. Should have, I guess."

"I'd have told you to mind your business."

"That says everything there is to say, E.J."

Silence followed for several minutes as she settled the rod in the holder and relaxed back into the chair. Thoughts of regret stirring, Emma Jewel wished she hadn't said those last words, but defensiveness had always been one of her faults. Sliding regretful eyes his way, she half grinned at Fate.

"E.J., you forget. I grew up with you. I know you better than anyone else around here. You should have then and you better now—go to the police."

"Humph, why haven't *you* gone to the police if you know so much?"

"Why haven't *you*?"

Pulling her bottom lip in, E.J.'s eyes shifted from side to side, "I thought about it."

Fate held up a finger. "One, you're an accessory. Two, you're scared of him. Three, at first you weren't sure and four, she's your daughter's husband—the last thing of hers you have to hold on to." He looked above his glasses and held her gaze. "You're still holding on to the past—am I right?"

"Possibly, but I've had all these months to think about it and we know for sure that he killed all those people—and he's living in *my* little cottage not paying any rent."

"Not paying any rent?"

E.J. nodded.

"Cute cottage. I always liked it, until…"

"I never meant for that to happen."

"I should have knocked first."

"Yes, you should have."

"You never did go after him for paternity, did you?"

"No. He wouldn't have made a good father."

They both sighed heavily and fidgeted with their fishing poles.

"Yep, that was a nice little place and the fishing up there was always pretty good." Fate said stiltedly.

"It *was*."

"What about an electric bill?"

"Generator, remember?"

"Money for food? I know he's not dipping into his bank account unless…" he glared at E.J. "don't tell me."

"I gave him my credit card last fall."

"Oh geez."

"That was before I knew!" Digging her bare feet into the sand, she rubbed her thighs, "E.J. Rosell, he signs it just fine and nobody's ever questioned it. I get the bill every month."

"And you pay it?"

"Yep."

"Fool."

"What about his houses and land?"

"Emma had me as her beneficiary and when she passed, I got half of everything."

"I'm surprised he hasn't come to—oh, I see. You do have a reason to be scared of him." He flicked the handle of the reel sharply making it spin, "you need to go to the cops, E.J. that man could try to kill you."

"I *do* have those two men sleeping with me every night." She grinned.

"Ha, ha, Smith and Wesson. I know. But could you do it? Shoot him, I mean."

"I've shot snakes, gators, and rats, one more won't hurt."

"No need to be flippant, this is life and death stuff. I still think you need to go down and talk with Lee at the station."

"They've had nine months to find him and in the first place, they didn't even realize it was him until he kidnapped that gal at the grocery store. And then, that damn detective lets him get away."

"You asked me here for a reason, I gave you my answer—my advice."

Standing to reel the line in, E.J. slid her eyes to catch Fate's, "Good advice, I appreciate it—I'll consider it."

"Hope you do more than that, Emma Jewel."

"We're all we got anymore, with my Emma gone and your daughter half way across the country." She tittered, "should have married me Fate."

"Can you imagine what the town would have done to me and you and our kids forty years ago? I was a married man then, and you were always involved with *somebody*—it just wasn't meant to be."

"Yes and now, about all we can be *is* brother and sister." She nudged him with her leg. "I'll settle for that."

"You'd have to." He chuckled.

"Do you mind?"

"Naw," reaching a hand to tousle her hair, Fate closed his eyes and breathed in the salt air. "So what are you going to do about Hank?"

"I'm not sure."

"You need to go to the cops, Emma Jewel."

"You keep saying that. You sound like a damn broken record."

"Just do it." Fate glared.

"Okay, okay—I know, I will, give me a couple of days to get my story straight and then I'll go."

"Get your story straight?"

"I don't want to go to jail."

"They aren't going to put you in jail."

"They could."

"But they won't. You were scared, intimidated, threatened."

"He never threatened me."

"You were *threatened*, hear me, that man *threatened* you. That's what you say. Okay?"

"I don't like to lie."

"But you don't mind harboring a killer."

"Okay. I was threatened."

****

Emma Jewel tapped "thank you" in response to Mindy's reply, a request to watch the animals for a couple of days. "Just make sure they have plenty of water and be sure to let Nicky out for a little bit. No need to spend the night unless you want. Sorry the A/C isn't working."

"That girl is a godsend," E.J. clucked as she packed the fishing poles in her SUV and slammed the door. Pulling the seat belt across her chest, she released a groan. She hated seat belts, but hated airbags more and was glad Fate had disconnected them for her. After her cousin Monroe suffered a broken collarbone and eye damage when one exploded in her face, Emma Jewel decided they were just too dangerous.

The corners of her mouth lifting, she thought of her cousin in Florida, living on a huge farm of orange groves.

She'd visited her a few years back, went horseback riding in the woods and picked wild grapefruit from trees. They'd had a good time talking about the old days on Topsail.

Even though there was a few years difference between the two, they'd shared many of the same experiences; hanging out at Barnacle Bills and Scotch Bonnet fishing piers, roller skating at the rink in Topsail Beach, and enjoying a place far from overpopulated areas.

After all those years, all the changes in both the island and themselves, Emma Jewel could say that Monroe was happy finally, after reconciling with her relatives in the Sunshine state.

Resting her hand on the edge of the cooler, E.J. pulled the pistol from her purse and pushed it into the side pocket. "Hope he doesn't act up." She backed out of the driveway and headed north.

Today she would confront Hank. Certainly he would give himself up if she talked to him. She could play on his heartstrings; remind him of Emma and what she would want.

"He's not playing with a full deck," E.J. muttered aloud. "He needs psychiatric help."

She was familiar with that sort of thing—mental illness. There had been long days and even longer nights that she and Fate had talked about his mother, Feona. Her mental woes had tortured him so much of his life.

153

'It's a different reality, confusing, debilitating,' Fate had confessed numerous times. 'You can't just throw them away like they're some kind of animal.'

"He needs help." As she pulled her lips in tightly, Emma Jewel tried focusing on the words she would say. She questioned if she could even rationalize with him. "And that woman—the one he called Emma? I hope she's not there."

*Maybe I should call him now, sh*e reached for the cell phone in her purse, *no, I think it's best if I just show up.*

The sound of her tires against the oyster shell driveway of the cottage brought back nostalgic memories of days past—ambivalent feelings of both joy and fear.

In the past the little house had been a carefree getaway for her, her daughter and various friends that had come and gone over the years. Memories of oyster roasts, shrimp boils, fishing on the dock and watching the deer come at dawn or twilight as they all relaxed on the porch, juxtaposed to the fear and knowledge of Hank's crimes, played havoc with her thoughts. She rested a hand on the cooler and felt the pistol through the material as she spotted Hank's car. No others were parked on the circular driveway or nearby. Emma Jewel nodded, *he's alone,* and pulled closer to the house.

Grabbing the poles and cooler she stepped lightly to the door facing the sound side of the cottage. "Hello!" she called. "Hey Hank. I've come to go fishing and collect some *rent*—ha ha. Just kidding."

She peered through the glass doors, making out the living room and kitchen area. *Neat as always, everything in its place. Not a stray glass or bit of paper anywhere.*

The cat, however, was sprawled along the window seat, its eyes closed to the morning sun beaming through the paned glass.

E.J. recalled the cat as a kitten, when Emma and Hank had first rescued it from certain death. Its mother, a feral cat, had just been struck by a car, leaving three kittens to fend for themselves.

Her own cat, Mildred, was one of the three they had rescued. She had been bottle-fed by Emma until at five weeks, E.J. couldn't wait any longer to take the kitten home. From the very start Mildred was affectionate, following her about from room to room.

There were such strident differences between her cat, Mildred, and Tango, Hank's cat. Mildred was loving and lazy. Tango was possessive, aggressive and always aloof.

The third cat, the male named Tom, she'd given to Fate. It still lolled around his house; she'd seen it now and then in passing.

Leaning the poles against the cottage, Emma Jewel looked out across the sound waters, *lots of good things, lots of not so good things,* she recounted the laughter and those horrible tears she'd shed when Fate had caught in bed with that young surfer. That was what she called, *the turning point* in her life.

E.J. looked in through the glass doors spying Tango sunning herself in the window. She sighed heavily brushing away the thoughts of those lost days.

"E.J. what in the world are you doing here?"

Startled by the words, she turned abruptly, her eyes wide, facing Hank, forcing a smile, she consciously made herself relax. "Just came up to see if

155

you want to go fishing on the pier. Not a thing's biting at Topsail, so I thought I'd give this old place a try."

Hank eyed her curiously for a moment, then reached for the poles and stooped to grab the cooler. "I'm glad you came. There are a lot of things I'd like to discuss with you."

She followed him out to the pier, watching as he settled the cooler beneath a bench.

"Did you bring bait?" Hank asked.

"Oh, just that packaged stuff that smells like shrimp."

"That's no good. I've got some bait in the fridge." As he neared her, Hank grabbed Emma Jewel suddenly with both hands, pulling her close to him. "I'm so glad to see you, E.J. it's been so long." His eyes scanning her features, he smiled. "It's so nice to see a familiar face."

Alarmed by the show of warmth, E.J. caught her breath, again trying to calm herself. "What's with the goatee and tattoo?" she asked as he walked toward the house. "And your hair, where did that go?"

There was no answer.

E.J. watched as Hank pulled open the glass doors and walked into the shaded living room. She could barely make out his silhouette pulling open the refrigerator door.

With her foot she nudged the cooler closer to her and bent to unzip the pocket where the firearm lay. *If I need it*, she opened the main compartment and retrieved a cloth napkin and tucked it around the pistol.

"Here we go, bloodworms—and I have a few shrimp here too, though they're not live. Live bait's always best." He met her eyes, "but then, why am I telling you that, the master fisher lady." He guffawed and sat next to her.

"I don't like sitting on the bench, why don't I get a couple of chairs?" he rose almost immediately.

Again, E.J. watched as Hank walked down the pier to the house and disappeared around the side. She wondered if he was searching for a weapon, if he was devising a way to hurt her, to kill her.

"Found them!" he hollered out, waving madly, his face beaming with joy. "I'm so glad you came to visit," again Hank wrapped his arms around his mother-in-law. "I didn't hear anything from you, from the texts I sent, except for that first couple of months." He searched her face, "I thought you might be mad at me. So I didn't want to just pop in on you—and there have been things." Turning away, Hank opened the beach chairs and settled them closer to the railings of the pier.

Emma Jewel examined the beard, the tattoo, the earrings and the baldhead. It was all so unlike the Hank she'd known all her life. "I brought some of my famous coconut cake, the one you like so much, or at least used to."

Reaching for the cooler, E.J. unzipped the top compartment to retrieve two containers of wine. She waved them in the air.

"And you brought wine—those little bottles of wine you know I like. "How thoughtful of you, E.J." His eyes softened, "but then you always were a kind soul, except—I know you never did like me a lot. You only put up with me because of Emma."

She shrugged, "You were good her, Hank. She loved you."

"I love her."

Tilting her head to the side, E.J. stared blankly at him for a moment, "You've changed." She felt her pulse quicken.

Hank patted his stomach and tapped the side of his baldhead, "yeah, I've changed, but not on the inside." He removed the lid from the tub of bloodworms and baited the hooks of his pole, then cast far out into the water. "Hope we catch something," he said, relaxing into the beach chair.

"You've changed so much, Hank. Why?"

He met her eyes for a second, but didn't answer.

"Here," E.J. handed a bottle of wine to him. "Goes good with the cake." she placed a paper plate of cake on his lap.

"Just like old times, huh?" Hank lifted his chin to quickly meet her eyes, then turned away.

As she cast her line into the water, E.J. moved to stand close to the cooler. "I heard, I *know*. I've talked with that gal from Grocery World and to the police. I know what you did Hank. It wasn't right."

"They were bad people. Every single one of them was selling drugs." Justifying his logic, he pointed a finger at her and began, "Everyone of them was contributing to getting kids on the island hooked on drugs, and they're killing the future, taking away everything that is bright and good. Those kids are going to die, they won't have babies, won't have families."

"It's not your job to seek vengeance, Hank."

"Then whose is it?" he shot back.

"God's."

"What did God ever do for me?"

She paused for a moment. "He brought you my Emma—your Emma."

"He took her, too."

"You had a wonderful momma, God rest her soul, she was a good woman; your daddy was a good man. They gave you a fine home, a loving home. I'm sure of that. I don't think you ever had to want for anything."

"Momma and Daddy *were* good people." Hank nodded.

"I know your parents and I had our differences; we seldom saw eye to eye on anything. But one thing I know for sure, your momma would tell you to get down on your knees and ask God for forgiveness. You did wrong, very wrong, Hank, vengeance is God's." She waited for some kind of response, watching as Hank dug his fingers into the wooden railing.

"Are you going to turn me in now? You've been hiding me for a long time."

"At first I didn't believe it. For a long time I didn't, I stuck my head in the sand—hoping you'd just go away. Then I *did* believe it and I thought about it, blaming myself. Thinking that if after Emma died, I'd been more conciliatory—but I was mad at you, blamed you and when I did get around to forgiving you for Emma's death, well, you were busy screwing everything with a skirt and if I was lucky enough to see you in town, you avoided me. Then I was worried about going to jail for harboring a fugitive, aiding and abetting, whatever you call it. But that doesn't matter anymore. Right is right."

"Have you considered that I could kill you too?"

E.J. breathed in, "Yes. But killing me won't keep you from going to hell—and that's where you're going—hell" She was surprised at the calmness with which she spoke and she stepped closer. "Turn yourself in Hank, or I'll do it—there's still time—you're sick—you can get help—you can be forgiven."

Reeling in her line, E.J. examined the baitless hooks. "Pinfish, they're everywhere." Re-baiting the hooks, she cast far out into the water. "This is a peaceful spot, I guess it lends to lots of contemplating and thinking about things that are important."

Hank jerked his fishing pole and wound the line in. "See, there's more than pinfish out here." He held up a nice sized mullet. "A couple more will make a fine super—you're staying for supper aren't you, E.J.?"

"No, just for a few hours. Just wanted to see you—see what you had to say about last year and I guess you said it. Now, everything's up to you. Will you come back to Topsail with me and turn yourself in?"

E.J. watched his jaw tightening, his shoulders tense as she moved to the cooler, bending close to the compartment where the pistol was.

"Yeah, I'll come with you. But give me until the morning, I want to get a few things in order."

He'd said the words, relaxed his frame and reached a hand to hold Emma's for a brief moment. "Sorry. Things have been so confusing."

The morning turned into late afternoon, both had caught several fish; they'd eaten the cake and drank the wine. E.J. didn't mention the killings anymore, she didn't talk about Hank turning himself in anymore either.

Hank talked mostly of the various fish he'd caught throughout the spring and the previous winter. He related joyful episodes with Emma, talking as it were taking place in the present, not the past. He never mentioned any other women; no other woman named Emma and E.J. never asked about her. She figured Fate was right when he said there were lots of women with that name.

"See you in the morning," she said, pushing herself from the hug they'd shared. "You're doing the right thing." As she drove from his driveway, she turned toward Beaufort. *No sense driving all the way home, I'll just get a room at the Holiday Inn.*

By midnight Hank had packed the few items of clothing he owned and put Tango in her cat carrier. But it wasn't until 1:30 a.m. that Estelle pulled into the driveway.

****

Mindy stretched her neck forward, eyeing the thermostat; it read fifty-five. She slid the tab back then forward, waiting to hear the unit stop the rush of cold air coming from the vents. No luck. "Crap," she thumped the apparatus with her thumb and slid the tab back and forth again. She pushed the mode button, changing from cool to heat and then to off, waited a few seconds, but nothing changed. Cold air still rushed through the room. "Damn, it's cold in here. I know Miss E.J. said her air conditioning didn't work, but I didn't think it was this bad."

She walked to the side door, opened it and felt the warm salt breeze blowing off the ocean; she slapped at a mosquito and quickly slammed it. "It's too hot and muggy outside and too cold in here."

Walking into the kitchen she called to E.J.'s pets laying curled on a blanked closely together by the door. "Waiting for Momma, huh? She'll be back tomorrow." Mindy sighed, then reached into a cupboard and pulled down the box of instant hot chocolate, prepared it, set the microwave and padded to the living room closet. She studied the stacks of blankets, the knitted hats and afghans. "Going to need these," she plucked a pair of earmuffs from a hook, "Oh, this is cute," she reached for a tan beret from a side shelf, "Miss E.J. wears this every winter." She then pulled down a multi-colored granny square afghan from the center of the closet and threw it, along with the ear muffs and hat onto the recliner. "It's cold, brrr," she padded back into the kitchen to retrieve her chocolate from the microwave.

With the earmuffs and beret positioned just so on her head, Mindy snuggled into the afghan and clicked on the DVD she'd chosen. "I haven't seen this movie in years." She sipped from the cup of chocolate as she read the title aloud, "Key Largo, this is going to be good." She leaned back a bit in the recliner, "just like winter—snug as a bug."

****

Pulling from the driveway of her sound side rental house, Estelle pressed the headlight switch to on. She drove slowly seven blocks and parked beneath a palm and scrub oak lined driveway. It was dark and vacant looking, as usual. She flipped the lights off.

"Red is the hardest color to see at night." She whispered, reassuring herself that her car and she, dressed totally in red, were as inconspicuous as possible. She walked another two blocks and turned back to view her Volkswagen; she could barely make out the silhouette of the car. Once again, at the top of a beach access, she turned to search for the car—it had become invisible.

Estelle pulled her shoes off and made her way north along the edge of the dunes.

In her hand was a plastic bag of cooked liver, chopped into tiny bits. Around the waist of her red jumpsuit, a leather belt held a sheathed filleting knife. She'd borrowed that from The Upper Deck.

As she climbed the stairway to E.J.'s home she unsnapped the cover and tiptoed to the kitchen door, tried it and grinned, realizing it was unlocked. Entering, she bent to pet the animals as she pulled the liver from the bag. *Damn, why is it so cold in here?* Estelle shivered. Peering into the living room she saw the glow of the TV screen.

There she is, Estelle walked stealthy toward the back of the recliner, pulled the occupant's head back sharply and slit the tanned neck.

Mindy's eyes rolled to meet hers.

"Hell, this isn't that old bitch." She completed the slit and pushed the young girl forward.

****

"What took you so long? I called you at nine."

"Had some car trouble. I think I'm going to have to trade this one in." Essa reached to pull Hank's face to hers. She kissed him deeply. "It was such a pain in the ass getting off of work early.

"I want to get out of here before E.J. comes back. She wants me turn myself in to the police."

"You're not doing that," Essa scoffed. "I'm taking my baby back to the land he loves."

163

"Darling, you're the answer to all my prayers—all the prayers I need, anyway."

Chapter Fourteen

"Nicky was barking his old tired bark. I knew something was the matter—thought a rat or a snake had gotten in." E.J. closed her eyes tightly and covered her mouth with her hand. "I don't like seeing dead people. And Mindy—that was the sweetest little gal."

Fate reached a hand to console her and glanced angrily at the detective. "Can't you do this later?" he asked.

"That's okay," Looking into the detective's eyes she nodded, "go ahead."

"Why was she here?" Detective Lev Gass asked, "Was she spending the night?"

"I told her she didn't have to, but that little gal loved watching those old DVD's of mine. I suspect that is what she had in mind. Whoever came in here must have thought she was me, with her wearing my hat and wrapped in that old afghan."

"May I ask you, Miss Rosell, where you went? Why you weren't home?"

Emma Jewel sucked in a long breath of air and released it slowly, "I may as well tell you now—I went to see Hank Butler."

"What the h--?" Lev checked himself. "Did I hear you say you were with Hank Butler?"

"That's what she said," Fate glared again.

Emma Jewel touched his hand lightly, "Shh, now." She looked back to Lev.

"Yes sir, you did. I was at my little cottage up between Havelock and Beaufort. I talked with him yesterday—we went fishing. I thought I made some headway—that he might come in with me this morning and turn himself in. But when I drove by there this morning, he was gone. My car was still there..."

"Your car?"

"Yes, I leave one up there for guests if they want to borrow it, but it was there, parked in the drive. So I called out and waited, but he never came to the door. I went in, it wasn't locked. His cloths were gone, everything was neat and put away—but, all his stuff is *always* neat and put away. Neatest man I ever met—but the cat—when I saw that Tango was gone I knew Hank had left."

"You should have taken me with you, Emma Jewel." Fate held her hand tightly.

"Mr. Bishop, I might have to ask you to leave if you keep interrupting."

"No! Please, Fate just let me answer what the police ask."

"Looks like he came to kill you, Miss Rosell."

She looked curiously at the detective. "Hank wouldn't do that. I'm his only link to Emma, my daughter. Hank wouldn't kill me."

"Don't fool yourself, as far as we know he's already killed three people. He's dangerous and he's not playing with a full deck. You don't know what he'll do."

"I know he's not all there. I know he belongs in a nut house."

"Ma'am, so you knew he was at your cottage?"

"Yes."

"How long had he been there?"

"Since last summer when he…"

"You've been harboring a murderer for nine months," Lev's jaw tensed, "I think you better get yourself a lawyer, Ms. Rosell."

"That will do." Fate scowled at the detective. "Are you arresting her?"

"I could."

"Come on now, you know this woman isn't dangerous. That man threatened her."

"Is that right? Did Hank Butler threaten to kill you if you told where he was?"

E.J. looked to Fate, then to the detective, "Yes, he said he'd kill me if I told on him."

"But you went up there to talk him into turning himself in? Is that right?"

She nodded.

"Really, you expect me to believe that."

"Yes," she turned to Fate once again.

167

"I know she had a stone cold killer in her house and never told a soul, but if my sister had've been scared she would have certainly come to me. She always comes to me in times of trouble." *Bullshit,* Fate chewed the last statement, *she's always been too proud.*

"There were reasons," E.J. justified. "It's much more complicated than you know."

Lev cast a cool look into her face; he turned to Fate, "Stay with her, either here or your place." He walked toward the door, "And I know I don't have to tell you to not leave the island."

Chapter Fifteen

She couldn't bring herself to call Don to tell him about Mindy. She imagined he'd heard anyway. Wouldn't Lev or someone on the force have contacted him?

Carrie texted the words, it didn't seem as real that way; she waited for a response. Carrie needed warm arms around her now. But she'd heard nothing in the three days since Mindy's death. *He must* know, she thought.

Studying the faces of the attendees, Carrie's eyes rested on Fern walking toward her. It was the first time she had ever seen Fern show anything less than stoic determination; tears poured non-stop from beneath her tortoise shell sunglasses. She leaned against Carrie, her hands trembling, a wad of tissues balled in her fist.

Paula, standing left of Fern, nudged her and handed her several fresh tissues, "Here you go, hon."

Slipping her arm across Fern's shoulder, Carrie patted her back. A thought flashed through her mind: *The old bat fired me last month. Why am I being so nice to her?* Instantly she reprimanded herself and stroked the older woman's shoulder and whispered, "She was such a sweet kid."

"She was dumb as a door knob, but had a real loving heart," Fern sobbed, pushing the fresh tissues to her nose. Searching Carrie's face, she asked, "Who could have done this to that young girl?"

Carrie and Paula shared a knowing glance.

The church was packed with friends and family of the murdered young woman. Mindy's relatives came from all over the state.

She'd even made friends with the people she called damn Yankees, the ones from up north that visited and moved to Topsail. And many came to pay respects to the sweet little southern girl at the grocery store.

Mr. Sanders, one of the locals who frequented Grocery World gave the eulogy at the funeral. He stood behind the pulpit, struggling to keep his composure. "Mindy had a loving heart, despite being involved in the goings-on around town—we all know Mindy loved to share a good story." He smiled. "And she liked offering her *advice*." His trembling voice cracked as he forced himself to continue, straightening his shoulders, he lifted his chin. "Her heart was in the right place and I don't know how many times that little gal came and helped my wife, when she was living, and me, 'cause I can't get around like I used to." He fell silent for a few seconds. "Those who got to know her, knew her to be a loyal and true friend. She'd give you the shirt off her back—she was always trying to be helpful."

Mr. Sanders talked a little more; then Mindy's boyfriend Robby rose to speak about her, about how he didn't know what he would do without Mindy's optimism and support.

By then Carrie and Paula were sobbing along with the rest of the congregation. They followed the crowd of mourners to the end of Surf City Fishing Pier where Robby tossed two-dozen pink roses into the water below. All that could be heard was the rushing of wind, blowing steadily from the south.

"Today is a blustery day, with white caps on the water." Robby began, I guess it's just like my Mindy—full of zest. There wasn't much that was calm about my girl. She loved living." His fingers grasped the lid to the urn and lifted it; he flung the contents into the wind and watched as it carried the ashes across the ocean.

****

"But why would Hank kill Mindy?"

"Why would he come back here?" Paula asked, her usual confident tone now replaced with uncertainty. "Are they sure it was him?"

Scott Abbott rested an arm against the steering wheel of his cruiser. "We're not sure who the perp is Aunt Paula, I mean Ms. Weldon. "The detective working the case is looking into it."

171

"Lev?" Carrie asked.

"Yes ma'am, Detective Gass."

Officer Abbott waited for more questions, looking from Paula's to Carrie's face. "Is that all, Aunt—uh ma'am."

"Yes Scott, I'm sorry to take up your time. Say hello to your momma for me."

Carrie and Paula watched the young officer pull from the Beach Bunny parking lot as they walked toward the entrance to the restaurant.

"I didn't know you were related to Officer Abbott."

"You should know by now that most of us around here are related in one way or another. Just about everybody is somebody's cousin or aunt or uncle, at least through marriage or somewhere down the line."

Carrie snickered.

"Hey, don't be judgmental. We watch out for one another."

"You mean like *Hank* watched out for Mindy?"

"I'm not sure if this is Hank or not."

"Why?"

"There haven't been any murders around here in decades and every one of those that were killed last summer were from up north. No local people were killed and it surely wasn't any relatives belonging to Hank, he'd never do that. Besides, he always did have this *thing* about Yankees."

"So do you."

"So do *you*," Paula snapped. "Anyone who works with the public knows how rude they can be—and how easy it is to dislike the tourists—their ways. Their attitudes are so opposite to ours."

Carrie nodded, "Sure are."

"You have to consider how our way of life here on the island has changed so dramatically by mostly northerners buying up land that we couldn't afford to pay taxes on after the hurricanes of '96. It was very devastating to us, Carrie. It happened to my family and to Mindy's family and lots of others here. So I suppose there's a bit of resentment combined with all the attitude problems."

Carrie settled her elbows on the booth table. "What's all this stuff then about 'letting it roll off my back—don't let it get to me.' What's all that then?"

"I don't let *them* get to me. It's *business.* You never did learn how to accept it as merely *business.* But I don't have to contend with it anymore. Do I?" Paula grinned sarcastically.

"No, I guess you don't. And I'm jealous." Carrie tittered. "I need to find something where I don't have to deal with the public. How about hiring me on as first mate on the fishing boat?

"Oh, if it was only so easy." Paula welcomed the waitress and ordered a cheeseburger with fries and sweet tea.

"The same," Carrie echoed. "How about that, I would love being out on the ocean every day."

"It doesn't work like that anymore." Paula folded her arms across her chest. "Why do you think I took the bridge tender job?"

"Oh yeah, regulations."

"It's just not profitable anymore, at least for me with such a small boat. I can't afford the gas, the regulations are prohibitive and just too much. Maybe I can save enough money to buy a bigger boat and move to where things are less restrictive."

"I'm going with you."

"It's a deal," Paula reached her hand to shake Carrie's.

"Me too, I want to go too," the waitress joined in as she set their orders on the table. "One more cutting remark from the tourons and I'm spitting in the salad."

"Tourons, that was Mindy's word," Carrie stared at her plate.

"Mindy was a good person, every time I waited on here she left, me a really good tip."

"We all miss Mindy."

****

"Nobody's going to recognize you, Hank." Estelle drew a brush through her long hair then wound it into a bun. "Go ahead and sit out on the dock, go fishing, do something. You've been moping around here ever since you came back. You're getting on my nerves."

"What's the sense in going out on the dock if I can't fish?"

"Why can't you fish?"

"If a game warden came by, he'd ask for a license. How would that look if I handed him a license with my name on it?"

"Humph, I guess you got me there—just go out and sit on the dock, go for a walk on the beach. Nobody's going to recognize you. After that picture you showed me when you weren't heavy and had that fine head of salt and pepper hair, you don't even resemble the man you used to be."

Hank's jaw tightened, "I know."

Shaking a tablet from a bottle, Essa held it out to Hank. "Be a good boy and wash this down, it will help you relax."

He obeyed, then smiled seductively, eyeing her as she wriggled free from a pair of shorts.

"I swear, I wish you'd never shaved that off. Honey, you had some fine hair." Essa rose to wrap her arms around Hank; she sucked hard on his neck, leaving a round red mark.

"I wish you wouldn't do that," Hank scolded. "I never did like hickeys, they look so trashy."

"Honey, *you* look trashy with that tattoo on your neck and that ear spike. The earrings—ugh. Well, it's what's in these days." She pulled her body in closer to his, "You look like a tough biker—like *my* tough biker."

"I don't like motorcycles."

Pushing away, Essa reached for the black skirt lying on the bed. She stepped slowly into it, "While I'm at work, please see if you can fix that leak in the bathroom sink."

"I'll try Essa, but I've told you, I'm not that good of a handyman."

"I've never met a man who didn't know how to fix things. Are you sure you're a man?" Her pursed lips rose slowly at the corners to form a smile.

Hank glared at her.

She blew a kiss to him and rubbed her breast teasingly.

Grabbing her wrist, he pushed Essa backward to lie on the bed.

"No, not now, I have to get to work."

"You don't need that job, I can take care of you. We can live in my house. I've got the money." He stopped, licked his bottom lip and tugged on an earring gently.

"You know, Miss Emma Jewel and I have been spending a lot of time together since you've been up at the banks. She says she likes me, that we could be mother and daughter. She's so nice." Essa pouted, her eyes teared. "I really missed you."

"Really? You and E.J.? You're friends?"

She nodded, "Uh huh. She likes me."

"You are a lot like …" He cupped Essa's face in his hands and swallowed hard, "you are—yes you are like her daughter, like my Emma."

"I just hope no one does to her what they did to that dead girl." Rising from the bed, Essa reached for her blouse.

"Mindy?"

"Yes, Mindy. What was she doing there anyway? It seems strange that Mindy would be all alone in E.J.'s house."

Hank shrugged, " Mindy sort of kept an eye on the dog and cat for her from time to time. Maybe that's why she was there."

"Well see, that could have been your lovely mother-in-law that got her throat slit instead of that young girl. I bet whoever killed her thought she was killing that old lady." Essa pushed her arms through the sleeves of her white blouse and began buttoning it. She tucked it into the waist of her skirt. "But it's odd that E.J. would be up around your place trying to talk you into giving yourself up. Now, why would she do that after all these months?"

Hank ran his fingers around his goatee, smoothing it against his skin. "Yes it is. Why would she want to have me in jail? I'm all she has left."

"What do you mean? She likes me. She's got me, at least she thinks she does." Pulling him to stand, Essa kissed Hank gently on the lips. "I will do anything for you, I'll have your baby."

Essa kissed him again, longer and deeper, more passionately. "We're like mother and daughter, Miss E.J. and me. I just hope that no one tries to hurt her like they did that girl Mindy."

Hank watched the door close behind Essa, his heart sank a bit; he'd come to care deeply for her. Leaning back on the bed, he folded his hands beneath his head. *There was no justification in killing that girl. Yeah, she could be slutty, yeah, she wasn't the hottest chick around, but she was clean. As far as I know, she never got into drugs.* "Poor Mindy, I hope she didn't suffer." He studied the ceiling as he lay on the bed, the bumps; little flecks of dirt and dust seemed to be everywhere. They appeared to multiply as he counted them, "eight, fourteen, twenty, twenty-six, thirty," they moved about, swirling, inhaling and exhaling.

Quickly, he sat erect. His feet firmly on the floor, he pressed the palms of his hands to his temples and closed his eyes tightly. Hank could feel his breath quicken, against his will it quickened even more. "Stop it!" he screamed.

The pounding in his head echoed about the room. Suddenly he felt lifted from the ground, as if his feet could not touch it. Hank balled his fists and slammed them into the sides of his head. "Stop it!" he screamed again.

Chapter Sixteen

He'd gotten the text from Carrie; he knew beforehand—Lev had called about Mindy's murder. Don stared through the windshield, his body tense; he lingered on feelings of guilt for not having responded to Carrie, but had told himself he couldn't deal with that loss, not at this time; he couldn't be there for someone who needed him, not right now. There was work to be done and there was no time for feeling sorry or for regrets.

"This is going too slowly," Don muttered as he lingered, still sitting in the car in front of Vera's. Frustrated with the ambivalent feelings of having to do his job and hurting another person's feelings, he groaned aloud then popped a few Tums in his mouth.

Grabbing the bags of groceries he stepped from the gray Dodge and made his way along the faux cobblestone walkway.

"Hi," Vera greeted him with a smile and smoothed her new bobbed hairdo. She looked past him to the Dodge parked in her driveway. "Is that it? Is that what you've been waiting for?"

"Yep, that's my baby."

She studied the vehicle for several moments, "I was expecting something a bit more flashy."

Shrugging, Don laid the bags on the counter. "Dependable, that car is always dependable."

"And that's why you've had it in the garage for so long."

"Nothing's perfect."

"You're right about that." Vera stood in the middle of her living room and twirled. "Like my new hairdo?" she asked. "New dress, too. Watcha think?"

"You look just like a picture, Vera—just wonderful."

He had to admit, she did look better without the big hair and too short mini skirt. If he wasn't somewhat attached, if he lowered his standards a bit and accepted all the cussing and drinking, he might even have been interested. "I've got French bread, fresh basil, some tomatoes." He held up a bottle of red wine, "and *vino*."

"Wine?" She grabbed the bottle and red the label. "Wow! This stuff cost you some bucks. But you didn't need to get all that other stuff I've got a jar of spaghetti sauce in the cupboard."

"You're in for a treat, I'm making it all from scratch."

Vera crinkled her nose and shrugged. "Suit yourself." She lowered her voice to a sultry purr and reached to pat his behind. "Ooh, trying real hard to impress me, aren't you? Real spaghetti sauce, wine...sounds to me like you think you're going to get some tonight."

Don felt the burn in his chest again; he popped another antacid into his mouth. "I've told you I have a gal, Vera. I'm just trying to show my appreciation for all you've done for me since I've been stranded here."

Vera poured herself a glass of the wine, "At least your hunk of junk is fixed and ready to go."

"Yes, it's nice being back with what's comfortable." Don opened a cupboard to retrieve a large pan, "How about a glass of that wine for me, my hands are kind of..."

"Yep, just like Hank. Didn't like getting things dirty, afraid you're going to mess up the wine glass." She shook her head as she poured wine into another glass then topped off her own.

"Where did you say this guy, Hank, was from?"

"Hell, I don't know. He said he'd traveled all over the place. He never got too specific. Why do you ask?" She turned to Don, her head tilted, her eyes hooded. "You're always asking about him."

"You're always bringing him up, comparing me to him. I'd just like to know what I'm being compared to and why it's such a big deal."

"Hope you brought two bottles of this stuff," Vera filled her glass again. "Mr. Hank Jordan is a big deal. He told me he loved me. He said he was going to take me to the Bahamas and Cozumel." She lifted her eyes sadly to meet Don's. "He was so tender when we did it...you know. Nobody's ever been like that with me."

181

Don felt sorry for Vera. Part of him wanted to pull her to him and comfort her. But he knew better. She would undoubtedly mistake his consoling for something romantic. *How do I keep from hurting this girl?* he asked himself. He watched her pour more wine into her glass. *How would she react if I told her that the way Hank treated her, the way he'd been with her in bed, was the way he treated all women?*

Surely Vera had been around enough to realize there were men out there who did that. Don had expected her to be tougher and she was, except when she drank.

As he turned the burner to simmer, and stirred the bubbling sauce, part of him felt like he was wasting a good meal on a drunk who would more than likely vomit it up later, and part of him felt like he was doing a kindness for a woman who had experienced few kindnesses in her life. "Let's go sit down," he led her to a chair, the one he'd slept in several nights before. He scooted an adjacent chair closer, "Sounds like he really hurt you. Want me to beat him up for you?" He smiled tenderly.

Vera rolled her eyes. "Yeah, like you could. He's got fifty pounds on you and looks tough as nails." She brushed the side of her neck, "Big ol' hammerhead shark tattoo here and earrings—little hoops."

"Doesn't sound like much of a looker."

"But he's got the most kind hazel eyes, I've never seen eyes like that. I mean, I feel like he is looking into my very soul when he looks at me."

"Do you know where he lives?"

"Yeah I know. He took me up there a couple times. And then I've driven up there, but the last time I did, *her* car was there."

"Can you give me directions?"

Already Vera was beginning to slur her words; "What? Why?" She poured the remainder of wine into her glass and shook her head, "You want to go now? What's so important about going there now?"

"I'm going to have a little talk with him."

"You don't have to do that for me. He's probably with that bitch anyway. I don't want to go. I don't want to see him." Vera's eyes searched the kitchen counter. "Where's that other bottle of wine you brought?"

Don grabbed the bottleneck and held the wine in front of Vera. "If you want more wine, you have to show me where Hank lives."

"Asshole, you snake in the grass." She snatched the air, trying to grab the wine.

"Nope. You have to show me first."

"Why are you so mean?"

"The wine, Vera, just show me where he lives."

They headed east on Highway 101, Vera still holding on to her glass of wine while Don drove the thirty or so miles to Hank's. He drove slowly since twice already Vera had instructed him to turn down wrong roads.

"Right here, turn down this little dirt road right here." Vera held her empty wine glass level with her chin.

"Are you sure this time?"

"Na na na na na, yes, I'm sure. Now give me that damn bottle or I'll knock you from here to next Friday." She stuck out her tongue and raised a middle finger to only a few inches in front of his face. "I need a drink."

Don turned slowly onto the oyster shell drive, still holding the bottle of wine against the door.

"I'd know that crunch anywhere. Them is oyster shells and they belong to Hank." Vera pressed an open hand against the window, "I told you someone was here. But it ain't *cuntusabundus*-that ain't her car."

Don slowed the Dodge down to below ten miles per hour and cut the lights. In the moonlight he could make out a dark blue Ford Mustang. Next to it was a car marked Carteret County Sheriff. An older model Chevy sedan sat parked to the side. "You stay in the car, I'll check this out." He handed her the bottle of wine.

"What the—what are you guys doing here?" He asked, staring in from the porch.

Lev stepped from the living room out to the dock. "Well, I'll be. Fancy meeting you here." He held his hand out to shake Don's. "All roads lead to Hank," Lev joked. "That lady, Hank's mother-in-law, has been hiding him up here since last summer."

"So this is Ms. Rosell's place?"

"Yep."

"That explains a lot. I never would have figured that sweet old woman would hide a murderer. She sure had me fooled, last year you'd have thought she hardly knew the man, talked as if she hated his guts, even though he had been her son-in-law at one time."

"You never know about people."

"Ditto, I never thought she'd do this; as long as I've known her she's been straight as an arrow."

"A mixture of fear and the loss of her daughter. At least that's what I figured. I don't think she meant to get herself so involved."

Don leaned against the dock railing. "Just goes to prove that nothing is ever as it appears."

"You should know." Lev kicked at the bench and glared disapprovingly at his friend, "So, you heard from the kid, from Phil?"

"Been too busy."

"Takes five minutes, bro."

"He's where he needs to be. I'm not too good at the parenting thing."

The wake from a passing powerboat sent ripples lapping at the pier pilings and to the shore. Don gazed into the water below at his hazy image. "Hank's changed his appearance. He's bald now, with a goatee, hammerhead tat on his neck and pierced ears." He stared deeply into the murky water, "Gotten fat, too."

"Ms. Rosell mentioned something about that—says she came up here the other day to talk with him. Thought she had him ready to give himself up."

"That was the night Mindy was murdered?"

"Same night."

"Why would he want to kill that little girl? She never hurt anybody—a little ditsy maybe," Don took a shallow breath. "But still a pretty good little kid. I don't understand. Rosell was up that night. Right?"

"Yes, said she stayed at a hotel in Beaufort—didn't want to drive all the way back to the island."

"Hank knew that, didn't he?"

"Maybe he didn't. Maybe he thought she drove back." Lev said.

"Did she tell him that?"

"I don't know."

"Because if he knew she was staying here, then he had the opportunity to drive down to Topsail and kill Mindy."

"*If* he killed her—we can't be sure it was him." Lev tousled his unkempt hair and yawned. "You coming back or you think there's more here?"

"I'm not sure. I don't think any of the "V" girls know anything."

"The "V" girls, oh yeah, you mentioned them once before. Who are they?"

Don snickered, "Twins and an older sister—all their names start with a "V."

"Hot damn, sounds like you've been *busy* up here. Is that one of them with her head out the window, puking all over the side of your car?"

"Yeah, that's the one who's got the hots for Hank. She'll probably pass out now. Vera—lovely girl. Yep, she was seeing our friend for a few weeks until a cousin of hers, Estelle, *stole* him away." Don guffawed.

"Cousin? Have you met her yet?"

"No. That's why I'd like to hang around. I'd like to see if she has any idea where he is, if she knows anything."

"Well, you enjoy yourself up here with all these "V" girls. Sounds like *fun*," Lev chuckled.

"Hardly. I did all my slumming in college, when I didn't know any better."

"Oh yeah, that's right. The one in Scotland, now, that's funny." Lev's chuckle stretched into another yawn."

"You need to get some rest, don't you buddy?"

"Yeah, I haven't slept much since the murder. Your girl, Carrie is pretty broken up about it. I've been trying to comfort her." He slid his eyes toward Don and grinned.

"You're sick." Don punched his friend's shoulder lightly.

"Yeah, I know. So how long has this thing with Hank and the cousin been going on?"

"I'm not sure. Sometimes it's difficult getting information from Vera. She spends more time passed out than awake." Don turned to leave, "And *you* keep you meat hooks off Carrie."

"You're not giving her much to cling to, old friend. People who care about *you* need to know that you care about *them* too—both she and Phil."

Don shrugged and turned to walk back to the cottage. Inside other policemen were dusting for fingerprints and searching for any telltale signs of the occupant.

"Any sign of a cat?" Don asked as he entered the doorway.

"No sir, and whoever was here wiped the place clean. It's spotless, not a print anywhere."

"Meticulous, Hank's OCD, always neat, with everything in its place. That's what surprises me so much, the Hank Vera talks about dresses sloppy, cut off shorts, old tees, tats—just not like our old Hank at all, except for this—the cleanliness." He swiped the window sill with his palm, "Cat hair, this is cat hair—the cat's been here and I know damn well he's not leaving that cat behind—he's gone for good."

Lev ran a finger along the sill, gathering loose hairs, "So where did he go?"

Chapter Seventeen

The photograph of Mindy on the nightly news made her death so much more real; Hank shuddered as cold shocked his body. He stared at the picture as the commentator mouthed words; he was disgusted that someone would even speak them.

Quickly Hank pressed the off button to the remote and laid it at his side. He pulled a pillow to his chest, hugging it gently as he listened to Tango's loud purring. *How many days did the reporter say it had been since her death? When did Essa tell him about it?* "Is this real?"

Mindy was the one who so often checked his groceries. He knew her—remembered her. *Did I take her to bed with me once?* he asked himself, struggling to recall whether or not he had. "Pretty little girl—well, not as pretty as Emma. All young women are pretty."

Sighing heavily, he rose from the bed and slipped on his shoes. *I've got to get out of here, Emma is right; nobody is going to recognize me.* He grabbed a ball cap from the rack, slipped it on his head and walked out the door toward the ocean.

Depositing his shoes at the base of an access, the image of the girl with the wispy blonde hair played in his mind. *Mindy, by no means was innocent. She liked to flirt, she'd been around.*

But there was something genuine that made her likeable, and Hank liked her as well as anyone else. He certainly didn't dislike Mindy.

He strained again to recall their sexual encounter, *I think we did, I'm sure we did.* "Couldn't have been earth shaking or I would remember it better." Hank looked up into the starlit sky, he inhaled, "so it is—we all live and we all die. How did she die?" He searched his mind, thinking he knew how, that he'd heard how. "Throat was cut. That little girl's throat was cut—what a waste."

He watched a ghost crab scuttle quickly across the shore toward the dunes. "Isn't her boyfriend a cop? Wonder if they have any leads on who the culprit is and I wonder about that detective--Don, that's his name. I bet he's out and about looking for the killer." He smirked. "It's not me this time."

The moon, hanging big and yellow in the starry sky, cast its shining rays upon the dark water. Hank stopped to relish the flickering light upon the waves; like silver it sparkled and danced with the ocean's to and fro. It drew him to memories of his wife and how they used to love walking on the beach at night. He could nearly hear her laugh as she skipped backwards along the frothy shore, teasing him, beckoning him to keep up with her. He watched as she chased a ghost crab back to its hole in the dunes then ran to the shore to kick seawater on him. Emma was so free, so playful, so real, unencumbered by the restraints and mores of the day.

Hank's steps seemed lighter as he thought of his wife; he quickened his gait and kicked at the incoming tide. "She'll be home any minute; I must get back to the house. I know, I'll make her dinner. There's got to be some fresh fish in the fridge. Emma loves Mahi Mahi."

Jerking the door open, Hank searched the contents of the refrigerator. Condiments on the side door, cluttered and smeared, stared back. He squinted. "Where's the fresh lemon and brine?" A liter of diet Coke, vanilla flavored coffee creamer, a giant tub of margarine and a tin foil covered can of spaghetti were among the items stored on the shelves.

He pulled open the freezer compartment. A couple of frozen pizzas and a T.V. dinner were all he found.

"I know I put fresh fish in here—I always have fresh fish." He held both doors open and studied the contents again. "Emma must have eaten it. But what's she doing with the pizza and this other *junk?* We don't eat like that."

His heart was pounding in his brain; Hank pressed his hands against the sides of his head, "Ugh, stop it." Striking his temples with balled fists; he called out, "Emma! Where's my fish!"

Tango wound her body in and out between Hank's legs, she meowed loudly at first, then softly several more times, looking up at him she seemed to be pleading for attention.

Hank followed her into the bedroom, where they both lay on the bed, the cat snuggling beside him, purring quietly. He stoked her thick fur and fell into a deep sleep.

****

Still in her robe, Vera opened the door to Don, "Hell, you don't need to keep coming around here. You know I can drink by myself just fine."

"You shouldn't drink so much," Don flopped down into the overstuffed chair.

"You again, the gentleman who cares? Bullshit. What's it to you?"

Don shrugged, "Sugar, if I don't care and Hank doesn't care, then who else but you is going to? If you don't take care of yourself, nobody else is."

"Don't beat around the bush, now. Say what you *really* mean." Vera lit the cigarette between her lips. "And I suppose I should stop smoking too?"

"That's up to you, but it's not a bad idea."

"Did you come over here to tell me how to run my life or do you want something? You sure as hell don't want to get in my pants, so what is it?"

"I'm glad you've finally realized that, Vera. Everybody doesn't want…"

"You *want* something." She interrupted. "What is it? Do you want to go back to Hank's? Want to beat him up for me? What happened with all that last night? I remember going over there with you, but that's it." She cast an admonishing frown his way. "You shouldn't have given me that other bottle of wine."

"You don't remember a thing do you?"

"Nope."

"He wasn't there. Neither was your cousin Estelle."

"They must have been out in *her* car."

"What does she drive?"

Pulling her robe tight, Vera sat across from Don on the couch, she inhaled from her cigarette and released a perfect ring of smoke. "Let's see, she's had so many cars—then there was that one year when it was trucks." She bit her bottom lip, "She just did get another one—a car this time—a small one I think."

"Do you know what make, model, what color?"

"I have no idea. All I know is it's little. Hell, I never go and check out what she's driving. And I haven't seen her in several weeks. It seemed it was dark red or orange—something like that." She shook her head. "Did you see a little car parked in front of Hank's?"

"No. The only one there was an old Chevy."

"That's what Hank drives."

Don scratched his head, trying to think, trying to find an excuse to have Vera introduce him to her cousin. *If I tell Vera I'd like to meet Estelle, she's going to go ballistic and think I'm interested in her. If I don't, then I've got to wait around until I bump into her. That could be forever, or never. I don't have time to worry about hurt feelings,* he thought. *Hank could be back at Topsail, he could have killed Mindy and he could go after Carrie.* He drummed his fingers on a side table, "I'd like to meet your cousin." He stood ready, waiting for the explosion.

193

It didn't come, instead he examined Vera's face, she seemed calm as she lit another cigarette, inhaled slowly and curled her legs beneath her.

"It's obvious that you're not interested in me. I mean, you've had so many chances and short of me throwing myself naked at you, well, I guess it's not going to happen." She looked at him; her lips forming a crooked smile. "But, you know, I'm kind of glad. I'm just not that attracted to you and…I guess I should get used to Estelle stealing all my men. She's been doing it since grade school."

"You've *tried* the naked thing." Don teased. "And it's not you, not anything you don't have or do have, or anything at all." He searched for Vera's eyes, meeting them confidently, "I've been stuck here for a while. You took me in until I could get a motel—nobody else did that for me. And like I told you before, I've got a girlfriend. I'm not looking for a romantic relationship or a POA. I needed a friend when I got stranded here— you treated me like one—so I'm just doing the right thing."

"The gentleman thing," Vera interjected.

"Maybe, but if you tell me where your cousin lives, maybe I could get up with Hank. He really should apologize to you for hurting you. And since I have nothing else to do, I may as well help you—my damsel in distress." Don leaned forward. "I bet you've been hurt a lot."

Tears welled in Vera's eyes, she ran the sleeve of her robe against them smearing mascara across the pastel fabric. Her body tensed as she drew another cigarette to her lips. "Sometimes life sucks." She shrugged, "I'll get over it. I always do. This time it just took longer. I had it bad for him, for Hank."

"Don't sell yourself short; you're a pretty woman, and you're kind hearted. Just quit going to bed with everybody. I know it's what all the magazines are touting these days, all the music and all the television shows. But don't be fooled, get to know someone *really* well before you hope in the sack with them."

"So you're my big brother now, huh?"

Hank grinned, "Where's Estelle live?"

****

He was glad he was no longer driving the rented Mazda; it would have been hell driving along the bumpy, curvy roads. At least with the Dodge he was comfortable.

Slowly he'd turned onto state road 101; he recalled Vera's directions: *On a big curve, right past the Cracker Barrel billboard,* he reminded himself again: *little dirt road, with tall pines on either side.* He slowed to a snail's pace as he neared one of many curves along the highway. Spotting the billboard, he turned onto the rutted path just beyond it.

This road too was curvy and full of holes; he bounced along in the Dodge. "And she's driving a *little* car. Seems you'd need something a bit bigger than that for this road.

His eyes scanning the landscape, Don stopped suddenly as several deer jumped in front of his car. He watched as they gracefully leapt from the clearing into the piney woods.

Ahead, nestled between a magnolia and several small oaks, sat a small wooden structure. Purple wisteria hung like juice-laden grapes from the spindly bushes interlaced among the other trees. The sweet aroma was intoxicating; it was almost too sweet.

The small house was nearly hidden among all the foliage and upon further examination, it appeared old, weather-beaten and in need of several structural repairs. One of the banisters was askew and a shutter hung loosely from a window. "This could be a nice little place, if it was fixed up," he spoke aloud.

Don scanned the front yard. "No cars, no trucks, no anything." He parked his car, exited and slowly began walking around the small structure. The greenery obscured much of the house, especially the sides. He strained to find a window as he made his way to the back. There sat an older model Volkswagen. Both doors had been spray painted with yellow peace signs; a purple flower was on the rear of the car; both headlights had been smashed as well as the windshield.

He studied the inside through the windows; beer cans and wadded fast food bags littered the floors. The cloth seats had been shredded.

Odd, he thought, *it hasn't been in a wreck. This looks more like the car's been vandalized.*

The smudged windows of the house made it difficult for him to see inside, but Don did make out a kitchen table cluttered with dishes and boxes of cereal and what looked like the living room area.

It was neat, if not clean, with a sofa, two chairs and a television. There were no pictures on the walls, no knick knacks, nothing that may have made the place look homey or cozy.

"Just a place to crash, huh." He tried the doorknob. To his surprise, it was unlocked.

He walked into the living room, then the kitchen. He stepped along the unpolished wooden floors of the hallway, peering into a bathroom and two bedrooms. Something was missing, though obvious that someone lived there, it seemed at the same time vacant. *With the way they were describing this chick, I was expecting more. Maybe frills and lacy curtains, a heart shaped bed or puppy dog figurines, a portrait of her nude body hanging on the wall, or something to indicate she is beguiling—that she has powers to steal men away.*

"The girls didn't ever tell me what she looked like," Don guffawed, "I can just imagine the raging, screaming and cussing that would have taken place if I had asked. Why is it that women think men can be *stolen* away?"

"Because they can."

The sultry voice startled him and Don turned quickly, reaching for the weapon he hadn't worn.

"My, but we're jumpy. And what was that? Reaching for a weapon—a gun? I don't see a gun. So you must usually wear one. So that would make you..." Estelle tilted her head slightly and pursed her lips. She leaned against the wall, crossing her long bare legs, "a cop—right?"

Holy shit, she is a looker, Don took his time studying her long frame, her perfect body. It was if Charlize Theron had walked from the movie screen— with all the composure of a self-assured accomplished woman. But this one was even more striking.

Initially he felt confused, surprised by being caught in the act. Then he felt defensive because of the woman's cool reaction. She had not shown anger or fear. She'd come across as if an old lover had suddenly materialized. "Are you Estelle?" he asked feigning his own confidence.

"Depends." She pushed her long hair to the side.

"Your cousin Vera told me where you lived."

"You haven't answered my question. Are you a cop?"

"Maybe," he retorted.

Estelle turned and walked into the living room, stretched her legs beside her on the sofa and pressed a cell phone to her ear. "Maybe I should call my cousins—or maybe I should call the police."

Don flipped open his wallet to display his badge.

"So you are a cop."

"A detective."

"You're not from here. What are you doing all the way up in Carteret County?"

"I'm looking for a man. His name is Hank Butler. Your cousins, mainly the one named Vera, told me you've been seeing a man that fits his description—sort of."

Estelle settled the phone in her lap, her eyes resting on his for a moment; she let them move slowly to his feet then back to his eyes.

Her blatant ogling unsettled him.

"I used to see a man named Hank—Hank Jordan. Tell me, what did Hank look like?"

"About six foot—fit—salt and pepper hair," He stopped.

"Doesn't sound like the Hank I know."

"He may have changed his appearance. How about hammerhead tat on his neck, pierced ears, bald, overweight."

She lifted her head and licked her lips, "Now that sounds like Hank."

Don suppressed a chuckle, as he exchanged a knowing look with her.

"I know, I've heard it before, what is a girl like me doing with a man like that—right?"

"Something like that."

"What kind of girl are *you* with?" Her gaze burned judgmentally as she clipped her hair atop her head.

Don thought of Carrie and then the image of Maggie, his druggie ex-wife, flooded his mind. He frowned and took a step back.

"I thought so."

"What can you tell me about Hank Jordan?" Don settled himself in an adjacent chair and leaned forward, fighting to focus on Estelle's face, not her voluptuous body.

Her long fingers caught stray strands of hair and pushed them from her eyes as she licked her lips again. "He treated me okay—at first. And like I said, he wasn't all that handsome, but he was nice—at first."

"At first?" Don echoed.

"Yes. He *was* what you might call a boyfriend— for a while and then things changed. He got too possessive and mean, he tried knocking me around some."

That part didn't sound like the Hank Don knew. Hank Butler was always kind to his women. When he was finished with one he simply quit calling, quit showing any interest. "So he was abusive?"

Estelle nodded, "I normally don't have much to do with guys like him—you know, tattoos and earrings. But I guess he just swept me off my feet with all his gentlemanly ways. That's what fooled me." She grinned shyly and swung her legs from the sofa to a sitting position. "He was a little too weathered for me. I usually go for the clean cut type—more like you."

Don ignored the reference, "A local man?"

She shook her head, "No, he certainly isn't local."

"Where is he from?"

"You know, I'm really not sure. We never talked about that." Standing, Estelle glided past Don, touching his shoulder, "Would you like a glass of iced tea?"

His eyes followed her into the kitchen; he watched as she reached into the cabinet for glasses, filled them with ice and poured tea into each.

"Here," she handed a sweaty glass to him, brushing his leg with hers as she walked to the sofa. "To answer your question, I think he may have mentioned something about Georgia or some place like that. I know he wasn't too fond of the ocean, said the land around here was too flat and sandy for him."

"Really?" He pondered her truthfulness—was she being honest? If she was, then *this* Hank was not his man. But if she was lying—. Or maybe she was telling the truth as she knew it.

"Did he have a cat?" Don asked.

"I'm not sure."

"Not sure?"

"I only went to his place once and I didn't see a cat, but then I didn't go inside. We were out on the dock, the pier, and we went fishing. Hank loved to fish."

"And he said he was from Georgia, right?"

"Um-hum, yes, that was it. I think he was from somewhere in the Georgia mountains." She sipped from the glass of tea, her eyes lifting to search his. "I don't know why I got involved with a man like that."

Don watched her eyes well with tears; as the lids closed, droplets poured down her cheeks. *I've always been a sucker for a crying woman.* He sighed and stretched his hand to hers.

It would have been easy to move to the sofa, wrap an arm around her shoulder to console her—he brushed the impulse away. "We all make mistakes, Estelle. It's not the end of the world."

Her hair, loosened from the pins holding it up, cascaded down to her shoulders, shrouding her face. Estelle lifted her eyes to meet his through the strands. Her lips, full and pouting, trembled. "I don't understand, I'm not a bad person." She giggled gently, "Oh, I know I flirt a bit, but—it's just that some men, because they think I'm pretty, take advantage of me."

"But you seem like such a confident woman. When you caught me in your house…"

"What was I going to do? If you were a bad guy and I had run, what would have happened? I read on the Internet that it's best to just keep calm." She touched the fingers of his still outstretched hand.

Damn, she is beautiful. Don felt himself swallow hard as he struggled to release himself from her gaze. Her perfect lips, shape of her face and dark blue eyes held him and he found himself wanting to touch the tiny flecks of brown dotting her almond complexion.

"Hank and I split about a week ago. I can't say I'm sorry."

The words startled him as he released his hand from Estelle's. Rising from the chair Don found his composure, straightened his shoulders and drew a breath. "Do you live here alone?" *Where did that question come from?* he asked himself before adding. "Are you afraid he'll come back and harm you?"

She shook her head, "Hank won't bother me. I saw him with another girl already."

"Where?"

"In Beaufort, at a restaurant. See, he's already forgotten me and found someone new."

Don found himself extending his hand to help Estelle rise from the sofa, "Good riddance to him then."

"Yes, good riddance. He sure did teach me a lesson, no more tattooed men, no more ear piercings."

He reached for the doorknob, smiled and asked, "Do you mind my stopping by if I have any further questions?"

"Call me," she jotted her number on a slip of paper. "Or come by, either one." She moved closer to him, slid her hand behind his neck, drawing herself near to kiss his cheek. "Thank you for being here. You're a nice man—a good man. I'd like to get to know you better."

He felt the stirring in his belly and the impulse to cover her lips with his. He swallowed again, pulled away, and walked to his car.

Before he knew it he was on the highway, gathering his thoughts, sifting through their conversation. Estelle's words still swam warmly from her clear pink lips, enveloping him. He wanted to touch her, feel her softness. "Hell," Don cursed, angry with his vulnerability.

****

Don rang the doorbell, and waited for Vera. "Hi, he muttered, walking through the door and slumping into his usual chair.

"What'd I tell you? She's something ain't she?" Did you two get it on?" She laughed and sat next to

202

him on the arm. "I don't stand a chance with her around. Men just seem to fall at her feet." Vera smacked Don lightly on the cheek twice, "Snap out of it, asshole. I swear, all you men—well, you know why your underwear has a hole in the front?"

Don stared curiously into her eyes.

"So air can get to the brain."

Tilting his head back, he laughed raucously. "She put me in a damn trance."

"But she is beautiful." Vera sighed.

"That, she is. She is one of the most beautiful women I've ever seen."

"Ain't fair—she did the lip licking thing, didn't she?"

"What?"

"That thing she does with her lips. Yeah, she's got those full gorgeous lips that look sort of translucent and she licks them when she's trying to be sexy."

A picture of Estelle sitting across from him on the sofa played in his head; Estelle licked her lips, her eyes suggesting both innocence and desire. "Some people get it all, Vera. Or a least appear to." He crossed his arms over his chest and slumped further into the chair. "God help us all, I'm not sure if she was putting on a show or telling me the truth. But I was actually feeling sorry for her. She was crying—said Hank had left her for another woman—and that he'd even hit her a few times. I think she's really hurting."

"Good, now she knows how it feels."

"It's not nice to revel in someone's else's misfortune."

Vera blew a raspberry his way, "It's not nice to nana, nana, nana," she mocked. "She's got you by the nuts, man. She's jerking your chain. You better believe she was lying, I'll bet a month of birth control pills that she's lying through her teeth." Vera rolled her eyes, "Tsk. Shame on you for believing her. Hank never hit me, so he certainly didn't hit her. If anyone would ever hit Estelle, she'd slice and dice them. She has never put up with anybody hitting her—that's for sure. And I find it hard to believe that anyone would leave Estelle. She's the one that leaves or finds a way to get rid of a man when she's done with him."

"How, how does she get rid of them?"

"There was the one who had a wife. Well, you can guess how that went. And then there was the one who killed himself because she wouldn't marry him. Or men just move away, never to be heard from again, heartbroken and distraught—makes me sick. But mostly, once she tells them to get lost, they do. They mope around town for a few months and that's the end of it."

"Wow, that is one amazing woman."

"All right, already. We know she's God's gift to mankind."

"What does she do for a living? How does she make ends meet?"

"Remember the one I just told you about that killed himself? He left that little house she lives in it now and then, most men she's with give her money."

"The house looks worn, no decoration, nothing."

"That's always been her way. It's sort of odd, her being so attractive. You'd think she'd want to pretty things up a little around that house of hers. Plant some flowers, paint the inside, the outside, clean it, but I don't think she knows what a vacuum cleaner is or even Dawn dish detergent. I've never understood that about her."

He understood now, a little more, the disdain for Estelle—it wasn't all jealousy. "Look, there's something I want to tell you."

"What? You're in love with Estelle and are going to ask her to marry you."

"I'm tempted, but that's not it," he chuckled.

"So, what is it?"

"I don't want you to get mad and I'm hoping we can keep this just between you and me."

"You're gay. I knew it. That's the reason you didn't try to get in my britches."

Don rolled his eyes. "No, I'm not gay."

"Then what?"

"I'm a detective. I'm investigating some murders that happened last summer at Topsail Island. I think the Hank you were seeing and whom Estelle has been with is the man I'm looking for."

Chapter Eighteen

"Nothing unusual?" Lev asked.

"Depends on what you call unusual. I see lots of strange things from my little nest. But you could say they're not what you'd call unusual for the island." Paula replied.

"Just keep your eyes open."

"I'm not exactly sure what you're looking for or what I'm supposed to report on." Paula pressed the speaker tab and laid the phone on the counter as she flipped a switch to raise the barrier arms for the swing bridge.

"Just something that doesn't look right or feel right."

Paula rolled her eyes, and exhaled noisily.

"Oh, don't act like you've got something more important to do. I know you've got to be bored up there all alone. Wouldn't you like some company?" Lev teased.

"No thank you, I enjoy my solitude." Watching as a lone car crossed the bridge and drove out of sight, Paula relaxed into a nearby chair.

"I could bring a bottle of wine and home baked bread."

"Are you trying to get me fired? It's against policy. Sorry Lev. And besides, this job I'm doing for you is strictly business, right."

"Did I suggest anything otherwise?"

Constantly. Paula pressed the phone to off and sighed, "What a piece of work." She opened the book she'd been reading and relaxed in a chair, propping her feet up. After a few minutes she closed the book and rose. "That man is so annoying. I don't even know what he wants me to look for.

It's the same old stuff here every night. One man is driving his secretary around in his wife's car at two in the morning. Some young kids are toking on a joint with all the windows rolled up, the car's full of smoke. Now, where's the cops on that one?

And then that little red bug with the eyelashes— Carrie's friend from The Upper Deck, zooming back and forth and back and forth in the wee hours of the morning. Haven't seen it in the last couple of days, maybe they went back to where they came from.

What the hell, it all looks questionable, but not nefarious. It's the same old crap.

She leaned against a table, studying the view—the road coming to the island—the road leaving the island. One car passed, then another. She checked her phone for the time, 2 a.m. "By now most people are sleeping, or passed out. If they're on the road at this hour, it's usually to do something they're not supposed to be doing."

A bright orange Volkswagen Bug passed beneath the metal stanchions of the bridge, reminding her of the red one. *Yeah, I haven't seen that red Volkswagen since* I met Essa and Carrie at the coffee shop. Now that is odd—I know she's still working at the restaurant. How's she getting around?" Paula looked north to where she'd seen the Bug turn. "There's something about that chick that's weird. Can't put my finger on it, and Carrie—she's not someone Carrie would hang around. Carrie's too low key, naïve—*nice.* Yeah, Carrie's too nice to be friends with this woman. I get the feeling she's some kind of player—with that wild hair and those boobs falling out of her blouse. There's something different about her—something I don't trust."

Paula heaved a sigh and picked up the book once again. She read a few sentences and set the book down again, "Mindy," the girl's image came to mind, a happy image, with her arms around both her and Carrie. "I'm going to miss that girl."

Once again, Paula rose to watch the comings and goings of late-night life on Topsail.

****

Carrie kicked her shoes off and crossed one leg over the other. Her fingers tenderly dug into the ball of her foot, massaging it deeply. "Oh, oh," she moaned, "my feet are killing me. I'm no more cut out to be a waitress than Joey is cut out to be a Seeing Eye dog." Pursing her lips she kissed the air, "But I love my wittle Joey."

The dog bounded to the couch and licked her wildly on the face. Bella followed suit as Carrie continued rubbing her feet. "And I know Blythe is going to can me after the summer. What in the hell am I going to do then?"

She glanced at her phone. "2:30, I can't believe I've been at that restaurant for twelve straight hours. When Blythe gets a cleaning streak up her butt, she really goes for it. She had me on my hands and knees scrubbing the baseboards—she's expecting the health inspector any day. Geez, what a slave driver." Carrie reached for her electronic cigarette and inhaled deeply and turned to again speak to Joey, "I've got to find something else."

The dog wagged his tail; Bella rolled on her back for a tummy rub.

"Alright, alright, I guess I've been ignoring you, but with Mindy dying, my mind has been elsewhere. I really miss her." She picked up her cell phone and dialed.

"Hi, thought I'd give you a call. I'm sure you're bored to death unless you've had a slew of boats come through in the last few hours." She stroked Bella's fur, then Joey's.

"Nope, dead as a door nail. Had one boat around one-thirty. Been trying to read a book, but can't seem to concentrate."

"I can't stop thinking of Mindy. I can't believe she's gone."

Silence ensued.

"Yep—dead as a door nail."

Carrie heard a light breath escape from the phone, and Paula had repeated her last statement. For a moment she considered that perhaps she shouldn't have called her friend.

Interrupting the thought, Paula's voice lilted, "You know, you mentioned once that you'd like to work on my boat—maybe it's something you should consider—you might really like it."

"Sounds interesting—sounds far more interesting than working with the public." Carrie tittered cautiously, "but I thought we were just joking around about that."

Paula exhaled noisily, "Having some help and someone to talk to might be just the thing—and things are getting too weird around her—with people dying left and right." Groaning, Paula added, "Mindy's death has me thinking that maybe I've missed some things—maybe I need to lighten up."

"This coming from *Miss I Want To be Alone, Miss Stoic*, herself. Doesn't sound like the Paula I know. Mindy's murder really has you rattled, doesn't it?"

Again Paula sighed.

"They'll find out who did this, Paula—they'll get Hank, and things will get back to normal."

"Normal, ha—what's normal?" Paula barked into the phone.

"Wow, you sound really pissed."

"Sorry about that. I just wish I was sleeping. This night stuff has me all out of wack."

"I *can't* sleep either, I'm so wound up from working at that damn restaurant. How about some company?"

"Bring the coffee."

"Decaf."

"You usually have it all together, always cool, always in control. Even when you're mad."

"When I feel like I'm losing it, I get in the boat and go. I haven't been able to do that lately."

Carrie held her coffee with both hands, sipping as she listened to her friend.

"The fuel, it's outrageous. I can't afford to fill my tank. Can't afford to fish—and for the last couple of years it's been difficult—doesn't seem to be as much as it used to be. Besides, it's always been just me going out fishing. I've never hired anyone on. I'd need a bigger boat for that."

"I didn't know you're hurting that much for money."

"Daddy sold his boat to my brother, he can't run it anymore, getting too old. He helped me get what I've got, but I can't afford to keep it up."

"What about helping your brother with shrimping?"

"That's not going to work either. He has a family to feed, Carrie. He can't afford to pay me too."

"So here you are a bridge tender. Sounds so romantic."

"If you like to day dream," Paula tittered.

"And what do you day dream about?"

"Prince Charming riding up on a big power boat and taking me away to Tahiti."

"Really?" Carrie laughed.

"I used to, but I'm not the prettiest girl and never had a lot of boyfriends."

"I always wondered about that, why you've never married."

"Not in the cards. Seems the men who wanted to wed me wanted me to give up the ocean. And the men who didn't mind about that, wanted to be my boss."

"I can understand that."

"I know I've gotten hard and cynical, but I have always felt I have my own path—even from a young age and when I tried to fit in, well, I was just too damn unhappy."

"What about Lev? He seems to be interested."

"Ha, Lev is interested in *all* women. You saw how he flirted with Mindy and even with you."

"That's a defense mechanism. He's not tall, dark and handsome and I think he uses his charm instead."

"His charm stinks." Paula turned toward the radio, messaging an approaching vessel. "Want to see the bridge open up close?"

"Wow, this is so neat." Carrie stood, watching as Paula pressed buttons, as the siren wailed, as the traffic barriers lowered and as the lumbering green bridge slowly turned to allow a trawler to pass. Lights from the vessel twinkled, reflecting in the passive waters of the Intracoastal.

Carrie rested her fingers on the table as the trawler glided past; its tall outriggers reaching high above the roadway. The men on board, bare chested, stood with their legs parted, balancing themselves with the miniscule sway, holding on to a boom.

"And you find this boring?" A grin rested on Carrie's lips as she listened to the siren wail the closing of the bridge.

"I've been around this my whole life and no, it's not boring. But I'd rather be on that *boat* than on this *bridge*."

"Me too, that one guy, leaning against the gunwale was—like Mindy used to say, a hunka, hunka burning love. Gosh I miss her."

"I do too."

Both women were quiet, watching the lights of the trawler, as they grew smaller; a faded white older model Saturn, still parked behind a barrier waited as it raised slowly.

"Isn't that Essa?" Carrie asked.

"What happened to that cute little Volkswagen Bug she was driving?"

"What's she doing out at this time of the morning? Carrie pinched her lips together. "I guess she has a lively night life."

"She didn't work tonight?"

"No, Blythe had to call in another girl, Essa called out—said she was sick."

"Maybe she went to Wal-Mart to get some medicine." Paula scoffed.

"Maybe, but she doesn't look sick to me—and she's talking on her cell phone."

"I've seen her several times with some bald guy in the Bug she used to drive. Maybe she's been to his house."

"Really? She was talking with some bald man at Gerard's when we went there together a few weeks back." Carrie watched the car pass onto the island and turn left at the next road.

"Has she ever mentioned a boyfriend?"

"No. But I know she flirts with everyone at The Upper Deck. She's always leaning forward showing everything off. I'm surprised Blythe hasn't gotten on her about it."

Paula let out a laugh, "You've got to be kidding me. Blythe shows everybody her boobs."

"Yeah, you're right about that, when I saw her at Gerard's she was taking it all off, singing or trying to. I swear, it surprised the heck out of me." Carrie flipped her hand in the air, "and then she walks around the restaurant like she's the queen of class."

"That's another one who isn't what they seem to be. Like Essa, there's something about her Carrie. I don't think she is what she appears to be."

"She has a hot temper, I know that."

"Throws things?"

"No, not really. She doesn't yell or blow up, like I do when I get mad, but I saw her push a plate off the prep table one day when a customer was picking on her—something about the food, I think it was the clam chowder. Anyway, she came back into the kitchen—was really calm—and then just wiped the prep table sending the plate flying to the floor.

Sammy had a fit. She apologized and then took the paring knife and stabbed it into the wooden top. He had a time getting it out."

"Whoa, I'd say that's a little strange."

"I just stay out of her way these days. When she first started working at the Deck, Essa was polite and invited me to go places, but then she'd ridicule me. You know, I was putting on some weight there for a while after I quit smoking. I don't deserve to be talked to like that."

"No, you don't." Paula agreed adamantly.

"And then after that time at the Daily Grind when she came up with some excuse to leave, I just told myself that she wasn't worth the hassle. I don't need all that negativity around me."

"Wonder what happened to the Volkswagen?"

"I don't know—I thought she still had it—never paid attention to what she drove to work. I guess it broke down or something and she had to get a different car."

****

"This cop, a detective, was asking about you. Evidently my dear, sweet cousin, Vera has been running her mouth." Estelle laid her feet in Hank's lap, "Rub them for me, honey. That restaurant job is killing my feet."

Hank pulled on Essa's toes gently.

"Harder," she cooed. "He was nosing around my house—I caught him, he'd walked in when I wasn't there."

"Don? What did he look like?"

"Tall—blond."

"Sounds like him. What did he talk about?"

Oh, he asked about you—about the man *Vera* has been running her mouth about. I told him that the *Hank* I had been seeing was from Georgia."

"Georgia. Good. You think you threw him off?"

"I don't know. But it's a good thing I ran into him, it will keep him there." She rubbed a foot along his thigh. "I'm going to go there for a few days, don't want him coming here and spoiling what you and I have."

"What do we have?" Stretching to lie beside her, Hank kissed Essa's neck. "I'll miss you terribly. I'm so in love with you—always have been."

"That's what we have, our love." She kissed him back deeply, pushing her body into his. "I want to see your beach house again. We need to make love there, so I can hear the roar of the ocean." Springing to her feet she pulled him up, "Come on, let's go over there now, you still have the key, don't you?"

Hank and Essa held hands as they walked among the scrub oaks to the road leading to the beach. For a moment they stood at the top of the wooden access; Hank breathed in deeply, Essa watched him.

"Last one with their toes in the water is a loser." She ran ahead, her long mane flowing, her long strides carrying her swiftly to the water's edge. From there she looked up to Hank, still standing atop the access. Essa laughed stridently, "Hey! Are you coming or not? Your Emma is waiting for you." She turned, racing along the shore. "I see one, I see two," she sped toward a ghost crab, "Come on, sweetie, let's chase the crabs."

As he made his way down the stairs, Hank kept his eyes on the woman dancing in the night air. He couldn't wait to hold her in his arms once again and love her.

Chapter Nineteen

"My friend the cop," Vera opened the door to Don. "Come on in and make yourself comfortable. "I've been thinking about all of this—you telling me all this stuff about Hank, maybe being a killer. About meeting up with Estelle the other day—I don't know. It seems pretty far fetched."

Don shrugged, "I could be way off base, but I'm curious to find out if this is the guy. And your cousin, you're right, I think she's smooth, a real player." He sat in his usual chair and watched as Vera pulled two classes from the cabinet.

"How about a root beer?" She grinned snidely from over her reading glasses.

"A root beer?"

"Hey, I'm trying."

"So when did you start wearing glasses?"

"I only wear them around people I don't want to impress."

"Should have –"

"I know—started wearing them long ago. Ha ha, you're funny."

"Okay, root beer sounds just fine."

"You know, I pulled up something on the net about those killings you were talking about—thought I might read up on them. Ugh. They were pretty grizzly. And then there was something else about a girl getting killed a couple of weeks ago. Did you know her?"

"Yes, I did."

Vera set the drink on the end table, "You think it was Hank?"

"I'm not sure. He had no reason to kill Mindy—as far as I know. Personally, I think the man's a raving lunatic. So, I guess he wouldn't need a reason."

"If he killed her in Topsail, why arc you way up here looking for him?"

"I'm not the only one looking. And I strongly suspect that your Hank and my Hank are the same person."

"But killing people just doesn't sound like *my* Hank. I mean, he's a bastard for dumping me, but I don't think he killed that girl. I find it hard to believe he killed anyone at all."

"Most people don't open doors to people they think are going to harm them."

"True, I guess you really never know someone. I mean, who'd have thought that Hank would hit Estelle, he never showed one bit of violence toward me, even that time I got mad at him and punched him."

"You punched him?"

"Yeah, he was late—half an hour late, and when he came in I called him a few choice words and punched him in that fat old belly of his."

"And he did nothing?"

"Nope, only he said he'd never be late again. I never saw him after that."

"That's the part that sounds like the Hank I know. He's known for stringing women along until he gets them in the sack and then dumping them."

"I don't think he's dumped Estelle."

"No?"

"Whenever Estelle is between men she always gets up with me and my sisters and we make a week of it."

"A week?"

"We party hardy for an entire week—drinking, driving up to Fayetteville, or down to Jacksonville and having a time with the soldier boys. Those Marines and Sailors love to spend their money, honey. And I ain't seen hide nor hair of her since she got up with that asshole, Hank, so that tells me she ain't done with him yet."

"Hmm," Don swirled the ice around in his glass. "She told me he left about a week ago."

"She's lying."

"Do me a favor, call her up and tell her you want her to keep her hands off of me. That she stole Hank from you and you're not going to let her take me, too."

"Are you supposed to be doing this? I mean, couldn't I get hurt or something being involved with a murderer?"

"I thought you said you didn't think Hank could kill anyone."

"You're making me want to pour some bourbon in this glass."

"Hell, woman. That would taste nasty—bourbon and root beer? You don't want to do that." Pausing, Don settled his arms on the rests of the chair. "I'm proud of you. This is the first time I've seen you without a drink—an alcoholic one."

She opened the drawer to the end table, pulled out her pack of cigarettes and placed one between her lips. "This is the next thing to go."

Is this the effect I have on women? Carrie was trying to quit smoking before I left the island. Wonder how that's going? "It can't hurt. But be warned, I have a friend that quit smoking who packed on quite a few pounds doing so."

Vera released a perfect ring of smoke into the air. "Yeah, Veda, my sister, quit and blew up like a balloon. She's still a chunky monkey." She shrugged, "I've got an idea. Instead of me calling and telling her to keep her grubby hands off of you, how about we both drive over to her place and confront her. What do you think of that?"

"No, better not. She doesn't know I've told you I'm with the police. She'll get suspicious."

"Umm, okay." Vera found her cell and dialed her cousin's number, "Hi. Watcha up to, bitch? Yeah you. You're still with Hank—so—I'm just calling to tell you that Don is mine. I want you to leave him alone." She pressed the speaker on.

"You're drunk again. Go buy a bottle of vodka or bourbon, or what ever it is you swill, and leave me alone," Estelle's retorted sternly.

"I'm just telling you that when you get done with Hank, 'cause I know you will, I'm warning you to stay away from my new boyfriend, Don."

"That idiot that was over at my house?"

"He was at your house—you've started already, haven't you?"

"If he's the same dolt, then sugar, you're in for a surprise. That man's a cop. He could give a flying fig about you; he's nosing around looking for some guy who killed someone down at Topsail. Now, get lost and leave me alone, bitch."

The phone blinked off. Estelle had hung up.

"Okay, so she told me you're a cop. I guess you told her not to tell me. La-tee-tah, proves she can't be trusted. And—did you hear what I heard?"

Don shook his head no.

"The ocean, she's at the beach. If she's at the ocean she's somewhere on the Banks. You don't hear the ocean on the sound. So that means she's at least an hour or so away."

"You want to go over to her place, huh?"

"Yep." Vera tittered. "You know this detective stuff is fun."

"She never locks the door," Vera walked into Estelle's living room, Don stepped in behind her. "If my house was full of junk like this I guess I wouldn't lock it either. There's not a damn thing in here worth stealing. That old television ain't worth fifteen bucks, I know, I was with her when she bought it at the flea market."

Don moved items around in the dresser drawers, peered into the closet and moved the few items of clothing about.

"What are you looking for?" Vera stood in the bedroom doorway, "Do you think she'd have anything important laying around if she doesn't even keep the doors locked?"

"Maybe nothing of value, but there might be something of Hank's here. Something that would suggest the two are together."

Estelle's unmade bed was piled with tangled sheets and pillows. A couple of magazines lay on the floor next to the nightstand; bending to pick them up Don noticed a couple more sprawled beneath the bed. "I didn't get to look around in here very well the other day, she surprised me." He knelt to reach for them. "Now, that's interesting." Brushing his hand against his khaki trousers, he picked at the tiny hairs accumulated there. "I didn't see a cat the other day. Does your cousin own one?"

"Estelle own a cat? I don't think so. If that cat's not going to be paying rent or doing something to earn its keep, that bitch ain't going to have it around. She never did like animals."

"Well, someone has a cat, its hair is all over my pant legs. Hank's been here, and he brought the cat."

"So where is he now?"

Don slowly perused the room, walking from the bed to the closet. "Your cousin doesn't have many clothes."

"She's a jeans and tee-shirt kind of gal—not too fond of shoes either."

"Hmm," Don kicked a pair of flip-flops and tennis shoes around on the closet floor. "Most women I know have at least ten pair of shoes."

"Thirty-five. I've got thirty-five at last count."

"I never understood that. What do you do with them all?" he asked, still examining the room.

"Blue shoes for blue jeans, black for special occasions, red for special occasions, I've got a cute pair of wedges with flowery yellow print that I wear with shorts, hell, gotta have matching shoes and clothes."

"Two pair, one black, one brown."

"You don't have tennis shoes?"

"They don't count, they're for comfort."

He pulled back the tangled sheets of the bed and pushed the pillows aside, "Ah ha," Don picked a wadded tissue from the bed, scrutinizing the folds, "blood—not a lot, but there's blood here."

"DNA? You're going to take it to a lab and get it checked. Right? Damn this is so much fun." Vera giggled. "I think we make a pretty good pair."

"We're not a pair."

"You're no fun. I've helped you a bunch. You wouldn't even be over here if it wasn't for me."

Don stuffed the tissue into a small plastic bag, then opened the bedside table drawer and picked up a set of car keys, ones he was sure were for the Volkswagen he'd seen in the backyard.

"Where you going?" Vera asked as he strode past her; she heard the back door open and watched from the window as Don slid into the driver's side.

Remarkably, the car started immediately; Don pushed the gearshift into first, then second and drove slowly around the house. "Nothing wrong with this car," he said, shutting the car door behind him.

"It looks like the one she was driving for a while. But it didn't have any peace signs and flowers painted on it and the lights and windshield weren't smashed out. Wonder why—wonder how." Her hands resting on her hips, Vera chuckled, "I told you she's got a hell of a temper. I bet my sweet cousin did all this herself. She got mad about something and took it out on this poor little car."

****

Carrie lay on the divan; Joey and Bella curled next to her outstretched legs. Picking up the remote control she flipped through the channels and settled on the PBS program from England, Grantchester. If the main character turned slightly to the side, he resembled Don—his thick hair, though Don's was blond—Don's lips were not quite as full. But the body, yes, the bodies were definitely alike—tall and long limbed. She felt the heat rise from her middle. "That's a good looking man. Don's a good looking man." She whimpered delicately then turned her gaze to the cell phone laying quietly on the end table. "I guess that's over. But then it never really began." She touched the phone, the time lit up the screen. "10:30. If he was going to call he'd have called by now. And I haven't heard from him in a week. But then, there were no promises."

Focusing on the characters of the television program, Carrie struggled to erase thoughts of Don.

Tanya's body lay sprawled on the floor of Rick's bedroom—the image of a dowdy British girl appeared on the screen; policemen knelt around her—Carrie thought of Mindy and flipped to another channel. Another dead body lay on a medical examiner's table. She flipped again to the news, politicians ranted at one another. "Damn, I'm going to bed." She pressed the remote off and padded toward the bedroom, Joey and Bella followed behind.

The buzz of her phone caught her as she brushed by the coffee table; Carrie hurried back to grab it. "Hello," she spoke, hopeful of hearing a man's voice.

"I'm not calling too late, am I?" Don queried

"I just turned off the television," she paused, "but it's okay—what's up?"

"Wanted to check up on you—make sure you're okay."

"Yes, everything is fine."

"Are you sure? You sound a little down in the dumps."

Thinking about you, wondering if there is an us. Carrie thought, "Just tired, had a long day—I really am tired."

"Okay, I'll let you go then, sleep tight."

"You, too." Carrie hung up the phone. *I'm forty years old now. I ought to see the signs. If a man doesn't call that means he's not interested. If he calls late, he's interested in someone else.* "But then, *we're just friends.*"

Carrie thought of the last time they kissed. It was tender and arousing and it was Don who had pulled away. *He said he couldn't get involved until he had things worked out in his life. That he didn't want to start something when he knew I was so vulnerable. 'We'll be friends, good friends,' he'd said.* And I agreed—but if a man can't be there when I'm down and out, then I guess I really don't need him at all. I need to quit hanging on to something that doesn't show promise.

Again the phone rang, "What?" An annoyed Carrie asked.

"Whoa, who licked the red off your candy?" Paula spoke into the phone. "I thought you'd be up, it's only a quarter to eleven."

"Sorry Paula, I just got off the phone with Don."

"That's a good thing, isn't it? Him calling?"

"It's the first time I've heard from him in over a week and then when he does call, it's always the same thing, 'wanted to check up on you,' well, isn't that what Lev is for. According to Lev, Don asked *him* to *check up* on me. I appreciate all the checking up, but some expression of fondness would be nice."

"You said y'all were just friends, Carrie. It's not his fault if you expect more."

"It's not as simple as that, Paula. You know how it goes—or was I fooling myself. Geez, he hung around me for eight months, he was there listening to all my blubbering about Hank—hell, I spilled my guts to that man. And I know when he kissed me—I know there was more than just *checking up on you* in that kiss. If he didn't have feelings for me he would have simply used me as a POA and moved on instead of hanging around for eight months and being my shoulder."

"Maybe he's just busy."

"Ha."

"If he didn't care at all, he wouldn't call—ever."

"You're no help. Really, you're supposed to be my friend. What makes a man act like that?"

"I think he cares too much to take advantage of you and needs to do his job without getting you involved. There's more to this Hank thing than we know—and we aren't supposed to know. That's what the cops are for."

Carrie sighed heavily. "I guess I was too hard on him. I kind of blew him off when he called. But I need more than *checking up* and if Lev is doing that, why does Don do it too. See, it's confusing."

"Hank is the only man you've had a relationship with other than your husband. Right?"

"Yes. Jim was horribly jealous. I don't know why, he never bothered to show me attention or act like he gave a damn. But I learned early to not make friends with other men."

"No brothers?"

"Not one."

"So your experience with the opposite sex is limited."

"I know."

"You're forty years old, have two kids and you're dumb as a rock when it comes to men. First you let Morgan Simpers give you gifts. And then you let Hank bed you—.

"Hey, I don't need it thrown in my face."

"I'm not trying to hurt you, Carrie, but you need to know that men are very different than we are. They think differently. So many of them hold their feelings inside."

"Oh, I'm so tired of trying to figure it all out. I'm tired of feeling, getting my feelings hurt, expecting things. Why can't men just come right out and tell you what they want?"

"I don't think they know what they want. But as for your detective, I think Don has a lot of baggage he doesn't want to burden you with."

"What makes you think that?"

"Little things he says, references Lev has made about him—his ex-wife, the boy. But isn't all of that his business?"

"If he cared about me he'd share his *business* with me."

"You worry too much, the man cares about you— don't throw him away yet."

"Look who's talking. You won't even give Lev a chance. I know he's sweet on you."

"Geez, *sweet*? Give me a break. My momma doesn't even use that term anymore."

"You know what I mean."

"I don't want to talk about it."

With one hand, Carrie scooted her jeans to her ankles, then kicked them off. Holding the phone next to her ear, she replied, "Ooh, I think I touched a nerve. Paula's got a sweetie," she sing-songed, and laughed aloud.

Chapter Twenty

"I need to get some eggs for tomorrow's breakfast, lover." Essa rolled to her side and wrapped a leg around Hank's.

"We can have Cheerio's, that's okay with me."

Looking tenderly into Hank's hazel eyes, she stroked the skin of his head gently. "No, I'd really like to fix an omelet in the morning. You know how I love my cheese omelets."

Hank grinned and pulled her close for a long kiss.

Essa pulled away gently, then rubbed his belly. "It's been so confusing with you moving in so fast. I was hoping I could get a bit more settled here before you joined me."

"I didn't expect E.J. to come for a visit—and then there were bound to be policemen around sooner or later. I had no choice."

Essa studied the confusion she saw playing within Hank's eyes. "Mom is just too nosy and she doesn't understand about last year. You, my dear," she kissed his tattooed neck, "did the cops a favor by getting rid of those scum."

He nodded, scowling as he clenched and unclenched his fists.

"E.J. will come around. I'll talk with her and before you know it, she'll be begging us to come over for dinner on Saturday nights."

Hank looked into her eyes, "I don't understand—Mindy—who would want to hurt her?"

"Probably another meth-head or coke-addict. Heroin is big now, all the low life are doing it." Essa moved her hands across his chest gently and rose from the bed. "I'm going to run down to the store and pick up a few things, eggs, maybe some milk; I won't be long." She pulled a long printed sheath over her head and slid on a pair of brown sandals. "You need to get your rest." Reaching into a drawer, Essa grasped a bottle, shook two pills from it and offered them to Hank with the glass of water. "You just haven't been the same since you left Carteret County. Maybe these will help you relax some, my love." She kissed him again, resting her cheek against his before turning to leave.

"Emma?" Hank called.

Essa stepped toward him, "Yes, baby."

"I really love you."

She smiled and walked through the door.

Hank heard the roar of the engine; his eyes grew heavy as he drifted off to sleep.

We have to go somewhere where no one will recognize the name. Essa thought as she drove north toward the high-rise bridge. *Georgia? South Carolina? Which is the easiest state to get married?* She drove slowly down the beach road, "Tennessee, I'll look that one up on the internet." Spotting E.J.'s house, she pulled the car to the side nearly a block south and killed the engine and lights.

I was careless last time. I need to make sure I've got the right person. Essa grinned to herself. *How can I make it look like it was Hank all along?* Leaning back in the seat, Essa twisted her hair into a knot and pinned to her head, "I'll get everything—his home, E.J.'s place, his land down by the sound and the boat. Shit, I'll be sitting pretty. I'll bet that old woman has land, too, lots of land." Squinting her eyes, she watched the shadows move across the curtains of E.J.'s house.

****

Fate propped his feet on the ottoman and slumped down in the chair, "I think I'll buy a recliner and bring it over here. I'd be more comfortable."

"I don't mind, me casa, su casa." Emma Jewel lifted her eyes above her glasses. "Are you moving in?"

"Oh, I don't think that would be a good idea, not now anyway. Besides, when I get a belly full of your stubbornness, I can go over to my place."

"I'm not quite as bad as I used to be."

Fate grunted a response.

"Oh yes, thanks for fixing the air conditioner."

"You're welcome." His eyes on the television show, Fate pressed a button, increasing the volume.

"I suppose you have pictures of Heidi still on the walls."

233

"She was a good woman."

"I agree, she was—and I'm glad you had a good marriage, Fate. If you and I had ever gotten things off the ground, I probably would have divorced you. You were always stubborn too."

"Well, we're old now and none of it matters." He pressed again on the remote, flipping through the channels.

"There you go, so I guess we're going to watch what *you* want to tonight."

"What do you want to watch?" Fate asked.

"I don't care."

Tossing the remote in E.J.'s lap, Fate rose and walked to the kitchen. "Want some pie? I brought over a blueberry pie."

****

Who's with her? Estelle stepped from the car, closing the door as quietly as she could. "Who's putting a crick in my plans?"

She walked to the side of the house. The windows were closed, curtains drawn. Her hand on the banister, she crouched, taking the stairs two by two and crouched beneath a window. *So that's it. That old man is staying with her. I've seen him around; he runs that little mart up the road.*

Essa eased quietly down the stairs and back to her car. "He's not there all the time. Most days he *is* at the mart." She jerked the gearshift into third as she sped along the darkened road. "Damn! Damn! Hell!" Curse words fell easily from her mouth as she pounded on the steering wheel. "That son of a bitch, that--" she breathed heavily, her shoulders tensed, "It's not fair.

That old bitch should be dead." Essa's eyes darted from one house to another as she drove the road back to the house.

Pressing hard on the brake, she stopped as a car pulled from a driveway. She took a long breath to relax herself, strummed the steering wheel and watched the car slowly pull away.

"But maybe this is good. Maybe I can do the marriage thing before I kill that hag off. Hank will probably want to tell her about it—she'll want to meet me. Hmm…" A scenario played in her head, calming her; Essa slowed the car down to below the speed limit. "Maybe he won't tell her—maybe we'll go to a Justice of the Peace. We'll drive over to South Carolina or Georgia or Tennessee—some little podunk town."

"I was thinking on my way to get the groceries, that we ought to get married." Essa sat on the bed next to Hank; his lethargic appearance did not surprise her.

"We're already married, Emma." Hank's glazed eyes searched her face.

"Renew our vows, my love. We could renew our vows." Essa wrapped her arms around his neck and licked his lips, "Don't you want to marry me again? Wouldn't it be so romantic to get married in the mountains? I love the mountains."

Hank slowly pulled the pins from Essa's hair, weaving his fingers into the tresses as they fell. "You are so beautiful. I would do anything for you."

"I would do anything for you, too, Hank. And I want to be with you for the rest of our lives."

"That would be nice, but things have gotten so out of hand, so messed up."

"Not really, nothing is so bad that we can't fix it."

"Last year—" His brow furrowed deeply as he shook his head.

"That was last year, give it a bit of time and I bet all will be forgotten. Even E.J. came to visit you at the cottage. She still cares for you. She's forgotten *things*." And I bet when we get back from getting married, everything will be back to normal.

Hank's lips turned upward as he closed his eyes.

Essa stroked his brow and kissed him gently, "My love, you rest."

The cell phone glowed 11:15 as Essa sat down in front of the laptop and typed: "It was wonderful last night, you're always do the right things, lover. Blythe called me in early, so I'll see you this evening. See you later, lover." Essa placed a salt shaker over the typed page and walked to Hank's side. *You should be out for a good twelve hours,* releasing a light breath, she walked out the door.

Don turned into the lane to Estelle's, driving slowly along the winding path. Nearing her residence, he found the front yard empty of any vehicles. *What about the back?* He considered driving around but decided not to. He slid his car into park and turned off the ignition; his eyes glanced toward the dashboard clock, *subtract two hours and add fifteen minutes,* "that makes it 11:30 a.m.," he said aloud, shrugging, then scolding himself for procrastinating about get the clock repaired.

He rubbed the back of his hand against the overnight growth on his face; *I need a shave, too.* Leaning back in the seat, he perused the windows and door, searching for any signs of occupancy. He reached into the glove compartment and retrieved a pack of crackers and cheese; his last meal had been lunch, yesterday.

As Don popped one of the squares into his mouth, he noticed a window curtain move slightly. *She's here, she's parked in the back.* Still, he sat relaxed in the car, waiting. *Let's see what she does, how she acts.*

He looked at the clock again, *11:35; she's taking her time.* "I've got to get that clock fixed," he mumbled to himself and popping another cracker in his mouth. Don reached for a bottle of water and chugged it half empty.

Finally the door opened, Estelle leaned out and hollered, "Aren't you going to invite me to your picnic?"

Don stepped from the car, "I wasn't sure you were home and I didn't want to intrude like I did last time."

"Oh, I never lock the door. Next time just come on in. I'm either here or I'm not. And if I'm not, just make yourself at home."

She wore a short summer dress, well above the knees. Her thick hair was braided and hung past her shoulders, touching her breasts. She stood mere inches away from him and licked her lips. "What can I do for you, Mr. Detective?"

"I just came by to ask you some more questions about Hank. I'm sure now that he *is* the man we are looking for.

Don studied the woman, well aware that he was ogling her. He knew Estelle liked that. She fed off of it.

Swept in her scent, he found himself thinking familiar compromising thoughts.

"After all, you are a man" he heard her say. He grinned in response to something he wasn't even sure he had heard.

"You do know what I mean, don't you?" Estelle walked into the kitchen. "If you'd like it, you're welcome to take it."

"I'm sorry, I must have missed something." Don shifted his gaze away.

"I said Hank left a fishing pole here and I know how men love to fish, you are a man aren't you?"

It was the way she said it, the way her eyes grazed his body, the way her lips pouted. It all said yes. Everything said *now*.

She leaned into the refrigerator exposing her upper thighs; she parted her legs.

Don moved closer. He felt his abdomen tighten.

Turning, Estelle held a bowl of strawberries in her hand. "Want some?" She held a berry to her lips and bit into it suggestively.

Turning abruptly, Don seated himself at the kitchen table, pushing aside an empty bowl crusted with cereal. "I think Hank Jordan and Hank Butler are the same person. I need you to tell me everything you can about him."

"You mean, I was having an affair with a murderer?" Estelle's eyes grew wide, color left her face. "Oh my, he could have killed *me*. I'm so glad he's gone," she grasped the edge of the table. "You've come here—to protect me." She toyed with the braids, un-plaiting them, running her fingers through the strands of hair. "What should I do, Detective?" Lowering her head, Estelle brought a hand to her trembling lips.

Oh, she's good, he thought, *or is this for real?* "He's gone now. I don't think he'll bother you anymore. You did say you saw him with another woman."

Estelle's eyes closed, her chest fell in heavy breaths as she seated herself at the table.

Don watched her for a few moments. "In Beaufort, you said you saw him in Beaufort."

"Yes."

"Then he's gone. He won't bother you anymore."

"How can you be sure the man who was with me is the same one you're looking for?" Estelle lifted her dark blue eyes; they seemed even darker filled with tears. "And how can you be sure he's gone? He could come back."

"He could. But we're pretty sure he's gone somewhere else. But I'm going to check in on you now and then to make sure you're safe."

"We're?"

"There are others searching for him."

"Who?"

"I'm not the only man on the Topsail Island Police Department."

Estelle sat quietly without moving a muscle as if his response had been expected. "Of course, I wasn't thinking. Certainly others from Topsail are looking for Hank." She leaned forward, "Tell me again what he looks like—what he *used* to look like."

Don recounted the description of a leaner, more polished Hank from a year ago. "He was quite a lady's man—had a reputation for it."

"That part sounds right, but the other—it's hard to imagine that he has changed so much. He must have been desperate to alter his appearance so radically."

Don thought of the blood soaked tissue he'd found in her bed—the DNA, there was no doubt the man was Hank Butler. *Should I confront her? No. I think she's known all along. But why the pretense? Why is she protecting him?* "And you say you never went inside his house."

She shook her head, "No, I've told you I only went out on his fishing dock."

"So, he came here when—"

Sliding her eyes to meet his, Estelle lifted her chin. "When we wanted to make love—have sex, yes, we came here." She paused, her eyes steeled, "he knows how to please a woman." She stroked the base of her neck and décolletage gently. "Mostly we met at the bar or drove to Beaufort or farther up the banks—you're getting a little personal, aren't you?"

"Murder is very personal." For less than a split second, Don could have sworn he saw flashes of anger in Estelle's eyes.

"He told me he was from Georgia, I slept with him a few times, went fishing and that's all I know about the man."

"How long has it been since you've last seen him?"

"I told you before that it's been a couple of weeks." Estelle crossed her arms and stretched her long legs out from the table. "On second thought, I don't think you need to come around and check on me. I can take care of myself."

"I bet you can." Don rose from his chair, "I will be coming around now and then and I may have a few more questions for you. Is that okay?"

"Suit yourself, lover." She looked up at him from the table, caressing the sides of her body, stretching;

she shook her hair loose and arched her back against the chair.

"You need to be careful with that." Don's eyes slowly grazed her body. "You have a very powerful weapon."

"It's loaded, lover—just needs someone to pull the trigger."

"Hmm, you make it difficult."

"Hard?"

Don blushed, "I have to go." His eyes drifting to the window, he noticed the white Saturn parked next to the red Bug. "New car?"

"Just something to get me around town. The Volkswagen blew up on me. I think it's the transmission or something."

"Oh. Want me to take a look at it for you?"

"No." She answered quickly. "I'm going to have Triple A tow it to the junk yard for me. But thanks." Bringing a strawberry to her lips, Estelle sucked gently on the fruit, then bit it in half. She licked her lips. "Sure is good, sure you don't want some?"

"No thanks, I've got to leave room for dinner."

Estelle watched as Don drove out of sight, she picked up her cell and dialed Hank's number. "Hey lover, I'll be off work in a couple of hours. Love you."

"I love you, too, darling."

She heard him yawn through the phone line.

"I just woke up. I must have slept for fourteen hours. I feel like I've been run over by a train."

"It's the weather, the pollen. You'll be fine." Estelle raced to remember if she'd taken the medication with her or left it with Hank. "Just be sure to take a couple of tablets from the bottle I left on the stand. It is there isn't it?"

"Um hum. But those things knock me out and I'm very tired of being cooped up in this house."

"I've told you to walk on the beach, or walk up to the IGA and get a few groceries. No one is going to recognize you, Hank."

For a moment he didn't understand the sentence. *What difference does it make if I'm recognized or not?* Mick's face flashed before his eyes, "Yes, you're right. I'll—think about it."

"The walk will do you good and I'd love to grill some steaks tonight. Why don't you pick up a couple of tenderloin steaks? Okay?"

His thoughts had been fuzzy for the last few days, ever since he'd come to stay with Essa. He rubbed his tongue over his teeth, they felt dirty.

In the bathroom mirror he studied his reflection. His eyes were still hazel, his nose was the one he'd had all his life. It was a familiar face. He felt as if he'd woken from a dream, one so real, it was hard to distinguish from it and reality.

The phone buzzed again and he raced to pick it up. "Hi."

"I forgot to tell you to buy a couple ears of corn, they're really good roasted. Bye lover."

Hank heard the whine of a kiss as Estelle hung up. *I love hearing her voice.* "Emma knows me. She'll get me through whatever is going on with me." *She makes things make sense.*

Chapter Twenty-One

"There wasn't a single print, nothing out of the ordinary, nothing disturbed. Not a single clue."

"It's as if a knife fell out of the sky and slit Mindy's throat." Don's eyes lowered to the table; he scraped a fingernail through the beer label and asked, "You think whoever it was came in through the door leading to the beach."

Lev set the phone on speaker and walked into the kitchen of his rental apartment. "That's what I think, with all the street lights on the road to her place, I think the beach is probably our best bet. The killer probably kept close to the dunes and simply walked up her steps." He heard the *humph* Don expelled; he opened the refrigerator door and selected a root beer from the side door. "That little gal didn't know what hit her. She had the television up loud—more than likely she didn't even hear the door open."

"She was a ditzy little thing." Don chuckled lightly.

"Yeah, she was that, but she didn't deserve what she got. It was the old woman they wanted."

"I agree. Mindy was just in the wrong place at the wrong time. But who would want E.J. dead? I'm not sure that Hank's our guy. If he wanted to kill her, he would have done so when she drove to the cottage—when they went fishing on his dock."

"The old lady says that her deceased daughter left everything to her. All of Hank's property was in both he and Emma's name when she died and her mom was listed as the beneficiary. That's a motive for Hank." Lev uncapped the root beer and lifted the cold bottle to his lips.

"But he can't do anything with it when he's in jail."

"Yeah, back to square one." Lev picked the phone up and walked to the living room. "How's it going up there? Any action with the "V" girls?"

Don rolled his eyes, "Vera's not a bad sort, I think she's trying to slow down drinking. She's actually been sober for the last few days."

"There you go, trying to convert everyone."

"I don't try to *convert* people."

"Ha—don't give me that load of crap. Everywhere you go you try to lead the sheep away from the slaughter."

A silence fell from the other end of the phone line; Don breathed heavily into the speaker. "Let's not go there."

"It's true bro, you may not mean to do it, in fact, I don't think you're consciously aware of your effect."

"I never badger people, never preach to them. And it's not like I've led a pristine life. I explained to you about my involvement with—"

"Yeah, yeah, but they didn't give you much of a choice and then you were trying to shield your son."

"Trying to save my ass. That's what I was doing."

"You tell yourself that. That boy has always been your main concern."

"Like I said, I don't do any preaching about what is wrong and what's right."

"No you don't. You don't have to. It's that demeanor of yours. Like, *I'm a good guy and you're not.* Like you always expect people to stop sinning— you're this shining example of the good guy—you make people want to be better, but then you go so far and then walk away. That first one, Maggie, she was already a user when you met her. She stopped, you got sent overseas and she went right back to it. And your kid, you got him, he was living with you—and from what I hear, you'd made some progress with the little juvie and then you ship him off. It's like you lead people to the water, but when they're getting ready to drink it, you walk away. Man, I just realized it—you're a tease." Lev waited for a response—there was none.

"Shit. He hung up on me." Lev pushed the half empty bottle of soda aside and walked out to the porch. "What an idiot."

Night was just settling onto the island, a mauve and indigo sunset streaked the sky, hazily reflecting in the sound waters. Leaning back in the wooden slat chair, he propped his legs on cement blocks before him and perused the cattails and marsh grasses. His thoughts reached back to the first time he'd met his friend.

That had been a long time ago—they'd both worked their ways up the ranks in the Marine Corps—developing a strong friendship. Both had seen action in Iran and Afghanistan. "Too much death, too much bullshit," he muttered. Rising from the chair, he scanned the darkened night sky. "Think I'll walk over to the bridge and pick on Paula."

"I shouldn't have let you in."

"No, you shouldn't have. I'm going to disturb your world, wreak havoc on the life you have so neatly tied into the proverbial bow."

"You're full of crap," Paula flipped a switch to turn the bridge. "Nobody gets in my life unless I want them there."

"You're going to want me there."

"Oh geez—tell me again why you came up here."

"Antsy—I've been talking with Don about Mindy—puzzling. I don't know why anyone would want to harm her."

"I'm sure you have it figured out, but she was killed by mistake, everybody knows that."

"Really?"

"And everybody who knows and loves Miss Emma Jewel is keeping an eye on her."

"She must be well loved by the community."

"What's left of it. There aren't many natives around anymore, most are transplants. They don't remember Miss Emma Jewel's family or even know who she is, but she is loved."

"A neighbor of hers, some man named Fate, is keeping an eye on her. He's even spending the nights, as far as I know."

Paula tittered, "Oh he's not her friend, he's her brother—they used to be lovers."

"Oh, that sounds interesting. A little bit of incest?"

"When they were teenagers, E.J.'s mom married Fate's dad. But they'd been sweet on each other since they were little kids."

"I'm sure it's a good story."

"Everyone has a good story, just some better than others."

Paula winked.

"And what is your story?"

"Nothing exciting there," she shrugged.

"Ever marry?"

"No."

"Ever almost marry?"

"No."

"And you?" she asked as a two trawlers passed beneath the bridge.

"This is pretty cool, watching the bridge turn up close."

"*Usually* it's quiet, too." Paula cast a snide glare his way. "You didn't answer my question, ever marry?"

"Once, in the Philippines—a mistake, a rebound from a girl who dumped me."

"Ooh, heartbreak for the heartbreaker"

"Me? A heartbreaker?"

"You're the one who's always flirting with everyone."

"Flirting makes girls feel special."

"And who told you that?"

"No one, but it's true. Every woman likes to feel pretty, noticed and wanted. When I compliment a woman her eyes light up, usually she smiles."

"You don't think it leads them on?" Pushing a button, Paula watched the bridge swing back into place, then lock.

"You have a point, flirting can lead a woman on. I've seen women lead men on by flirting. Wouldn't you say the lie goes both ways?"

"Point taken."

"I think a little bit of fun led you to get hurt a lot and that you don't let anyone in anymore."

Paula turned away, refusing to respond to the statement.

"Maybe you've tried a couple more times, but were led on again. Maybe your expectations were too high, maybe you let your own self down. So now, you've carved out this life for yourself where there's no room to trust anymore. You don't even trust yourself."

"I suppose you expect me to pay for this insight into my psyche. Let me guess, you're not really a detective, you're a shrink."

"I took a few psych classes—have to for the kind of work I'm in. I find it comes in very handy when trying to solve problems."

"Look, let's get past all this crap. I know you're up here to see if I've seen anything suspicious—sort of, but I also think you're making your own brand of *pass* at me. So if you want to ask me out on a date, then ask me. I don't feel like playing any games."

"You take all the fun out of it."

"Well?" Paula stood facing Lev, her hands firmly on her hips.

"I'll put the gas in the boat, I want you to take me fishing."

"And this is the date? Well, I guess at least you know what I like."

Chapter Twenty-Two

"I'm sorry ma'am, but the restaurant can't help it if the white heron isn't out in the marsh today."

"It was there yesterday, and at the same time it is now, and it was on the brochure too."

"Well—it's kind of nature and…"

The customer's head cocked sideways, her mouth dropped open. "Nature? You're just trying to come up with excuses. If there aren't herons here, you shouldn't advertise them."

She looked up at Carrie from the table, her face drawn into an angry scowl, "And the sharks, what are sharks doing in the water? There was nothing online or in the brochure about there being sharks here. If I'd have known there were sharks, we wouldn't have come."

For a moment Carrie stood confused, unable to process the customer's inane statements.

"Don't you get it?" the woman barked, then turned to her companion. "These people down here…"

Carrie sighed, hearing the familiar words; At *least at Grocery World I could squeeze the bread. Here there's not much I can do.* She grimaced and walked into the kitchen, exasperated, she slammed the tray onto the prep counter.

"I take it that one of the customers said something rude." Sammy scooped a bowl of lettuce into a large plastic bag.

"Not rude, stupid. That lady's upset because we have sharks in the water."

Sammy burst out laughing, "Now that's a new one—as if we have any control over the fish of the sea."

"I know, can you believe that *these* people think we have any control over what birds fly here or what fish swim in the water?"

Sammy laughed, "They're from the city, they're not used to seeing animals in the wild, only in zoos. Actually, I feel sorry for them."

"Sorry my ass." Essa stepped from the dishwasher, "There's no excuse, when someone is rude to me, I make sure they pay for it."

Carrie and Sammy exchanged looks.

"What? You spit in their food?" asked the cook.

"No, I don't do anything here at the restaurant. I wait until they leave and check out which car they get into."

"I would think it's hard to follow them home." Carrie said.

"No dummy, I can't very well follow them home."

"Then what do you do?" Sammy sneered.

Essa, scraping food from plates with a steak knife, viciously stabbed a morsel of food, then grinned. "Oh, I was just kidding. I don't do anything at all. Like

Sammy says, they're from the city and just don't understand the way things are." She grinned and wiped her hands on her apron. "I'm finished with my part of the cleanup and I think the only people left in the dining room are your idiots, so I'm going to split." Untying her apron, Essa wadded it into a ball and stuffed it into her bag. "See y'all Saturday."

Carrie and Sam watched as she closed the door behind her; they heard her car move across the graveled parking lot.

"That is one weird chick."

Carrie nodded in agreement, "I'm glad you said that, I was beginning to think it was only me who thought she was strange."

"At first I just thought it was her womanly time, but hell, nobody's on it for that long."

"Womanly time?" Carrie teased.

"You know what I mean."

"Yeah," she chuckled, "When she first started working here, I thought we'd be friends, at least that's how she came across. But then she'd act nice one minute and the next minute bite my head off. She's moody."

"She's nuts."

"Hell, I just try to stay out of her way now."

"What was that all about—saying she gets people back for being rude?"

"You did that—I heard about the bread." Sammy chuckled.

"Guess I shouldn't have done that but sometimes…"

"Yeah, sometimes it all gets to you." Sam laughed, continuing to wipe down the prep area, "Come on, help me a little," He threw a cleaning rag to

Carrie. "Finish up by the dishwasher. Essa never does her job."

"Why don't you tell her about it."

"Hey, I'm not getting on the wrong side of that bitch. You saw how she handled that knife, she might slash my tires or something."

****

Lev cast the line onto Paula's fishing boat and hopped aboard; "So how far are we going out?" he called above the sputtering engine.

"Maybe fifteen miles, there's an artificial reef south of here and we should be able to pick up a few Spanish mackerel."

"Anything else?"

"If we're lucky, maybe albacore or kings. We'll just have to see—we may have to go a little farther out."

"That would be fun, I've never been out in the ocean."

Oh geez, now he tells me. "You know how to tie a rig onto a line?" Paula asked.

Shaking his head, Lev cast a puzzled look.

"You think it all appears magically or did you expect me to do all the rigging?'

"Sorry, what do you need me to do?"

Paula grabbed a pole, pulled out a length of monofilament and began instructing Lev in the art of rigging lures. "There's a difference between salt water and fresh water fishing."

Lev studied her as she spoke, guiding, teaching curtly but not impatiently.

"Got it, you wind the filament several times, slip the end through the loop--" her fingers dexterously wound the opaque material to secure it. "And then, since it's the middle of summer and hot, we're going to use a plane to drive the lure deeper where the water is not so warm." She turned to him and grinned, "Fish don't like hot weather either."

"The only ocean fishing I've ever done is from Jolly Roger and Surf City piers, when I lived in Arizona, my father took me fishing on Lake Havasu. I caught a three pound bass there once." Lev bragged.

"We've got lots of three pound bass here if you want to do some bottom fishing, but I thought we'd do the real thing and troll for something bigger."

Paula noticed his eyes growing wider, the curve of his lips as they grew into a smile, he seemed boyish; she suppressed a giggle.

"That would be great." Leaning against the gunwale, Lev propped a leg up on the side of the boat, relaxing as he studied the scenery of marsh grasses and tiny islands dotting the Intracoastal Waterway. "I don't see how you could give this up."

"You paid for the gas, imagine dishing out that everyday without the promise that your catch would pay for it."

"How do you do it—with a pole, that's a lot of poles or do you use a net?"

"Traps, I set traps—put them out then gather them up. They're tied to buoys—I make a huge circle and then go back and pick them all up. Sometimes, if the fishing is good, I do it again. I've caught so many fish, I've been shin deep in them and then other times catch only a few dozen. I never did make a lot of money at it; that's why I've always needed another job—and a bigger boat would be nice, too."

"You've done this your whole life, haven't you?"

"I worked with my father, and Daddy did well, but now my brother's taken over for him."

"Why didn't you take over for your father?"

"Long story."

"I'm listening."

"My brother Tom is a man—I'm not. And Daddy is old fashioned. He thinks a man should call the shots, make the decisions."

Lev listened as she continued.

"Daddy said that if I got married, my husband would want to run the business, he'd start trying to butt in." She shrugged. "That's about it."

"Kind of old school, isn't he—your dad?"

"Yes, but I understand his way of thinking. I got over being mad. And then he helped me get the boat I have now and he supports me as best he can—I can't ask for more than that."

Paula pointed to an osprey nest atop one of the markers as they passed it portside.

Lev nodded, "Can't beat the view, that's for sure." He was quiet again as they motored toward the inlet.

"It's going to be a little choppy going through, but once we're past things will smooth out. We might rock a bit today, but it's not bad."

He held on as the thirty-foot fishing boat made way past the small breakers to open water between Topsail Island and the little uninhabited piece of land, Lea Island. He breathed a sigh, turned to Paula at the wheel and fell in love. His heart seemed to burst, seeing her in a different light, as if she was truly part of the ocean and sky and all he beheld.

Her back to Lev, Paula focused on the expanse ahead; steering southeast, she followed the same course she had for over twenty years. Glancing back, she met his eyes, they held for several seconds before she turned away.

For nearly twenty minutes Paula motored southeast; she'd heard nothing from her passenger, and turned to find him, snoozing against the gunwale. "Hey," she called loudly to wake Lev. "You wanted to go fishing, so you have to do your part. Or do I need to let the line out for you, too?" She slowed the boat to a few knots and walked to the transom.

Embarrassed, Lev scurried to the fishing poles, clutching one; following Paula's lead as she attached a spoon to the line and let it flow into the water. Her hand guiding the line from the reel, she watched as it trailed behind to about seventy-five feet and settled the rod in a holder.

"Got it? Do just what I did." She turned to man the steering wheel and adjust the speed.

"What do I do now?" Lev eyed the line as he released it into the ocean, trying to have it match the same distance as Paula's.

"Sit down and wait."

Lev settled into the chair and swiveled from side to side. His hand resting on the arms, he turned to study Paula once again. He felt so helpless, so inadequate next to her. He didn't like that feeling, but for some reason, it felt nice.

Another twenty minutes rolled by and there had not been a strike. Lev called to Paula, "Are you sure that lure is still on there?"

"Lures don't disintegrate and if something hit it, you'd know—be patient," she called back.

Lev heaved a sigh, watching the water as it rolled. Hypnotizing him, he found himself swaying with the movement of the waves.

"How are you doing out there?" Paula asked.

"Okay, just wish we'd get a bite."

She slowed the boat to trolling speed, a few knots, keeping her eyes on the horizon. Another ten or so minutes passed. Turning to Lev, she saw his body sway with the movement of the boat, he looked pale.

Paula set the steering on autopilot and walked to the transom. She stared down at Lev. "You look a little green around the gills." She chuckled. "You getting seasick?"

Straightening himself in the chair, Lev shook his head no.

"You sure?" Leaning to check the other pole, Paula wound the reel a couple of times. "I think we might as well go out a few more miles—might have a better chance of getting something. It is pretty hot today." She looked over to Lev, color was leaving his face, she knew the signs and was sure the man was fighting a churning stomach. She grinned and patted him on the shoulder, "I've got some crackers, eat a couple, might make you feel better."

"I'm fine." The words spilled from his mouth along with the contents of his stomach. Quickly Lev leaned over the side of the boat and heaved again."

"Feel better?"

He shook his head and heaved once more. Reaching into the ocean he scooped a handful of water to wipe his face. "I don't think I have anything else inside."

"So you're done?"

Lev groaned and nodded slightly, raised his head to find Paula then wretched again, the yellow bile spewing on the deck. Now he really felt ridiculous. He couldn't meet her eyes. "Damn, this is horrible." He grabbed his aching stomach, waiting for the next wave of throw up to spew from his mouth. "Sorry."

"It happens."

How can she be so blasé about this, Lev looked into her eyes.

"You poor pitiful thing," Paula rubbed his shoulder, then sniggered, "I've been sick one time, and I felt like I wanted to die—I prayed for God to take me—I felt so horrible."

"That's how I feel. Does it stop?"

"Ha, sometimes it does and sometimes it doesn't. Like I said, I've only been sick once in my life. But I've seen plenty of hard-core fishermen upchuck on rough days. It just depends." She handed him a pack of saltine crackers, "This is about the only thing that works once you get sick. The whole idea is not to."

Lev chewed on a cracker and sat back in the chair. "I think I'm okay now—stomach still hurts though."

"Quit thinking about it, you'll only make it worse. And get that bucket over by the winch, fill it with water and wash that slime you puked up off the deck."

Following orders, Lev scooped water from the ocean and threw it toward the vomit. He watched as it oozed slowly toward the scuppers and out of the boat. Filling the bucket again he splashed the slimy area once more.

"We can go in if you want." Paula offered.

"No, I'm fine."

"First, don't go to sleep. Next, keep your eyes on the horizon or the land. Keep yourself busy, your mind off what's going on in your stomach."

He shot her an angry glare, "I'm feeling better. It won't happen again. I've never been on the ocean before."

Paula nodded, grinned and rolled her eyes. "Whatever you say—so if you're feeling fine, reel in both those lines and we'll head out a few more miles." Paula pushed the throttle up; the boat sped ahead, hitting the water in rhythmic pulses as it moved through the ocean.

He thought he was going to get me out here and woo my britches off. Hardy har har. We'll see how tough a man he is. She looked back, watching as Lev reeled in the lines, grasping at them, missing, then grasping a spoon as it swayed in the wind. *Should I tell him how to secure it,* Paula thought, *or let him figure it out himself.* Still gazing at him —studying Lev as he maneuvered the spoon into an eyelet, Paula felt a pang of guilt for her lack of compassion. *I know how it feels, it's hell."*

She slowed the vessel to a few knots and pulled a couple of Pepsi Colas from the cooler.

"Here, this might help your stomach a little too."

"I'm fine," Lev refused to meet her eyes. "Don't let up for me."

"Getting seasick is…"

"It's the worst feeling I've ever had in my life. I hope I never have to go through that again. His eyes stared strongly into hers, embarrassed, he turned away.

"It happens to the best of us, Lev. Don't worry about it. And if you start feeling sick again, eat some crackers—stay busy."

"You're not busy, you're just standing at the wheel."

"Remember, I said just once—and I've never been sick again. I learned how to control it." Paula sniggered and folded her arms across her chest. She studied his face and moved a finger to the corner of her lips. "You got a bit of vomit still hanging on your chin, Mr. Tough Guy."

Instantly Lev's hand swiped his chin and mouth.

Paula smiled broadly.

Lev returned the smile, "I'll be okay. I think it's over."

Paula moved to the helm, pushing the throttle forward once again.

Lev followed, Pepsi in hand. "Sure is a pretty day." His eyes following the contours of her profile, Lev felt his stomach flutter once again. His hand drew quickly there.

"Sick again?" Paula asked.

"No."

"Next time you come out with me, get one of those patches. It helps."

A softness exuded from her now—a gentleness that surprised Lev. He moved closer, sipped from the cola, keeping his eyes on the horizon. "So, you've been doing this all your life."

"Most of it."

They were quiet for another moment, focusing ahead.

In his peripheral vision Lev studied Paula's features—she was not a gentle looking woman, there were already lines etched in her brow and around her eyes. But there was calmness about Paula—and something more too, that pulled him to her. "How far are we going out?" Lev asked.

"Maybe another five miles or so." Her eyes still focused ahead, she asked, "Have you found out anything more about Mindy—any ideas who could have…?"

"No, it's gone cold. No one saw anything, no foot prints—but then the wind would have blown any prints on the beach away."

"I still can't believe it. Mindy was such a good kid—a pain in the ass sometimes, but she was a good pain in the ass. She just wanted to have fun."

"I only met her a couple of times, but that's the feeling I got from her too—just a kid wanting to have fun."

"What about Hank? Is there any chance it was him?"

"We don't know. But we're following leads north of here." He grabbed her arm gently, "That can't go any farther, okay."

"Don's working on it, huh?"

Again they stood quietly as the boat moved through the water.

Lev turned his head a bit and stepped back to view Paula. He noticed her long lashes, her nearly perfect mouth. Breaking the silence, he spoke, "Other than her case, there's not much going on this summer. It's been pretty quiet, relatively little vandalism except for the elusive tire-slasher."

"What tire slasher? Is somebody going around slashing car tires?"

Chortling lightly, Lev popped another cracker in his mouth and washed it down with the Pepsi. "Every few days someone will call up with a complaint that one or more of their tires has been gouged beyond repair. And the funny thing about it is, all the cars are from out of state—mostly from New York, New Jersey and then one guy was from Texas."

Paula couldn't help from laughing aloud, "My gosh, if I didn't know better, I'd think it was Carrie."

"Why do you say that?"

"I guess you had no way of knowing, but earlier this summer she got fired for squeezing a customer's bread at Grocery World. In fact, it was a pretty common practice with her—and a few others in retaliation for rudeness they have to endure with some people—one guy crushes the eggs." She giggled, "I can't blame them, sometimes its just overwhelming—the rudeness and arrogance."

"And you?"

"Being out here is how I handle stress." Paula tilted her head slightly to meet Lev's eyes and was caught off guard as his hand caressed the nape of her neck pulling her into a kiss—a long slow kiss; Paula lingered, lost in the sensuous feel. She felt the blush covering her cheeks as her eyes opened to his, "You know, I don't always kiss men who have just vomited."

"Oh damn, I forgot!" Color filled Lev's face as well. "It just came over me, I had to." He apologized, "I guess that killed the romantic mood I was shooting for."

"No, it was nice," Paula's face glowed," and I really couldn't taste it."

They both laughed.

Lev brushed the little stray hairs away from her face; the breeze blew them back, "You're a pretty neat gal, Paula."

"You think so, huh," She tittered. "You ain't so bad either."

****

"So how'd it go, your date?" Carrie inquired teasingly.

"I hate using that term—date, at my age. Makes me feel like a teenager."

"Did *he* make you feel like a teenager?"

Paula felt her cheeks tingling, *they must be red,* she thought, lowering her head.

"Ahh haa, there it is, you're blushing. Tell me about it. I have to live vicariously through people who actually have a love life."

"Carrie, it's not as dramatic as you make it out to be. We simply had a nice time."

"You didn't—" Carrie raised her eyebrows in exaggeration.

"Who do you think I am, Mindy?" Immediately Paula regretted her words, she bit her lip. "Geez, I feel so badly for saying that."

Carrie laughed, "Yes, but it is something Mindy would have asked. She loved to talk about *lovin'*." She touched Paula's hand gently, "Sorry, it's none of my business. But he's such a flirt—he flirted with me at first, he flirted with Mindy."

"He flirts with everybody," Paula started, "But I kind of understand the type." She laughed. "He's harmless, believe me, he's totally harmless—but I do like him."

"I thought you did—always so stoic—so uninvolved with men, well with most people, but I thought I recognized a spark when you two met at Gerard's."

"Yeah," Paula grinned broadly, "He's a good guy, but one crummy fisherman."

"And how did that part of the date go?"

"First we went out to fifteen mile reef, no luck." She hesitated for a moment considering whether or not to disclose the vomiting episode, decided against it and continued. "So we went out about five or seven more miles. He finally got the hang of things; we caught a couple of albacore, a king and three mahi mahi. I filleted some for you."

"Thank you, which one?"

"The king mackeral."

"Yum, I'll fix it tonight." Carrie thanked Paula again, her brow furrowed as she changed the subject. "Does he know anything more about Mindy's killer?"

Paula shook her head, she closed her eyes for a moment, "He says it's already gone cold—that there isn't the first clue."

"Nothing about Hank?"

"Nope. But I'm sure something is going on—" Paula stopped.

"Don, huh?"

"I think so."

"I hope he's finding something. I hope he finds Hank." Carrie brought a fingernail to her lips.

"I thought you stopped that."

"I did, I really did." She reached for the e-cigarette in her purse. "I want to quit this too. I don't want to be dependent on anything—or anyone." Her face clouding with despair and annoyance, Carrie drew on the vial and released a stream of vapor. "So what else did

265

detective Lev have to say about our little town and its nefarious events?"

"Nothing much, just that there is someone slashing tires on the loose."

"Slashing tires?" Carrie thought of the other night when she, Sammy and Essa worked late at The Upper Deck and the comments her co-worker had expressed. "That's funny—slashing tires."

"What's so funny about that."

"Essa—The other night we had some rude customers in, and she said she gets back at people like that. Then Sammy made a joke about her slashing tires."

"Does she?"

Carrie shrugged. "All I know is she's weird."

Chapter Twenty-Three

"Come on, baby. Just swallow this one last pill and the pain will go away." Essa placed the tablet on Hank's tongue and handed him a glass of water. She'd been feeding him the oxycontin since he'd come back to Topsail. Now, he was hooked and needed them every day, two and three times a day. *It's going to be so easy—little lamb wants to please his Essa—his Emma, and will do just what I want him to do.*

She kissed Hank's baldhead, stroked it and waited for the words she'd come to expect.

"You're so beautiful, my dear Emma."

The transition, moving him from an awareness of she and his late wife's resemblance to believing she was Emma herself, had been easy as well.

In fact, getting what she wanted had been easy for Estelle most of her life. Men had always come easy and with them, money or at least gifts. Now, all she needed from Hank was a marriage certificate, after that the rest would fall into place.

"Let's go for a walk," she cooed in Hank's ear.

He smiled at her, wrapping his arm in the crook of hers. "Whatever you want, darling."

"Tomorrow's the big day." Essa leaned into him as they closed the door behind, "A renewing of our vows."

"I'm so damn lucky."

You are do damn ignorant, you bald bastard. Lifting her head to meet his eyes, Essa giggled, "Everything is going to be so perfect."

"We should have mom come with us."

"E.J.? I asked her if she'd like to come to the mountains with us and be part of everything but she was adamant about not going," Essa smiled back, pleased with how well Hank swallowed her lies. "She said she couldn't stand the mountains and that she'd have a nice party for us when we returned—champagne, clams, shrimp—all kinds of good food."

Hank nodded, "It's probably for the best. We sure as hell don't need a *third* party along." He cupped her buttocks in his hand and gently squeezed. "You're body just does not stop."

Essa pushed back as he pulled her in tightly. "Oh baby," she ran her fingers along his inner thigh, "it's going to be so good."

They crossed over to the beach, walking north, letting the water wash over their feet. A crescent moon hung low in the indigo sky; Hank held his breath as he scanned the horizon. "Sure is warm." His fingers wound tightly with Essa's, he tugged for her to come closer.

"It was ninety-five today, a really hot one." Pulling his face to hers she kissed his mouth, the image of Don, the detective she'd met in Harlowe, danced in her thoughts, his bare chest pressed against hers, his arms encircled her body, holding her the way she wanted. Essa slid her tongue into Hank's mouth, imagining the tall blond detective against her.

Breathing heavier, Essa's chest rose, heat filling her body. She pushed Hank into a sand dune, tugging at the zipper of his shorts.

****

"It is what it is."

"And that's all you have to tell me?" Don hissed into the cell phone.

"It's far fetched I know, but Carrie says this waitress she works with, besides being wacko, has a thing for knives."

"So what. What has she got to do with anything?"

"Just hear me out." Lev insisted.

"Did this waitress know Mindy?"

"Like I said, I don't know anything. It's just a feeling both Carrie and Paula say they have about her. Paula says she used to drive a red Volkswagen—now she's driving a white Saturn."

"Interesting."

"Could be but I've got absolutely nothing here on the island, may as well check this out."

"No, this is good. Anything else?"

"The waitress's name is Essa."

"Essa? Not Estelle?"

"Just Essa, that's her name. Paula says most of the time she has a fat bald guy with her."

"What's that?"

"A fat bald guy."

He could feel the tingle, the one he felt when things were coming together. Don pulled his shoulders back; his mouth drew into a line as he pictured the red Bug behind Estelle's house. *The name, Essa—Estelle—could be the same.* Scenarios, images burst in and out of his thoughts, "When's the last time she saw Essa or the guy?"

"She hasn't seen either in a week. But then she's had the last week off."

"A whole week, huh. Must be nice." Don growled the words.

"Hey buddy, everyone deserves a few days off. Don't sound so angry about it."

"Sorry, just want to get this thing wrapped up—so, she's had the whole week off, how fortunate for her."

"We went fishing…"

"We?" So it's we now. What's been happening since I've been gone?"

"Uh, we just went out and caught a few fish on her boat." Lev explained awkwardly.

"Is that all—just fishing?" Don teased. "You starting something down there?"

"Hey man, we just went out on the boat."

"That gal isn't going to put up with any of your crap, old buddy. She's truly a no-nonsense kind of person—she'll eat your lunch if you screw with her. Maybe take you out about fifty miles and dump you."

"Maybe—maybe not." Pausing, Lev changed the subject back, "She'll be at work this Monday, she'll be keeping an eye out, but Paula seems to think Essa is going over the high-rise bridge at the north end of the island, that's why she hasn't seen her very much."

"What does Essa look like?"

"I haven't seen her. She's never been on her shift when I've been at the Deck. I'm just telling you what the girls told me."

"Find out." Don pressed the off tab and slid the phone in his pocket. He stepped back into Joyce's Bar and Lounge, his eyes focusing on the "V" girls perched on bar stools, flipping their hair and laughing too loudly. Slowly he walked up to them.

"Ooh, long time, no see." Vela fluttered her lashes, her eyes ogling his body. "You've been spending too much time with my older sister."

"Where is she?" Veda asked.

"She's at home, I guess."

"You sure she's not in school? She told me she's going back to school, but I don't believe it." Vela added sarcastically.

Don shrugged.

"You didn't ask her to come along?"

He considered telling the twins Vera was at an Alcoholics Anonymous meeting, but didn't. "I have no idea where your sister is."

Veda eyed the empty glass next to her, shifted her gaze to Don's and smiled, "Would you, honey?"

Don caught the bartender's attention and ordered drinks for the two women.

"Thanks," Veda cooed. "You do know that she's going to go to medical school?"

"Just that she's taking some classes at the community college."

"Vera always was a little snooty. Now she'll be even worse."

"Yeah, she's been acting like she's got a burr up her ass or something—like she doesn't want to be with us—hung the phone up on me the other night—her own sister." Veda punched Don's arm gently. "What did you do to my sister? Y'all ain't in love or something and trying to be uppity, are you?"

He pushed his hand into the pockets of his trousers and grinned, "Not today."

"Let's go sit at a table." Gabbing her bourbon and coke, Vela slid from her stool and led the way to a far booth. "She says she's going to be one of those nurses that takes your blood—icky."

"A blood sucker," Veda giggled.

"Phlebotomist," Don corrected.

"What's the big deal about that?" Veda rolled her eyes.

"She ought to go back to school for bartending." Vela guffawed.

"I really don't see what the big deal is. So what if she's going back to school," Vela snorted. "It's not as if she's getting married or won the lottery."

"I think Vera has turned a corner, she's made up her mind to do something good for herself." Don broke into the conversation.

"We'll see."

"Yeah, we'll see just how long it takes her to drop out of school and pick up a bottle of bourbon."

"It wouldn't do either of you any harm to try and better yourselves." Don regretted the words the moment they left his lips.

"So we're not good enough for you," Vela turned to Veda, "get that, and I knew it all along, he's uppity, just like Hank—acting all polite—the gentleman, and at the same time looking down his nose at us."

"Vera is doing something good for herself and that's the end of it. If I offended earlier, I apologize—how about I buy you two a round of drinks and we can all be friends again."

Veda and Vela always seemed to be more forthcoming after a few drinks. Vera usually did too, but tonight, and according to her word of honor and oath to God, she was abstaining from alcohol, going to AA. He hoped she kept her word.

Why it is always so complicated, he thought, listening to the banter between the twins. *Why do I care, it would be so much easier if I didn't care what happened to people. I could get answers, better ones than from these two bozos, from Vera. But I can't go there, she gets so bent out of shape when I bring up Hank or Estelle. And she's trying so hard to stop drinking.*

He swallowed from the bottle of beer, nodding as he continued listening to the twins. With good luck Vera was where she was supposed to be and he could get what he needed from them. They would have to do.

"So, your cousin Estelle—is that the only name she goes by?"

Veda pinched her brows together, "What kind of question is that?"

"Ha!" Vela raised her hand high in the air, "I know the answer—sometimes we call her *bitch!*" Vela swilled the remainder of her mixed drink. "And then there is my favorite, *cuntusabundus.*"

"No, no, I have it," Veda giggled, "*Whore*ndous!"

"Giant genital!"

"Thief!"

"Don't tell on Estelle." Veda growled. "That's what she always used to say when we were kids, but let me tell you, buddy roe," Her words slurring even more, "I learned to stay away from that cow, *who doesn't have enough dirty words to describe her*, real fast." Pulling her blouse up over her bra, Veda exposed a long jagged scar, reaching from the center of her chest nearly to her armpit. "She did this to me when I was fourteen years old 'cause I told on her for shoplifting at Wal-Mart."

"Really?" Don listened intently as the girls espoused the dirty deeds and antics of Estelle, her untrustworthiness, lying, and deceit. But then, he'd heard all that before; he was interested in new information.

"Sounds like she has a bad temper."

"Not really a bad temper, she doesn't yell and throw things, she just gets you back. This," Veda pointed again to the scar, "she *tripped and fell*, that's what she said the day after I pissed her off—the day after she said she'd get me back— she tripped and fell and just happened to have a knife in her hand when she did it."

"No, you don't want to cross my cousin and if she wants something you better let her have it or she'll make you pay—one way or another." Vela said self-consciously, almost as if she had sobered from the conversation. "She's mean Don—and it's not just because she stole Hank from Vera. She the one who pulls wings off of flies—she even drowned some puppies my dog had because she couldn't find a home for them."

"I think she and Hank deserve one another, both are selfish and manipulative as hell. I think he uses women and maybe he really doesn't like them as much as he wants you to think."

"Same thing about Estelle, she's in whatever she's in to get what she can."

For a moment the table fell quiet, then the girls whispered something between themselves, igniting the loud giggles.

Don mulled over whether or not to continue the questioning, then rose as if to leave.

"Well now, don't go on my account," Veda tittered.

"No, just go." Vela mocked.

They had become drunk, ugly drunk—slurring words, spilling drinks drunk.

"I'm just going to the can, be back in a second." He turned and left, still hearing their raucous laughter as he walked toward the restroom. "I'll be so damn glad to be able to get the hell away from here." He mouthed the words as he opened the stall door.

"She's tall, six feet, I'd say. Too tall for a woman." As she turned to her sister, Vela contorted her face, sticking out her tongue and poofing her hair. "She's always got that tongue hanging out of her mouth."

"She thinks it sexy to always be licking her lips," Veda added.

"I've met your cousin, I know what she looks like. What I want to know is—things about her personality. What is she like—as a person?" Don asked, as he returned from the restroom.

"That hair."

"Now, she does have some pretty hair. I always envied that hair." Veda grunted.

"It ain't fair to have that hair," The twins giggled in unison.

"We know she has hair. What else?" Don asked again.

"It long and curly and used to be red, then it got faded red and now it's sort of blond, not really blond but kind of blond highlights," Veda shifted a glance to Vela. "Wouldn't you say that?"

"So her hair color is not the same as it used to be? It's more blond." *Like Emma's.* He thought.

Chapter Twenty-four

Holy shit! Lev's table at The Upper Deck gave him a spectacular view of the sound and marsh life of Topsail Island. But the expletive, still reeling in his brain, was not in response to Mother Nature, it was to Essa—the long, tall, sultry waitress who'd skirted his table with a tray full of food for an adjacent table of customers. *How could I have missed that when I was here before?* he thought. *Carrie's description of her falls short, to say the least.*

He picked up his cell phone, and snapped a quick photo of the waitress as she laid plates of food on the nearby table of customers.

"If there's anything else I can get you, just wave you hand, I'll see you," Essa ran a finger along the letters of her name tag pinned conspicuously on her right breast, "I'm Essa," she winked at the two men seated there.

The waitress's eyes hurriedly scanned Lev as she brushed by.

Essa would tower over him; a self-deprecating grin played on his lips. Yes, he could feel intimidated by a woman like her and not just because of the height—the way she carried herself, the way she'd slid her eyes over his physique—so quickly, yet so efficiently, added to the aura of confidence and power she exuded—plus, she was beautiful.

Lev felt a nudge against his shoulder and looked up to Carrie, settling a glass of water on the table.

"Wipe the slobber off your chin," she chided. "Every damn man that comes in here goes gaga over her. I've seen more spilled water glasses than I can count, from men not paying attention to what's on the table, when that Amazon walks by."

"She is striking."

"I can be striking too," Carrie drew her hand back as if to slap him. She laughed gently. "Poor men, always thinking with the wrong brain."

"Yeah, yeah," he rolled his eyes and reached for the cell phone next to his plate. "How about I take a picture of you and send it to Don, I'll be talking with him in a bit. Anything you'd like to say?"

Her eyes lowering, Carrie shrugged, "Just tell him I said hi. He called the other night, we talked for a bit."

"Ah ha, that's a good sign."

The corners of her lips curled, "sort of." Changing the subject, Carrie asked, "Did you see the rock on her finger?"

"Wedding finger?"

"Yeah, it looks like a wedding ring."

Shaking his head no, Lev asked, "Is it new?"

"It wasn't there the last time I saw her and that was about three days ago."

"She hasn't mentioned it? Usually when women have a new wedding ring, they can't wait to brag about it."

"You have experience with this?" Carrie taunted.

"A long time ago."

"My turn to *ah ha,*' she crinkled her nose. "So, who, when, where?"

"Nothing you'd find interesting," Lev waved his hand, "Did you ask her about the ring?"

"She hasn't been all that friendly to me this evening. Every time I get ready to ask her something she zooms past me with an order or flashes me this look, this stare that makes the hair on the back of my neck stand up."

"She never mentioned anyone to you? A boyfriend, fiancé—anyone?"

"Never. She flirts a lot with men, but the only one I've ever seen her spending any time with at all, is that man I saw her with when she and I went to Gerard's."

"The bald guy—do you have any idea who he is. Ever see her with him again?"

"I've got no idea who he is. I've never seen him again, but Paula says she has seen Essa with someone like that in her car."

"Maybe she married the fat, bald man."

"Maybe."

****

"That's her. That's Estelle. She goes by Essa, at Topsail." Don tapped the letters into the phone.

"That's right. Can't believe I missed this gal, I would have remembered seeing her before. And get this, she's wearing a wedding ring. Carrie says it's new—she married somebody in the last few days."

"Fifty bucks, it's Hank."

"I don't bet."

"You don't do anything fun."

"No, we just have different opinions of what fun is."

Lev could hear the smirk from the other line, "You're going to love this next bit."

"What?

"Carrie says she's never seen Essa, *Estelle*, with any men, except the one she saw her with a few weeks ago at Gerard's—he's bald, fat—has a tat on his neck, with a goatee. Now who does that sound like?"

"No wonder you wouldn't bet."

"Doesn't matter, I wouldn't have bet anyway." Lev chuckled. "I think we've got our man."

"I'll be down there tomorrow."

Chapter Twenty-Five

She liked Hank. Estelle had always liked Hank, and when he was gone, she might even miss him for a while. But she'd thought everything through; there were things that had to be done. There were always things in life that had to be done, necessary things one had to do that weren't pleasant—that's just the way life was—hers anyway.

No longer having Hank in her life would be like getting rid of an old worn sweater that didn't fit anymore—that she'd gotten used to, that was comfortable, but nevertheless, had to go. That was Estelle's rationalization for just about everything in life.

Estelle crossed her legs and studied the frame resting on the sofa. Hank was snoring gently, his arms folded over his belly. She considered giving his bald head another shave before the night was through, prickly hairs were starting to grow there.

"No, it won't matter," she shrugged thinking of the sweater analogy, "No sense picking off the little balls of yarn if I'm just going to throw it away."

Glancing at the bottle of dilaudid on the table, Estelle took a deep breath and leaned back in her chair. The dilaudid had certainly done its job. Hank was out of it just enough for her to carry out what she needed done. Shifting her thoughts to Emma Jewel, Estelle thought of the flubbed murder and how much of a mistake it had been. She did not like making mistakes. Everything from now on had to be perfect.

The old woman would have to go, eventually, but not now, she'd wait. The right time would present itself sooner or later. If something happened to E.J. now, it might look too suspicious.

Now, everyone suspected Hank for Mindy's murder. *After tonight they'll know for sure he killed her.*

Watching his chest rise and fall, Estelle thought of the words *he* would use to explain things. The words would have to be perfect, as if Hank were saying them. She thought of his cadence when speaking, of his emphasis on what he found important.

She must convince the reader that it was Hank's letter—that he was distraught over events, that he felt justified in all of his actions.

"How to begin," she whispered, recalling his words. "Emma Jewel is the one that must believe he wrote this." She placed her fingers over the keys, still pondering the many times she'd heard his rant about the island changing. It seemed a broken record; the recounts of the way things used to be, the huge sand dunes, the fishing piers, the slow lifestyle; she'd heard it and heard it until she couldn't stand to hear it any longer.

The past was gone, as far as she was concerned. Topsail Island had never been a part of *her* past, why should she care. And even if it had been, well—things changed, life changed and if you didn't get what you needed before the changes affected you, then you were up shit creek. Besides, she never did like the beach—too much sand, and it all stuck to you as you sweated in the hot sun. Fishing was a bore, as were most fishermen.

No, life with Hank—going fishing, laying in the sun, going out on the ocean, would not be bearable—it would never be her lifestyle. But his land would fetch a good price—so would the boat and ocean-front home.

Then where? Thoughts of the mountains—hiking through the woods—brought a smile to her face.

Estelle's eyes twinkled as she recalled the worn phrases Hank used so often to describe his displeasure with present day Topsail. She pressed down on the keys and began:

To my Mother-in-law, Emma Jewel Rosell and others whom have been part of my life,

E.J., the day you visited me at the cottage was special. We talked about old times; happier times and I apologize if I did not show my appreciation for all you've done for me. I wish now that I had come back with you as you requested. But I think it is too late for me.

I want you to know that I loved your daughter, Emma, more than anything. She was my whole life and has been even since that horrible day on the sloop. I have never recovered from her loss and I accept responsibility for her death. It is a torturous existence living with the knowledge that because of my actions, beautiful Emma is no longer part of our lives.

That day when you and I sat on the pier, fishing and talking, you mentioned I should repent, that God would forgive me. Maybe this is true. But I cannot forgive myself. I have caused too much pain to you and everyone else.

As for the three people whose lives I took last year, Sarah Chambers, Reggie Bourne and Mick Boles, they all deserved to die. They were selling drugs to young people on Topsail, a place I have loved my entire life. People like them have brought so much destruction to the island—they have changed it from a humble and friendly town of caring souls, to a heartless tourist trap. People like Sarah, Reggie and Mick have helped to destroy the hometown atmosphere that once permeated the island. I've seen our sand dunes destroyed for houses where nobody lives, but a few weeks a year—

Pausing, Estelle settled her fingers over the keys of the computer, "what other blather can I write about?" She tapped the side of the Toshiba, glanced at Hank and began typing again:

Mindy was one of those that were so affected by all the changes, she was using cocaine and methamphetamine and selling it to other young people. I watched her change from a sweet young kid to a drug-peddling whore.

It pained me to take these things into my own hands, especially that lovely young girl, but it all has to stop! I knew of no other way than to do things myself.

I know the police are close now, I know they will find me and lock me away and I could never bear being far from the ocean. I hope what I have done will help the people I grew up with and that my local friends and family will understand why I did what I had to do. Perhaps after this, things will go back to the way they once were. The police should make more of an effort to rid Topsail of drugs. And they need to do it now.

I have met someone, a new love who is kind and loving. She is one of the gentlest souls I've ever met. Her name is Estelle Bottoms and she is my darling. Recently I made her my wife. She has helped to soothe some of my sorrows and I feel beholden to her, she has brought me peace and sadly through that peace I have come to realize I can no longer hide from the sins I've committed. Estelle, my Essa, is one of the wonderful gifts of my life that I do not deserve. Please be understanding and good to her—make her feel welcome. I hope you, Emma Jewel, will welcome my Essa and treat her like your own daughter. My wife knows nothing of my sordid past or any of the events of last summer or even this year. Help her with the sorrow I know she will go through after my body is found.

Essa read the pages, corrected a couple of misspellings, then clicked "print" and watched the letter slide from the Epson 300.

"Here, babe," she shook Hank gently, rousing him to a lethargic wakefulness. She helped him sit upright, then slid an ink pen into his hand. "Would you write your name for me? Be careful now and make it really pretty. Use your best penmanship."

Hank looked into her eyes, "I'm thirsty," he slurred.

Essa drew the pages back and studied his groggy appearance. "Sure baby, you need to wake up." She walked to the sink and poured tap water into a glass. "Here you go." Watching as he drank, Essa rubbed his stubbly head. "Good boy," she said, pulling the empty glass from his hand. "Now let's try this again."

Hank's handwriting was sufficient—not his best, but good enough. It would certainly pass as his signature.

Folding the paper, Estelle slid it into an envelope and encouraging Hank once more, had him write, To Whom it May Concern, on the front.

"Come on now, it's such a lovely night for a walk by the sound." She tugged on the waist of his shorts, helping him stand.

He buried his face in her hair. "You're so beautiful, my darling Emma."

She kissed his neck, leading him through the door and down to the paved road leading to the water. Holding both hands she walked backward, "It's so warm. It must have been ninety-eight degrees today. The water feels like a warm bath" She stepped back a few more paces, leading Hank farther.

Essa sat down in the soft sandy bottom and pulled him against her, his back to hers. "Feels lovely doesn't it, baby?"

She could feel his head nodding up and down against her breasts. Holding his torso with her long legs she rubbed his arms, resting them on her knees. "That's a good baby, just lean against me, relax against your Emma. I'll take care of you." She pulled a thin scalpel from her shirt pocket, waited as Hank eased back into the dilaudid oblivion, and gently ran the blade along his wrists.

One at a time she gently eased them into the brackish water. In the moonlight she could just make out the reddish tint seeping near her legs.

Stroking his head, she bent to kiss it, "Bye, bye baby, baby good bye." Estelle rose from the water, pushing Hank farther out into the Intercoastal Waterway, watching his body move with the current.

Chapter Twenty-six

Lev unzipped the bag holding Hank's body, then peered into his friend Don's face. "Got the call early this morning about thirty minutes ago. I was hoping you'd be back—knew you'd want to see this. The "V" girls didn't hold you up any, did they?" His lips drew into a smirk.

Don rolled his eyes, "Thank God, that's over." Inhaling a deep breath he added, "Thanks for calling; I would have hated to miss this, wish I would have known sooner that he was here at Topsail. I would have liked to have had him alive." He looked at the swollen face, the tattoo on the neck. "A far cry from the man I once knew. I'd have never recognized him. You're sure it's him?"

Holding up a wallet, Lev nodded, "and her," he motioned toward the woman sitting in the ambulance.

"Um," Don studied the tattoo on Hank's neck again, the spike and earrings in his ears." *The bastard is dead.* "Sure has changed." He spoke the words as casually as he could. Inside he screamed, he ached with freedom, struggling to compose himself. *"That's it, it's over, no one else knows now. No one can pin anything on me now. I'm free."* He reached a trembling hand to search the beast pocket of Hank's polo shirt. "Just what I need to start my day, another bloated body."

"Wonder who killed him."

Lev nodded again toward the ambulance parked nearby, "She says her *husband* left a note."

"Ah yes, her husband?" Don's eyes squinted against the morning sun; he strained to make out the figure in the passenger seat. "Why am I not surprised?"

"Essa. That's how we know her, she works at The Upper Deck with Carrie."

The two men watched as the woman opened the ambulance door and walked toward them.

"Is this your vacation home?" Don asked snidely.

"It's my home away from home." Estelle ran her fingers through her long loose hair. "You know how life goes, sometimes you just don't know where you belong. Sometimes you just need a break to find yourself."

"You never mentioned you were engaged. And I thought you said you hadn't heard from Hank in a while."

"I hadn't. But out of the blue, he called me up, said he couldn't live without me and wanted to get married." She licked her lips, "a couple days ago we drove over to Tennessee and got married." Stretching her left arm forward, Estelle flashed a one-carat solitaire diamond ring. "It's not much, but he loves me." Her shoulders quivered, Estelle lowered her eyes, "I mean, he *loved* me."

Extending an arm to steady herself against Don, she suddenly broke into sobs, "I woke this morning and found a letter—a note. I—I didn't know what to do, so I called the police station."

Lev met Don's questioning gaze. "We were here already. The bridge tender called in, she said she saw the body at sunrise—it was washed up over there."

"Paula?"

Lev nodded, "She said this man," he nodded toward a thin wiry man wearing a straw hat, "was in a boat near the body."

He gestured again toward the wiry man. "Buck Butler, that's his name. Says he knows you—said he found a body last year, too."

Hearing his name, Buck moved closer, "Yep, I found him floating near that little point in the marsh." He pointed to the piece of land jutting out into the water.

"Hank's your cousin, isn't he?" Don lifted his chin and eyed Buck disapprovingly.

"Yeah, but I didn't turn him over, didn't even touch him—from where I was at, I couldn't tell who in the hell it was and 'bout the time I got out of the boat, the cops were here." Buck scratched his head beneath his straw hat. "I wasn't sure it was him, until this lady showed up anyway. She's the one says he's Hank Butler. Besides, he's the other side of the family—we never was close." Buck stood self-consciously with his hands in his pockets.

"You were here last year, with the other floater, weren't you?" Don resisted the urge to grin.

Buck nodded his head, "Damn it all, I just want to go fishing and Hank, over there, he always was uppity and then all them people he killed last year." Lifting his shoulder, Buck's mouth twisted into a grimace. "And he killed that little gal, Mindy, too, didn't he? She always used to check my groceries at the store." Buck tugged at the hat atop his head.

Don turned toward the marsh, muffling another laugh; *doesn't he always keep a roach in that headband?* Recalling how he'd toyed with Buck the previous year, he succumbed to the urge again. "Is that a new hat?"

"Nope," Buck grabbed it from his head, and displayed the inside, "See, see all that sweat, look at that headband—it's old." His eyelashes fluttered.

"Why are you showing me the inside? I don't want to see it when you've got nothing hidden in there." Meeting Buck's gaze, Don pulled out a note pad from his hind pocket.

Nervously Buck settled the hat back on his head and began, "I ain't got—"

"Settle down, Mr. Butler. I'm not after your little stash of weed I just want to know more about your cousin all zipped up in the bag."

"I don't know nothing else—everything I know, I just told you. All I wanted to do was go fishing this morning. And you know early morning is the best time, so I come over here. And just like last year, there's a damn body floating face down in the water."

"And you had no idea it was your cousin?"

"I told you I didn't—besides the Hank I always knew didn't have a tattoo or a bald head. It doesn't look like him at all. But like everybody's been telling me, the Hank we knew as kids, ain't Hank no more. That man's gone."

Estelle walked toward the men, "Y'all talk about him like he was some kind of monster. He may have had his ways, but the Hank I knew was kind and generous—he wouldn't have hurt a fly." Her eyes steeled as she stared into the faces of Lev and Don.

"You told me he hit you," Don glared at her.

"Oh, that was just a little shove, and then, I was so upset about him leaving me at the time that I may have exaggerated."

"Really?"

Lifting her head, Estelle inched closer to Don, "You know how lovers get."

Don reached for her arm, "Why don't you come down to the station with me and tell me just how that is, Mrs. Butler."

She pulled away, "I'd rather come later, if you don't mind. I want to go with my husband, and I need to make arrangements for him."

"Okay, but stop by later. I want to talk with you about the note Hank wrote."

"I've got it," Lev said, "Got it from her this morning, first thing."

Don carefully perused Estelle's expression; she seemed one second distraught, another second playing coy—seductive. Now, tears welled in her eyes, she trembled. He felt disgusted with himself for falling prey to her, and turning to Lev he snarled, "I want to see that note."

****

293

"Looks like he confesses to it all," Lev propped his feet on the desk. "She's going to get his entire estate."

"Half—she gets half. Emma, Hank's first wife left her part of their property to E.J., her mother. Estelle Bottoms Butler gets half of everything."

"You think she'll move into his house?"

"I think she's throwing a party right now."

Lev nodded, "We need to keep an eye on our widow, and keep a close watch on Emma Jewel Rosell. Estelle wants it all."

"There's no way of proving she had anything to do with Hank's death and I seriously doubt he killed Mindy. That widow bitch did that."

"Proving it is another story."

Chapter Twenty-Seven

"So how are you going to prove it?" Cupping her face in her hands, Carrie leaned forward.

"I don't know. But one thing I've learned in all my years as a cop, is that if someone kills once, they'll kill twice." Don brushed a finger against a few stray strands of her hair. "Always did like that red hair of yours."

"Thank you."

He leaned across the table and pulled her face to his, kissed her gently on her lips, then again on a cheek. "I've missed you—more than you know." Holding on to her hand, he gently squeezed, "I want to start again."

"I didn't ever stop."

"Okay, you two lovebirds, don't tell me you haven't even ordered our drinks." Lev shoved against Don. "I'm not going to have to watch a bunch of googly-eyed mushy crap, am I? I came here for dinner not a show."

Paula rolled her eyes. "Shut up," she slid next to Carrie in the booth. "You've been *googly*-eying me all day."

"I must confess, you're right." Lev responded with a grin.

"It's the fishing," Paula taunted. "He's *crazy* about the boat. That's all it is. He just wants me to take him *fishing* again." She stared seductively into his eyes.

Lev rested against the booth, his lips pursed. "Yep, that's it, I'm after your money and your boat and I love to fish."

"I love to *fish*, too."

"What kind of *fish* do you like?

"Fishing? What the hell?" Don interrupted.

Carrie laughed, "Going fishing doesn't always mean catching fish."

"I gather that, and they're accusing you and me of being mushy. Sure you two don't need a room?"

"We already had one, thank you." Paula tittered.

"Um-hum, already had dessert. We're ready for a good meal now." Lev strummed his fingers on the table.

"Didn't see that one coming," Don's eyes widened. "I thought they didn't like each other."

"Me, either." Carrie turned to Paula.

"Me, either," Paula held onto Lev's hand, "blindsided me."

"Me, too."

Exchanging knowing looks, Don and Carrie both shrugged, then chuckled.

"Well, ain't love grand?" The waitress startled the couples as she placed menus on the table.

Carrie raised her head to thank her. "Essa?" She glanced at the name tag above the waitress' breast pocket. "Estelle? What—why?"

"I left The Upper Deck—too many bad memories. I decided to try this place, The Shrimp House—and beside, it offers a great ocean view."

"But you don't like the ocean." Carrie interjected.

"It's growing on me." She settled four glasses of water before her customers. "I'll be back for your orders in a few."

"What the hell is going on?" Lev queried.

"This throws a wrench into our nice quiet evening out." Pushing the menu aside, Carrie shook her head.

"We all know she did it—killed Mindy."

Don sat quietly, his head turned toward the ocean, his fingers running across his jaw line.

"What in the hell is she doing here? You'd think she'd be home counting Hank's money."

Estelle seemed to appear from nowhere, "I haven't gotten it yet, sweetie. Those things take time and I have to have a job to make ends meet—for now." She stood tall, her hair swept into a bun; shifting her hips she laid the pencil against an ordering pad. "So, what will it be?" she smiled.

.